GETTING CLOSE

WARREN FLYNN

HOWLING WOLF PRESS

ISBN: 978-1-961703-15-5

Acknowledgements

For Brittani, who gives me the freedom to write uncompromising work, and for Beckett, who doesn't care what I write as long as he gets fed.

Chapter 1

Rain tapped rhythmically against the windshield, each drop scattering the muted glow from the distant streetlamp into abstract patterns. Callan sat motionless in the shadowed interior of his black sedan, eyes fixed on the once-grand apartment building across the street.

Room 304 had been dark for hours. Its occupant unaware of his impending end.

He flexed his fingers, the leather gloves tightening across his knuckles. The sensation grounded him. Memories stirred. Killing had always come naturally. His first time remained sharp in his mind, like initials carved into oak. He hadn't been careful back then—impulsive, curious. It had been messy. But also raw. Exhilarating.

He'd grown since then. Now, his work was defined by discipline and calculation. Callan provided a service. People with means needed problems removed, and he had a reputation for doing just that—quietly, efficiently, without mistakes.

The man inside Room 304 was one of those problems.

Callan had studied the file. He believed in knowing every detail.

Daniel Holt had once been a rising star in real estate, until someone dug up his past. Not just shady business. Worse. Women had come forward with stories of manipulation, coercion, violence. Charges dismissed. Settlements paid. Lives ruined. One woman had disappeared entirely. No consequences.

Until tonight.

A faint glow flickered behind the apartment curtains—movement. Callan leaned forward. Pulse steady. Gaze sharpening. The job was simple. It paid well. Even though this was business, he couldn't deny a certain poetic symmetry in helping men like Holt meet the consequences they'd always evaded. Men who thought they were untouchable.

He stepped out into the night. Rain slid lazily off his coat as he crossed the street. Callan moved with ease—a predator returning to the hunt.

The building, once prestigious, had fallen into disrepair. A distracted delivery driver masked Callan's entrance, arguing with his GPS about "recalculating routes."

The outdated security system and a disinterested doorman absorbed in cat videos were practically an invitation.

Callan's breathing remained steady as he climbed to the penthouse—a testament to his rigorous training. At forty-six, he prided himself on meticulous physical maintenance.

The dim stairwell smelled of mildew and cheap cleaning products. Wallpaper peeled like shedding skin. He paused at the landing, listening, then moved toward the apartment door marked *Penthouse.*

The lock gave in under thirty seconds. He knew it well. He'd done his homework. Inside, darkness greeted him like an old lover. The air reeked of cigarettes, expensive whiskey, and regret—like every office party he'd ever tolerated.

The coffee table was littered with empty bottles and overdue bills. A faded photograph sat crooked in its frame. Callan's gaze snagged on the image: a younger Holt with a woman and a child. Smiling. Frozen in better times.

A cough from the bedroom yanked him back to the present. He shook off the thought. Refocused.

He moved with precision. Every footstep deliberate. His gloved hand brushed the handle of the knife beneath his coat. Knives were his preferred tool—quiet, clean, intimate.

The bedroom door stood ajar. Streetlight sliced across Holt's profile, revealing him hunched at the edge of the bed. Smoking. Unaware.

Callan considered a quip— "Surprise." But professionalism won out. He stepped forward with trained grace. Holt turned too late. Eyes wide.

Callan clamped a hand over his mouth and drove the blade into his heart.

The light left Holt's eyes quickly. It was cold. Automatic. And yet—there it was again. That flicker of something. Not guilt. Not even regret. Just a mild, creeping annoyance at how predictable all this had become.

Lowering the body gently onto the bed, Callan wiped the blade on the sheet. He stood for a moment, calming his heartbeat.

The penthouse was silent. Designer furniture sat in dust. Fast food wrappers. Neglect. He scanned the space again. His eyes landed back on the photo. It tugged something in him. He turned away.

Exfiltration was as easy as getting in. The alley door used by tenants for garbage disposal was down the same stairwell.

He'd left his trash upstairs. Still warm.

The rain still fell as he stepped onto the street. It always seemed well-timed—nature's way of deleting browsing history.

His car was untouched. No ticket. He allowed himself a small breath of relief. It would have been an embarrassing end to an otherwise impeccable night.

Chapter 2

The drive to the airport was uneventful. As Callan navigated sparse early-morning traffic, he mentally ticked off the checklist for dropping off the rented sedan—registered under a fake identity. He laughed, imagining a world where fake credit cards could earn cash-back rewards.

As the car purred along the highway, his thoughts drifted. The melodic hum of the tires softened his focus. Picking up cat food. Paying the house cleaner. An upcoming condo board meeting. The mundane rotated through his mind until it settled on an old, familiar memory—his second kill.

It had occurred two months after the first. Unlike that impulsive burst of violence, this one had been planned. Every detail accounted for—not just out of necessity, but out of a growing hunger for control. And the undeniable thrill.

Kevin had been an insurance broker, infamous for beating a prostitute to death and escaping punishment on a technicality. The kind of man who left pain and injustice in his wake. Callan had trailed him for weeks—learning his routines, his favourite restaurants, even his jogging route through the park.

The second kill was art compared to the first. Surgical. Executed in the shadows of a parking garage. Kevin never saw Callan's face. Never sensed danger until the garrote closed around his throat. No struggle. No mess. Just cold efficiency. Overdue justice.

The exhilaration had felt different this time. Controlled. Cleaner. When it faded, Callan went home, ordered Pad Thai, and watched a documentary about Patagonia—marvelling at how ordinary his evening would look from the outside.

The memory made him smile.

Then—*ding*.

A sudden warning chime jolted him back. He blinked, momentarily disoriented, before realizing the car was alerting him to low fuel.

Even agents of dark justice couldn't outrun basic car maintenance.

A gas station appeared ahead, its neon signage flickering in the dim pre-dawn haze. Grateful at the timing, Callan pulled into an empty fuel lane.

As he exited the car, his gaze drifted toward the neighbouring pump. A woman—attractive, sharp—was fuelling a vehicle identical to his own back home. Something about her presence threw him. A flicker of unexpected nervousness caught him off guard.

I should say something. The car return can wait. Don't blow it. He pushed the feeling aside, reassuring himself with a sardonic grin. *If I can kill people, I can handle small talk.*

"Nice car," Callan remarked casually, flashing a polite smile as he reached for the pump. Smooth one, he thought, wincing inwardly.

The woman glanced up, startled, as if shaken from her own thoughts. Then she returned a warm smile. "Thanks. You know what they say—great minds think alike."

Callan raised an eyebrow. "What do you mean?" His tone stayed light, genuinely curious.

She chuckled, shaking her head. That sparkle in her eye. The asymmetrical smile. "I was thinking about saying hi first," she said. "But you beat me to it. Seems you're quicker on the draw."

Callan smirked. "Well, I like to keep my reflexes sharp. You never know when a surprise duel might break out at a gas station." He mimed a little finger gun.

She blinked at him, then laughed out loud. "What the actual fuck?"

So much for not blowing it.

He recovered quickly with a shrug. "I mean, you never know, right?"

"Callan, by the way," he added, giving a small wave

She replaced the nozzle, giving him a thoughtful look. "Look, Callan, I've had a rotten week. But you made me laugh. I want to give you my number. So don't be a stalker, okay?"

Callan grinned. "I'd never. Stalkers are the worst!"

She rolled her eyes and gestured for his phone. "Come on, let me add my number before you say something even weirder."

Callan hesitated a moment. "Phone's dead. Can I write it down?" He never brought a personal phone on jobs. Too many risks. Too many ways tech could betray him. It was a rule.

She rummaged in her car for a moment, returning with a business card and pen. Flipping the card, she scrawled her number on the back.

As she handed it over, their fingers brushed. Just slightly. Callan flipped the card. His breath hitched.

Beneath her number, in clean, professional font:

Detective Tricia Langley,

Key Biscayne Police Department.

She worked in a small, wealthy bedroom community just outside the city.

"There's something about you, Callan," she said, tapping her finger to her lips in mock contemplation. "I think I might have to keep my eye on you." She pointed two fingers at her eyes, then at him, laughing.

Callan bit the inside of his cheek to keep from laughing himself. Of course. The one time he flirts with a stranger, she turns out to be a cop. Maybe the universe had a sense of humour—just a cliché, a twisted one.

They lingered for a moment, both of them awkward in the way two people are when neither wants to leave first. Tricia finally rolled her eyes, gave a small head shake, and climbed into her car. One last glance. A two-finger wave. Then she pulled out of the station, disappearing into the haze.

But that look she gave him just before leaving—it stuck.

Not flirtatious. More like... curious. Measuring.

He'd seen that look before. Usually in mirrors.

She was watching him. Not just because she liked his face.

And whatever was behind that gaze—it made him shiver.

CHAPTER 3

Callan unlocked the door with a smooth twist of the key, stepping into the peaceful sanctuary of his condo. The scent of wood polish and faint traces of expensive bourbon lingered in the air—remnants of a life curated to appear unremarkable.

Off-white walls and caramel-toned cabinetry were relics of a bygone aesthetic. Dated, but inoffensive. Marble and wood floors gleamed under the dim glow of recessed lighting, luxurious finishes at odds with the beige palette. The previous owner had considered it sophisticated. Callan, for all his precision, had never bothered to change it.

He kicked off his shoes and set his car keys in the small dish by the door—a habit more about control than convenience. Everything in his home was intentional, from the minimalist furniture to the lack of personal photos. No clutter. No sentiment.

Crossing into the living room, he exhaled and settled onto the sleek leather couch, eyes drifting to the city skyline beyond floor-to-ceiling windows. The high-rise view stretched westward, the last hints of night still clinging to the horizon. Headlights and streetlamps bled into each other like a watercolour painting.

He ran a hand through his hair—no gloves, just skin on skin. Last night had been another clean contract. Another life taken. But his thoughts weren't on the body he left behind.

They were on Tricia Langley.

Her number sat in his pocket—just a business card, but heavier than it should be. Naturally, the first woman he'd casually flirted with in years was a cop. And not just any cop—a detective from a wealthy suburb where people liked to pretend crime didn't exist.

He pulled out the card, flipping it between his fingers.

Detective Tricia Langley.

Would she recognize him if they met again? He'd been careful, just a guy at a gas station with a dead phone and a bad joke. But cops have instincts—and instincts were dangerous.

He should toss the number. That would be the smart move. Rational. And Callan was nothing if not rational.

Except... she'd laughed. Not polite. Not fake. Real.

He hadn't had a girlfriend since university. Romance had no place in his life. Too complicated. Too risky. Back then, he was just a finance student with a casual interest in death. Now, he was something else entirely.

Miami, he kept things simple. No attachments. A rotating cast of women who shared his outlook: No strings, clean exits. It worked. It was clean.

Yet, here he was, staring at a phone number like some teenager with a crush.

He should shred it. Burn it. Instead, he set it gently on the table beside his wallet.

Curiosity gets the cat arrested for life, he thought. Then he spoke aloud to no one in particular. "Speaking of curiosity—where is my boy?"

He rose from the couch, rubbing his jaw. Something felt off. Not wrong—just... too quiet.

In the bedroom, he found Beckett sprawled across the centre of his pristine bed, methodically grooming his massive white paws. The Norwegian Forest cat, pushing twenty pounds, looked up briefly and resumed cleaning, unimpressed by Callan's arrival.

Arms crossed, Callan watched him work.

"Nice to see you're hard at it."

Beckett paused mid-lick, flicked an ear in Callan's direction, then returned to the task without a single fuck given.

Callan shook his head, grinning. "Good talk."

Satisfied, he pulled off his hoodie and hung it in the closet. *Don't put it down. Put it away.* Beckett remained in his domain, perfectly at ease, utterly unconcerned with the world.

Callan sat at the edge of the bed, watching the cat's tail twitch. He ran a hand over Beckett's thick fur— soft, luxurious, with an untamed roughness. From the start, Beckett had been like this: wild, indifferent, untameable. Callan hadn't planned on adopting him. Just like he hadn't planned on keeping that number.

Plans had a way of changing.

Maybe that's why Tricia lingered in his mind. She wasn't predictable. Just like Beckett.

And he thought back—back to the day he met the damn cat.

***

Ten years earlier...

The wind howled across the parking lot of the town's only animal shelter. Snow clung to the edges of the squat brick building. Above

the door, a faded sign read: Swift Current Animal Rescue—Every Life
Matters.

It was just another dull Saturday. His target was working out of Regina. Callan's cover kept him nearby, stuck in Swift Current—close to
civilization but far enough away to be a hassle.

Out of boredom more than interest, he had Googled "Things to do in
Swift Current." After dismissing an alarming number of curling links,
he ended up at the shelter.

The air inside was thick with disinfectant, sawdust, and wet fur. Dogs
barked in the back, almost deafening.

The teenager at the front desk greeted him with the tired cheerfulness
of someone who'd seen too many broken promises.

"Looking to adopt?" she asked.

Callan hesitated. "Just looking."

"Cats or dogs?"

He shrugged. "Cats."

"Cool. Cats are in the back."

She waved him down a hallway lined with small wire enclosures. Each
one bore a handwritten tag—name, age, and a short personality blurb.
Callan passed cage after cage until he reached the last one.

The tag read: *Beckett—8 months old. Difficult.*

Inside, a scrappy, long-haired brown and white kitten glared at him.
Ears too big. Oversized paws. Tail flicking in irritation. His golden-green
eyes locked on Callan with unsettling intensity.

"He's been here a while," the girl said, appearing beside him. "Most
people want lap cats. Beckett... well, he's not exactly a people person."

Callan raised an eyebrow. "How difficult?"

"He bites. Doesn't like being held. Knocks stuff over for fun. I love
him, but my mom won't let me have another cat."

Callan turned back to the kitten, who was now tearing into his cardboard bed with precise violence. He seemed fully aware of being discussed—and was choosing to ignore it.

"Most people want something affectionate," she added. "That ain't Beckett."

Callan watched Beckett tip over his food dish, then look him dead in the eye. *What are you gonna do about it?*

Something about that defiance was... very impressive.

"What's the adoption process like?" he asked.

***

A decade later, Beckett head-butted him, snapping him out of the memory.

"You bastard," Callan muttered.

The cat sighed, stretched, then flopped on his back and offered up his belly. When Callan reached, he got a swat for his trouble.

"Still difficult, huh?" Callan chuckled and walked back toward the living room.

Some impulsive decisions had a way of sticking.

CHAPTER 4

Callan woke up hard, blinking up at the ceiling, groggy but alert. The bedside clock read 11:07 AM.

He exhaled, rubbing a hand over his face. Eight uninterrupted hours—no tossing, no nightmares, just clean, guiltless sleep. For a man who killed for a living, he rested suspiciously well.

"If you love what you do, you'll never work a day in your life," he mused. "Guess that applies to murder, too."

Most people lie awake, haunted by bad choices, Callan thought. I sleep like a baby because I make mine with conviction.

It should've been mildly alarming how well-adjusted he was. Meanwhile, somewhere, a barista was losing sleep over foam art.

He groaned and stretched, swinging his legs over the side of the bed. Beckett, perched on the dresser, observed him with a look that could only be described as supervisory.

"Don't start," Callan said. "You'd nap through an apocalypse."

Unbothered, Beckett yawned.

Callan smirked. "Yeah, yeah. Do what you love."

He padded to the kitchen, flicked on the lights, and was met by the sterile neatness of his condo. Minimalist to the point of austerity. One coffee mug in the drying rack. A fridge stocked like a survivalist with taste.

Beckett leapt onto the counter, violating every rule. Callan didn't bother enforcing them anymore.

"You're bold," Callan said, grabbing a can of gourmet cat food. "At least pretend to be grateful."

Beckett sniffed it, gave him a look of aristocratic disdain, and walked away.

Callan exhaled. "Typical."

He poured himself coffee and leaned against the counter, letting the silence settle. Tricia's card loomed in his periphery, daring him to make a mistake.

Callan traced the rim of his mug with his finger. She's a cop. A charming, insightful cop. His rational mind was already drafting a list of ways this could implode. Spectacularly. Jail, dead, married. All equally undesirable.

And yet...

"You're getting sloppy," he muttered.

The moment with Tricia had felt... natural. And that was the problem. Callan loved his work, but lately, it was starting to feel routine.

Beckett, now mid-groom, lifted his head and stared with muted judgement.

Callan rolled his eyes. "I know."

Pondering what to do with his day, the opportunities were endless: Beach? Cuban food? Oil change on the motorcycle? All fine options, but his thoughts were interrupted.

His phone vibrated.

Not the burner. The personal line. The one reserved for a select few.

He answered with practiced neutrality. "Yeah?" The voice on the other end was unmistakable—airy, casual, tinged with mild exasperation.

"Oh my God, Callan. You sound like a shift nurse contemplating their own mortality."

He laughed despite himself. Isabelle. His stepsister. Spiritual enthusiast and perpetual disruptor of his calm. "Morning," he said flatly.

"Barely," she replied. "Did you do your affirmations?"

"My what?"

"Affirmations. You know, 'I am light, I am love, I am manifesting abundance.'"

Callan blinked at his coffee. "I regret picking up this call."

"Wow. So much blocked energy."

He could practically see her waving sage and shuffling tarot cards. "Night person," he offered.

"No," Isabelle said matter-of-factly. "Emotionally constipated person."

Callan sighed. "Skip to what you need."

Her tone softened. "It's about Maggie."

Callan stilled. Cold pooled low in his gut. *Maggie.*

He tightened his grip on the coffee mug. A faint pulse thrummed behind his temple. "What about her?"

"I ran into her sister yesterday," Isabelle said. Her voice had lost its usual floaty calm. "She's still... shattered, Callan. You know how it is. She's carrying around this hole. No closure."

Isabelle didn't know. She didn't know that Kevin—the man who'd beaten Maggie to death—had been Callan's second kill. That Callan had made damn sure Kevin never saw the inside of a courtroom.

"I just..." Isabelle exhaled.

"It was a long time ago. Kevin paid for his sins. Isn't that enough?" Callan asked, studying his nails. Need a mani, he noted.

"You're so cold. Her spirit needs to heal."

Callan reset his focus. "I feel like twenty years is a long time to carry a torch."

She laughed softly. "Still an ass."

"And yet you keep calling."

"Because you're not hopeless," Isabelle replied. "Just heavily repressed."

He exhaled. "Anything else?"

"Yes. Breathwork."

He hung up. Beckett, still on the counter, blinked in typical cat fashion.

Callan sipped his coffee. "Don't say it."

Beckett flicked his tail. *She's not wrong.*

Callan exhaled. Too early in the day for this. Time to hit the shower.

CHAPTER 5

Callan stepped out of the shower, rubbing a towel through his damp hair. Steam curled around the mirror, briefly obscuring his reflection. He wasn't in the mood for self-analysis.

Still towelling off, he finally glanced up. His reflection stared back.

He was often called good-looking in a rugged sort of way. Broad shoulders. Strong jaw. Deep-set blue eyes. Features that made people assume he was thoughtful.

A five o'clock shadow darkened his jaw—a mix of brown and the first hints of grey. His hair, permanently tousled, was still mostly dark, though a few silver strands glinted under the lights. It suited him, he supposed. Aging without softening.

His gaze travelled downward. He kept himself in peak shape, but not out of vanity. Strength was a necessity. The muscle across his chest and arms was functional, not excessive. No use being built like a linebacker if you couldn't sprint up a fire escape.

And yet, he thought—bland. Average height. Average face. Nothing striking. Nothing memorable. The kind of guy you'd see in line at Starbucks and forget by the time you got your drink.

It had served him well—handsome enough to avoid suspicion but not so remarkable that he stood out. He knew how to blend into the background, a talent that kept him out of prison.

Callan exhaled and ran a hand through his hair. "All right. Enough narcissism." He stepped into the closet that adjoined the bathroom and bedroom.

Dressing was efficient. Habitual. A fitted black T-shirt, Lululemon shorts, and a pair of well-worn flip-flops—comfort over intimidation. Fitting in meant dressing the part.

In the bedroom, Beckett sprawled across Callan's pillow, tail flicking lazily. Indifferent as ever.

Callan laughed. "Glad to know you're emotionally invested."

The cat didn't budge.

"Well, my boy, I'm off to rejoin the real world."

He picked up his phone from the dresser and checked the time: 2:42 PM. His favourite coffee place shouldn't be busy.

Time to visit Wanda.

***

Callan grabbed his keys and slipped out of his condo, flip-flops smacking against the tile. The elevator ride down was uneventful. Just him and a guy in sweatpants who smelled like poor decisions were made the night before.

"Gotta love the MIA," Callan muttered, stepping off.

The afternoon air was warm, the city humming to life. He liked this hour—early afternoon. Just enough motion to feel alive, not enough for small talk.

When he stepped into Java Junction, the scent of coffee and whir of the burr grinder hit instantly. Comforting. Familiar.

A few regulars held down their spots. An elderly couple shared a newspaper. A tech bro hunched over his laptop. A woman in yoga pants appeared to read but was clearly eavesdropping on the barista drama.

And behind the counter— Wanda.

Wanda had been running the place as long as Callan had lived in Miami. Early sixties, sharp as hell, and a professional flirt. She could make a triple-shot latte while maintaining eye contact and dishing out innuendos. It made Callan briefly wonder if she's had a past life in adult cinema.

She made a point of keeping Callan on his toes.

She glanced up and smiled slow and wide. "Well, well, well. If it isn't my favourite dark and brooding customer."

Callan shrugged. "Figured I'd stop by before you put up my missing poster."

Wanda leaned on the counter and looked him over, unapologetically. "I was worried you had run off with some young thing who doesn't appreciate you like I do."

Callan chuckled. "Wouldn't dream of it."

She snorted, already reaching for a cup. "Half-sweet mocha, whole milk, no whip? Or are you finally gonna let me add something sweet to the black little heart?"

"You know me too well."

"Oh, I do, honey. More than you know." She scribbled on the cup. "Muffin? They're fresh. Like me."

He leaned on the counter. "Define fresh."

"Well, they arrived this morning. Unlike me, they don't come with years of experience and untapped potential," she teased.

He considered it. "Fine. Blueberry."

"Living dangerously today," she said, dry as dust, sliding the cup and muffin his way. "I like a man who knows how to treat himself. You deserve it."

Callan pulled out a bill and dropped it into the tip jar.

She raised an eyebrow. "You feeling generous, or just trying to butter me up?"

"Both," he said, taking a sip of his mocha. The warmth and sweetness hit immediately— comforting and indulgent. The muffin, despite his usual no-carb discipline, was exceptional.

Wanda gasped, hand on her chest. "If only I were thirty years younger! But, hey—if you ever tire of yoga moms and twenty-somethings with commitment issues, you know where to find me."

Callan chuckled. "Noted."

As he turned to leave, she called after him.

"See you tomorrow, handsome."

He gave her a mock salute and headed out.

CHAPTER 6

Outside, the Miami heat was already intense. Callan took his time walking back from Java Junction, savouring the last sips of his mocha as he wove through the afternoon rush. Horns blared. Cyclists cut between cars like daredevils with a death wish. The city pulsed—chaotic and loud.

Callan found it soothing. Background noise. Organized chaos.

He wandered into his high-rise, tossing the empty cup into the lobby trash. The elevator was mercifully empty.

Back at the condo, his device buzzed.

Ellen.

One of the few people Callan would still call a friend. She was like the city itself—fast-moving, unpredictable, and impossible to ignore.

He answered. "Ellen."

"Oh, good, you're awake," she said, relieved but vaguely annoyed. "You're coming to a concert tonight."

"I—wait, what?"

"Nathaniel Rateliff," she continued, barrelling on. "Sold-out. You're taking my brother's ticket because he's useless and bailed. David's out for work. That makes you my new date. I can't go alone—I hate being the third wheel."

Callan blinked. "Ellen, I—"

"Eight o'clock. Texting you the details now. Wear something nice. Kay byeeeeee."

Click.

Callan stared at the phone. Somewhere deep inside, a warning bell rang. Not because of Ellen—but because every time he tried to live like a normal person, it felt like tempting fate.

Beckett, perched on the couch, flicked his tail and gave Callan a pointed look.

Callan exhaled. "Yeah, yeah."

The cat hopped down and rubbed against his legs. Pity, Callan decided. Or mockery. Hard to tell with cats.

"I should've let it go to voicemail."

Still, irritation aside, there was no denying Ellen had a gravitational pull. She didn't make polite requests. She issued mandates with charm and swagger and somehow made people glad for the inconvenience.

There were too many parallels with Callan's employer, which he had no interest in unpacking.

And, for reasons he didn't want to name, he never quite told her no.

She flirted with everyone like someone adopting a stray—amusement, half challenge, with no real expectation of success. It disarmed. Which was dangerous.

Ellen didn't *examine* people. Maybe she just didn't flinch when she saw the cracks in their armour.

Callan exhaled and headed for the closet. Another night playing the role of a functioning human being, surrounded by beer, music, and a woman who saw him as salvageable.

He knew better.

Chapter 7

The Uber deposited Callan into the chaotic mess of people swarming toward the concert venue. He took a deep breath, letting the atmosphere settle around him. Music pulsed from inside the building, the deep bass vibrating through the pavement under his feet. The packed street teemed with people—laughing, half-drunk, teetering in heels and optimism.

The scent of cocktails, sweat, and humanity hit his nostrils like a wall. He scanned the crowd.

And there was Ellen.

Standing out from the crowd, not because of her height, sun-kissed blonde hair, or those stunning blue eyes—but because of her outfit.

Callan exhaled through his nose.

A fitted black dress clung to her figure in a way that suggested either adhesives or a miracle of physics. The heels could double as weapons. She looked like she was auditioning for a music video, not showing up at an indie folk concert.

He shook his head and made his way toward her, dodging a cluster of Gen-Zs taking selfies mid-sidewalk.

Ellen spotted him. Her lips pursed as she gave him a once-over, scanning his presentability. "Look at you," she teased. "Wearing something that doesn't scream 'brooding assassin.' I'm impressed."

His blood ran cold—just for a moment.

He lifted an eyebrow, keeping his expression easy. "Does Dave know you left the house looking like you charge by the hour?"

Ellen gasped, one hand to her chest. "First of all, rude. Second, David *loves* this dress."

He didn't argue. He knew better.

They moved toward the entrance, joining the throng near the bar line. Callan kept his hands in his pockets, his posture relaxed—at least to the untrained eye. Always assessing. A few drinks. Some live music. Then back to the condo, where Beckett was likely already judging him.

"Ellen!"

A woman broke through the crowd and threw her arms around Ellen. *Tricia.*

Of course. The universe wasn't even pretending to be subtle anymore.

The detective he'd flirted with—briefly, foolishly—was now wrapped around Ellen like an old friend.

His body didn't tense. It shifted. A subtle recalibration. Not fear. Just... calculation

Tricia pulled back, laughing. "It's been forever! I'm so glad you could still make it."

Ellen grinned. "I know, right?! Oh, my *God*, girl, how are you?"

Tricia looked around. "So, who'd you drag with you?"

And then, as if she sensed him, her gaze slid sideways. She locked eyes with Callan. A flicker of recognition passed over her face. Confusion, then memory. Then—

Shit.

A slow grin tugged at the corners of her mouth. "Well, well, well." Her voice rose with teasing amusement. "I told you I'd keep an eye on you, mister."

She made the same finger-to-eyes gesture she had made that night.

Double shit.

Callan kept his face neutral, offering a casual nod. "Detective."

Ellen looked between them, confused. Her gaze bounced like a ping-pong ball. "Wait... you two *know* each other?"

Tricia chuckled. "Kind of. We met in passing." She folded her arms, giving Callan a long look. "Though, I must admit, I wasn't expecting to see you again. Since you didn't text me."

Her pout felt a little *too* convincing.

Yeah. Me neither, Callan thought.

Ellen, now fully invested, turned to him with a gleeful grin. "Oh. Oh, this is fun. Spill!"

Callan didn't flinch. Kept it cool. "Tricia and I bonded over high-quality fuel and my impeccable taste in cars."

Tricia laughed. "He made some weird joke about duelling at a gas station."

Ellen howled. "That is *so* on-brand for him."

Tricia's eyes sparkled, her attention now razor-sharp. Playful, but cutting. "Yeah, I can see that."

Callan felt the shift. The static in the air. Curiosity, not suspicion. Not yet.

Then salvation. Or complication. Depending on how you looked at it.

A stocky guy with a damp forehead and forced confidence elbowed into their circle, slipping an arm around Tricia's waist like he'd claimed something.

"Hi, I'm Dwayne," he said, aiming his grin at Callan. "And you are?"

His tone was off. A little too pointed. Too challenging.

Callan flicked his gaze to Dwayne's hand. Back to his face. His pulse didn't waver. Not a threat. Just noise.

Callan offered the kind of smile that lived comfortably in corporate boardrooms and crime scenes. "I'm just the plus-one." Smooth as glass.

Tricia arched a brow, clearly enjoying herself.

CHAPTER 8

Drinks cost too much, but killer-for-hire was a very lucrative profession. And a fourteen-piece band on a summer evening made it worth it.

Callan took a sip of his eighteen-dollar canned cocktail, letting the burn settle in his throat as he observed Dwayne who, on the surface, appeared to be the human equivalent of a damp towel. Tall, heavier than Callan, he crowded Tricia, one hand hovering near her waist like a possessive claim.

Interesting.

Tricia didn't react, no leaning in, no pulling away either. Callan couldn't tell if Dwayne was her boyfriend, a first date, or just someone who assumed too much. Ellen, meanwhile, appeared delighted by the entire situation.

"Callan?" Dwayne's expression was unreadable. "You and Tricia go way back?"

Tricia snorted. "We met at a gas station."

Dwayne's brows furrowed, clearly thrown.

"Uh... what?"

Callan shrugged. "Classic love story."

Ellen choked on her drink.

Tricia tilted her head, eyes sparking with amusement. "You know, I was wondering what happened to my dashing gas station stranger. Turns out he's friends with Ellen." She smirked. "What other secrets are you hiding?"

"Oh, so many," Ellen teased.

Callan took another sip, his gaze sliding back to Tricia. She was playful, relaxed, and yet, the way her eyes flicked over him when she thought he wasn't looking suggested she might be more perceptive than she let on.

A guitar strum from the stage signalled the opening band's arrival. Tricia perked up.

"We should probably find seats before we get stuck in the worst section."

Ellen slid her arm through Callan's, pressing up against his side with a smirk that was just shy of scandalous. "Oh no," she purred, eyeing Tricia and Dwayne. "Looks like we're all in this together. Rush seating, baby."

She gave Callan's arm a slow, deliberate squeeze that felt too intimate to be innocent.

"Wonderful," he sighed. "Forced proximity. My favourite."

"Oh, I know it is," Ellen said, dragging him forward. She revelled in his discomfort.

They weaved through the throng, eventually claiming a row of seats off-centre. Callan sat first, Ellen next to him, then Tricia, and finally Dwayne.

As the opening act took the stage, the hum of amplifiers and chatter blended into a kind of musical current. Callan relaxed, at least outwardly. He loved live music, the way a talented band could captivate a room—controlled chaos, something he could lose himself in for a moment.

Half a minute into the first song, Dwayne leaned over, stage-whispering. "Seriously? These guys again? Did the venue lose a bet?"

Callan said nothing, though he noticed Ellen's eyebrow twitch in annoyance.

Tricia sighed. "Dwayne."

"I mean, they're fine in a bar."

Ellen, who was swaying with the beat, turned and stared. "Do you just... hate fun?"

Dwayne scoffed. "I have taste."

Callan bit back a smirk. *Jesus.*

Ellen shot Callan a meaningful look. *Can you believe this guy?*

Callan responded with a shrug and another sip of his drink.

The band segued into their next tune—upbeat, a little rough around the edges, but a crowd favourite. People nearby were already moving in time.

Except Dwayne. "Man, their timing's off. Drummer's sloppy."

Callan turned his head, voice low and unimpressed. "You in a band?"

"What? No."

"Then shut up."

Smooth, Callan.

He reminded himself to stay inconspicuous, but Ellen's fiendish cackle virtually drowned out the music. Tricia grinned ear to ear, eyes gleaming with an approval that caught Callan off-guard. Dwayne looked like he'd just swallowed battery acid.

Ellen leaned in toward Callan, laughter still in her voice. "What's gotten into you, mister?"

Callan played it off with a slow sip.

Tricia seemed to forget Dwayne was present. Her gaze lingered on Callan's face, a small flicker of curiosity and something else he couldn't quite name.

Determined to recover, Dwayne muttered, "People should demand better from live music. Raise the bar, you know?"

Ellen groaned a little too dramatically. "Dwayne, please, just let me enjoy this in peace."

Callan leaned back, noticing that Tricia made no move to defend Dwayne. If anything, her attention kept drifting Callan's way.

A new song started, the lights dimming to a cozy glow.

Ellen jumped up, grabbing Callan's hand.

"Oh, I love this one! You're coming with me or I'm dragging you like a corpse, your choice." She tugged him out to the aisle, where the crowd was dancing.

Tricia stood. Then Dwayne—rigid, arms folded.

Callan closed his eyes, letting the percussion thrum through him. His phone buzzed in his pocket.

Of course, just when I relax. He slipped it out:

Isabelle.

Ellen frowned in question. He shook his head.

"I'll be right back," he yelled into Ellen's ear.

He stepped outside to a quieter corner near the concessions. Tricia's gaze followed him, her brow knotting—not suspicion, exactly. But something else. Like she'd just spotted a crack in an otherwise perfect mask.

"Yeah?"

Isabelle's voice was breathy, eager, maybe panicked, hard to tell over the noise. "Callan! So, I found an old photo album of Dad's. But you sound busy. Call me when you can, okay?"

"Fine. Talk later."

When he turned back, he caught Tricia watching him from a few steps away. Far enough to be polite, close enough to overhear. Her lips parted as though she were considering following. Her posture was casual, awkward, like someone caught between minding their own business and intruding.

"I'm going to grab another bevvie. Need anything?" she asked, keeping her voice pitched low to compete with the music.

Callan slipped the phone back into his pocket.

"All good." He forced a half-smile. "My sister has shit timing."

Tricia didn't buy it. Not entirely. Her gaze dipped to his pocket, then to his stance. How his body stayed angled toward the nearest exit. A flicker of realization crossed her face. She masked it with a casual shrug.

"Right. Your sister." She stepped forward. "Drink?"

"Sure."

The line was short. Soon they were back with their group, cocktails in hand, the band playing a slower song now, the lights shifting to a warm amber.

Ellen arched an eyebrow in curiosity but didn't pry. Dwayne sulked in his seat, arms crossed.

Callan reclaimed his spot next to Ellen, aware of Tricia's occasional glances.

"Everything okay?" Ellen murmured.

Callan nodded. "Yeah. Just a quick call."

Ellen relaxed, her attention back to the stage. Dwayne muttered something under his breath—a complaint about the band's tempo. Tricia said nothing, though every so often, Callan felt her eyes on him, like she was cataloging every detail. Filing it away.

He took another sip of his fresh drink—each one tasting better than the last—while letting the saxophone solo rumble through his brain.

Sure, Dwayne was a nuisance, but Callan had bigger concerns: A detective whose focus was growing more personal. A stepsister he needed to catch up with.

For a night built on chaos and canned cocktails, human interaction wasn't half bad.

CHAPTER 9

Callan leaned back in his seat, letting the music wash over him. The band was hitting its stride—guitars tight, drums solid, energy building. The crowd pulsed with movement, caught up in the performance's raw energy.

Ellen was in her element, half-dancing in her seat, laughing at something Tricia had said. She was having the time of her life.

Callan was buzzing—the band was killing it, and for once, he was almost relaxed.

But Dwayne?

Dwayne was drinking like he had something to prove.

Callan cast a glance sideways. Dwayne had been knocking back drinks too fast for someone clearly not enjoying himself. His whiskey—of course he was a whiskey guy—was already gone.

It struck Callan then: The guy's overconfidence might not be simple ego. It had that edge. Hitter's swagger. He'd seen it before—back home, after deployment. The stiff posture. The tight jaw. That low simmer of frustration. Some men never adjusted to peace.

Callan made a mental note to watch him more closely.

Dwayne kept darting glances at Tricia, waiting for her to look his way. She didn't. Not once. Her focus was elsewhere—more specifically, angled toward Callan.

Callan exhaled, taking another slow sip of his drink.

It would be easy to defuse the tension—step back, ignore Tricia, play it safe. He had nothing to gain from a scene. His life was good. He loved his work, had more money than he needed, and a clean slate. Why jeopardize that over some half-drunk poser with a chip on his shoulder?

The answer came to him as clear as the Gulf breeze.

He didn't want to ignore Tricia.

He wanted to impress her.

And that, he realised, was a problem.

Chapter 10

The concert ended in a mess of cheers, stomping feet, and spilled drinks. The final notes rang out through the venue as the crowd roared, the energy still electric even as people began shuffling toward the exits.

Callan took one last sip of his drink and stood, stretching out his back. He had to admit—it had been a solid show. The band had delivered, and for a couple of hours, he'd actually enjoyed himself.

Then he looked over at Ellen and Tricia. They were giggling like drunk sorority sisters, arms slung around each other, swaying as they sang an off-key, and lyrically incorrect version of the encore chorus.

"Youuu were the liiiight in the daaaaaark!" Ellen howled, throwing her arms up dramatically.

Tricia doubled over, wheezing. "Oh my God, that was *so* bad."

"You know what's bad? You not singing!" Ellen grabbed Tricia's hands and twirled her like they were in a bad teen rom-com.

Callan watched, unimpressed. "Christ."

Ellen whipped around, pointing at him. "You have no soul."

"Correct," he said flatly.

The irony wasn't lost on him. What did catch him off guard, though, was his own laughter.

Tricia turned too fast and grabbed his arm to steady herself, her fingers lingering longer than necessary.

"Nooo, he does," she slurred. "Deep, deep, *deep* down." She squinted at him, then tapped his chest. "Like... real deep."

Callan arched a brow. "That an official detective assessment?"

Tricia grinned. "Maybe."

Ellen snorted. "You should frisk him. Just to be sure."

Callan exhaled, resisting the urge to walk straight into traffic.

Dwayne loomed behind them, arms crossed, his mood dark enough to suck the rest of the fun out of the night. He hadn't said much in the last thirty minutes—not since his third or maybe fourth whiskey. His jaw was tight. Expression unreadable.

But he'd been watching. Watching Tricia lean into Callan's space. Watching her laugh. Watching her not once look his way. Her interaction just now? Harmless, maybe. But to Dwayne, it was public humiliation. A joke. And he was the punchline.

It was eating him alive.

Callan sighed, already predicting the mess about to unfold.

"You're a cocky fuck," Dwayne slurred. "Someone oughta take you down a peg."

Callan held his ground, his voice even. "Spent ten years in the infantry. Sometimes I act up. No hard feelings, man?" He extended a hand.

But Dwayne didn't want peace. He squared his stance like he was more interested in throwing punches than shaking hands. He'd had some time in the ring, Callan noted. Filed it away.

Tricia, now in full drunk girl mode, stepped between them. "God-damn it, Dwayne. Chill *out*."

"This prick's ragged on me all night," Dwayne snapped, slurring over his whiskey and Coke.

Tricia's face flushed red. "This is why Lydia won't let you see your fucking kids." The words landed like a brick.

Dwayne froze.

Then shoved her.

It wasn't hard, but she was drunk—she stumbled, nearly falling, and Callan caught her, steadying her with a hand at her waist, easing her out of range.

"Easy," Callan said, voice low, calm, controlled. "It's been a good night. Let's not fuck it up."

Then he leaned in just enough for only Dwayne to hear, his voice like a scalpel—quiet, precise, deadly.

"Don't hate *me*," he said softly. "Hate that she looks at me like she's already forgotten your name."

A pause.

"And you're pissed because, deep down, you *know* she should."

Dwayne's pupils blew wide.

Callan saw it—the crack, the fracture—his control collapsing.

Then Dwayne exploded.

Chapter 11

Even though Callan saw it coming, Dwayne shifted his stance, settling his weight on the balls of his feet. The guy was fast. He'd clearly fought before. Drunks threw wild punches, but fighters aimed.

So, this wasn't just some drunk swinging from his asshole. Dwayne had form.

The first strike came fast, clean, precise.

Callan reacted on instinct, years of training kicking in. He slipped most of the blow with a head turn, but the fist still grazed his jaw hard enough to send sparks to his vision.

Dwayne surged forward, not wasting momentum. The second strike was sharper, aimed low. Callan evaded it, but Dwayne adjusted mid-strike, twisting his weight to slam a knee into Callan's ribs.

A real shot. A real fucking shot. Pain tore through his side. Callan gritted his teeth and pivoted, deflecting the next strike.

Dwayne was good.

Callan let him come again, measuring now. Dwayne's stance was tight, his strikes controlled—but he was fighting angry.

Callan caught one punch on his forearm, absorbed the impact. The next, he redirected, nudging Dwayne's wrist just enough to throw off his aim.

Dwayne hesitated.

Callan didn't. A hook to the liver. A brutal right to the solar plexus.

Dwayne's body locked. His breath hitched. A strangled gasp as his knees sagged. He refused to collapse, but clutched his stomach, wheezing.

Tough. But not unbreakable.

For a second, all Callan could hear was his own breathing.

Around them, the crowd had shifted. A few onlookers stopped to gawk. Some sidestepped the scene entirely, giving it a wide berth.

A few shouted out, "Hey, cut it out!"

"Grow up, you idiots!"

"Is someone calling the cops?"

A couple of half-drunken voices even cheered, like they'd stumbled into a street fight on pay-per-view.

But as Dwayne staggered, the scattered jeers and taunts fell away. A charged hush settled over everything—the kind that only comes after the violence ends. Then Tricia's voice sliced through it, sharp and furious, "What the hell is wrong with you?"

Callan wasn't sure if she meant Dwayne or him.

Across the pavement, Ellen hurried over, her earlier buzz and flirtation gone in a rush of alarm.

"Oh my God, Callan—are you okay?" she asked, scanning him, ignoring Dwayne completely. Concern etched her features as she reached out to touch Callan's arm.

Dwayne coughed, still doubled over, rage burning in his eyes.

"Fuck you," he rasped, spitting out each word. "Fuck all of you." Callan watched him wheeze, twitching like a wounded animal. Poised for something. Anything.

Callan tilted his head slightly. "That went well!"

Seething, Dwayne glared up at Callan.

Callan sighed and brushed off his jacket like it was nothing more than spilled beer. "Are we good?"

Dwayne's hands twitched, but he didn't lunge. He turned and stomped away.

Tricia stared at Callan with an unreadable expression. Ellen stayed close, her hand still hovering near his arm. For once, she had no snark—just worry.

"Callan, seriously. Are you hurt?"

He shook his head, even though his ribs screamed otherwise. He forced a shrug.

"I'm fine."

Tricia stepped beside Ellen. Something twisted her features— glee, maybe. Elation. Her fingers twitched like she might start dancing.

"Fuck that guy. First round's on me."

A wash of headlights interrupted them. The Uber Callan had summoned earlier rolled to a stop, the driver not even glancing up from his phone.

"Time to go," Callan said, mostly to Ellen.

She nodded, reclaiming some composure.

"If you're sure you're okay, I'm going to catch up with Trish." The prospect of the former model reliving some of her glory days was clearly overriding her concern for Callan.

He let out a laugh that turned into a wince. His ribs flared white-hot. "All good. I would if I were you." He glanced at Tricia, couldn't help himself.

As he pulled open the door to the Uber, something flickered in his peripheral vision—bright light. A phone flash.

Someone near the venue entrance, wearing a hoodie and a beanie, was holding up a phone. A red recording dot blinked, steady and accusing.

Fuck.

Act cool. Nothing to see here.

Callan didn't break stride. He slid into the backseat like nothing had happened, even as tension knotted in his shoulders. The SUV doors locked with a soft click.

The driver—middle-aged, tired—met his eyes in the rearview. A strong weed smell clung to the interior, woven into the seats. "Callan?"

"Yeah."

The car pulled away from the curb. Callan leaned his head back, exhaling as the city scrolled by outside the window.

Someone had recorded that fight.

In a few hours, it wouldn't just be a drunken scuffle.

It would be content.

And content doesn't disappear.

CHAPTER 12

The city lights flickered through the SUV's tinted windows, streaking yellow and white across Callan's vision. He barely noticed.

Someone had recorded the fight.

How many people had seen? Just the guy in the hoodie? Or was he part of something bigger? A cop? A journalist?

Callan exhaled, clutching his ribs. The pain was sharp, but it wasn't what unsettled him. It was the feeling that, for the first time in a long time, someone else might have the upper hand.

He didn't like that feeling.

He forced himself to think logically.

Best-case scenario: The guy was just another clout-chaser, racking up views. In that case, the video would hit social media, get some attention, and disappear into the abyss. A hundred street fights happened every day in Miami. No one would look twice.

Worst case? Someone recognized him. Not as Callan—the unremarkable finance guy—but as someone who should never be caught on camera.

He pulled out his phone and started searching. Twitter, Instagram, TikTok, Reddit. Anywhere the video might've landed.

Nothing.

No clips. No blurry footage. No breathless commentary on a brawl outside the venue.

It should have been a relief.

It wasn't.

It was suspicious.

A slow, rolling heat crawled up his spine, searing his chest like a live wire. *This shouldn't have happened.*

He saw it coming.

Callan balled his fists, nails digging into his palms. The muscle in his jaw twitched, his teeth grinding hard enough to ache. His own stupidity burned—a violent thing clawing behind his ribs.

People like him were supposed to be disciplined. Calculating. Not some bar-fighting meathead massaging his ego.

And yet, he'd stood there. Let Dwayne make his move. Like some punk with something to prove. Like an undisciplined child. Arrogant. Untouchable.

A red haze edged his vision, pulse hammering in his throat. His fingers twitched against his thigh, itching to wrap around something—someone.

He wanted to break something.

To break *someone.*

He wanted to go back and put Dwayne down hard.

A muscle in his neck twitched.

Breathe.

His nails had pressed so deep into his palms they stung. His breath came slow, deliberate. He forced his hands to open. Not here. Not now.

The haze thinned, leaving him cold. Controlled. The steel wire pulled taut again. The rage coiled back—contained, not gone.

One slip-up. That's all it took. One second of carelessness, and now he was digging through the internet, wondering if his face was about to star in someone's viral reel.

A low chuckle from the front seat pulled him out of the spiral.

"Long night, hey boss?" the driver quipped. Oblivious. "Looked like you were dealing with some guy back there. Reminds me of my glory days." He laughed—abrupt, self-deprecating. "Used to throw a mean right hook. Got me into a lot of trouble. Thought I was unstoppable. Now I'm an old man driving an Uber."

The words were light, but they landed heavier than they should've. A soft warning. No agenda.

Callan didn't answer at first. He just let the silence stretch.

Then finally, low. "Yeah. Glory days."

That was all he said.

Silence fell again, broken only by the engine's hum and the dull hush of city traffic outside. The driver, apparently satisfied, refocused on the road.

Callan leaned back. The wire inside him still pulled tight.

When he closed his eyes, he didn't see the lights. Didn't see the driver.

He saw Dwayne's face.

He saw the lens of the phone.

The SUV rolled on through the night. Somewhere in his memory, Diego's voice echoed—cold, clipped, sharp as broken glass.

"Control the room, or the room controls you."

Tonight, the room had won.

And he *fucking hated* that.

CHAPTER 13

Lying in bed, he stared at the ceiling as if expecting it to look different. His muscles were locked in rigid tension, his body demanding rest while his mind refused to comply. His night of mistakes left him wired.

This is how it starts, he thought. *One night. One moment. One loss of control. That's how monsters are made.*

It shouldn't have happened. He *had* to be in control—because without it, everything he'd worked for was in jeopardy.

The sheets were cool against his skin, but he was running hot. His condo was silent, except for the faint hum of the city beyond the window. Normally, that stillness calmed him. Normally, he slept without trouble. Deep. Dreamless. Like a man without regrets.

But tonight, sleep wouldn't come.

His ribs ached—a slow, pulsing reminder of his stupidity—but the pain wasn't what kept him awake.

It was the feeling of *losing control.*

Not just losing it. *Giving* it away. To adrenaline. To anger. To the part of himself he pretended didn't exist.

He rolled onto his side, eyes fixing on the dim outline of the bedside table. His phone sat there, screen dark, waiting. He had checked it a dozen times before forcing himself to put it down. Still no sign of the video—no leads, no movement. Just silence.

That was the part that gnawed at him. If it was online, there was nothing he could do.

He remembered reading an article—some woman whose ex posted revenge porn years ago. She got the original post removed. A decade later, her kids could still find it.

He remained restless. Wanted to get up. Move. *Do something*. But all he could do, was wait.

Delay isn't a strategy, he thought. *It's surrender.*

He exhaled, forcing himself onto his back, eyes closed. He started counting his breaths—a technique he'd mastered over years of training, a way to force his mind into submission.

But every time the darkness edged closer, a flicker of rage surged through him, dragging him back to wakefulness.

Dwayne.

The moment replayed behind his eyelids. The way he'd let it happen. And once it was happening—the way he'd enjoyed it. The undisciplined, reckless indulgence.

It wasn't justice. It wasn't a clean extraction or neutralization. It was personal. And worse—it had felt right. Like he'd been waiting for an excuse.

All for what? For Tricia? To impress her? It made no sense.

Callan opened his eyes again, exhaling hard. His pulse had steadied, the rage bottled tight. But his mind kept turning.

He shifted on the mattress—and felt a weight land beside him. Something moved. Shifted. A second later, warmth pressed against his side. A familiar, lazy vibration filled the quiet.

Beckett.

Callan didn't move.

The cat stretched, kneading the blanket with purpose before settling in. His massive body leaned against Callan's ribs with muted righteous entitlement. Then, a contented sigh. Beckett tucked his head against Callan's arm and purred.

Callan blinked at the ceiling, and some of the tension in his chest loosened, despite himself.

Beckett didn't care about codes. About control. About lines not to be crossed. He didn't need Callan to be good.

He just needed him to be here.

Beckett wasn't affectionate—at least, not often. And never on command. If he was here, it was because he chose to be.

Somewhere deep inside, a flicker of honest gratitude stirred—for his little man.

Callan lay there, letting the sound of the purring fill the silence. Letting the warmth settle against his side. Letting his own heartbeat slow to match the cat's rhythm.

The storm inside him didn't disappear. But it dulled.

A low, barely-there smile ghosted across his lips. "Love you, my boy," he murmured.

Beckett, unmoved by sentiment, let out a sigh and stretched one massive paw over Callan's chest—claiming him.

Maybe that's what he needed. Not to win. Not to clean up every mess. Just to be needed—even by something that didn't ask for anything.

And just like that, Callan finally slept.

CHAPTER 14

He wasn't sure what had woken him. The condo was silent, midday light filtering through the curtains, casting sharp streaks of gold across the floor. Beckett stretched like a king in his rightful domain, his front legs still draped over Callan's ribs, and his tail flicking in contentment.

The faint vibration of his phone on the nightstand caught his attention. He exhaled sharply and reached over, grabbing the device. The screen lit up.

Twelve missed calls.

A slow, sinking weight settled in his chest.

They weren't from Ellen. Or anyone who would call just to annoy him.

They were all from Ellen's husband, David Crawford. A high-strung personal injury lawyer, David never texted—it left a trail. He was a riot at parties, a train wreck everywhere else.

Callan sat up. Beckett protesting with an irritated flick of his tail as the sudden movement disturbed him. He swiped the screen open and scrolled through the timestamps. The first call had come at 7:42 AM. The last one, just a minute ago.

David was dramatic, so Callan wasn't concerned. He hit redial and brought the phone to his ear. It rang once before David picked up.

"Callan?" David's voice was tight. Urgent. Not his usual, carefully controlled tone.

Callan swung his legs over the edge of the bed, pressing a hand to his face, forcing himself awake.

"Sorry I missed your call. Sleeping," he said flatly.

"Well, that must be nice," David snapped. "What did you idiots get up to last night?"

Callan hummed in response, stretching. His ribs were a mess.

"Yeah," David continued. "Ellen threw up so hard she thought she burst a blood vessel. She demanded Tricia and I take her to the hospital."

Callan laughed, sharp and probably inappropriate—which made it funnier. Of all the things he expected to wake up to, this wasn't one of them.

"You're a real asshole, you know that?" David growled.

He dragged a hand down his face, the grin lingering. "You're telling me Ellen nearly drank herself to death?"

"No, I'm telling you she threw up so hard she fucking near burst a goddamn blood vessel and had to be dragged to the ER. I practically carried her in. Tricia was just as shitfaced. She crashed at ours."

The image of David—always composed, five-foot-five, and built more for comfort than speed or power—carrying his six-foot-tall, ex-model wife anywhere made Callan laugh again.

He sighed and stood up gingerly. Pain lanced through his ribs the moment he straightened. He clenched his jaw and breathed through it.

Dwayne had done more damage than he thought. "It's a long way from her heart."

"Yeah, yeah. She'll live. She's already bitching about the hospital food, so you know she's fine," David grumbled. "But that's not the only reason I called."

Callan frowned, stretching his back as he walked toward the kitchen. "Then why the hell did you call twelve times?"

David hesitated—just for a second.

"Tricia. She wants your number."

Tension hit like a hammer. He swallowed. Throat tight. Dry.

He exhaled through his nose. "Did she say why?"

"No. But she mentioned the fisticuffs, and I know a cop digging for answers when I see one."

He stared at the floor, jaw tight.

So. Detective Tricia Langley was looking for him.

His head spun. The walls closed in. Breath caught. He closed his eyes, letting the emotions flood him. Then he let them go. A practiced calm washed over him.

It wasn't the first time he'd thought he was fucked.

***

Twenty years earlier...

The neon glow of a rooftop bar flickered against the night sky, broken reflections rippling across the infinity pool. Callan sat near the glass railing, nursing a whiskey he had no intention of finishing. He wasn't here for the view.

Grant Hathaway, hedge fund royalty, lounged at the far end of the pool deck, roaring with laughter beside a woman young enough to be his daughter. Maybe she was. Maybe she wasn't. Either way, she looked too expensive to be here on her own dime.

Callan had watched him for weeks. The world saw Hathaway as the genius behind a billion-dollar empire. But the clients who'd lost their life savings to his schemes knew better. A fraud. A parasite. A man who ruined lives and walked away untouched.

Callan was here to fix that.

The job—more hobby than mission back then—had gone smoothly. Hathaway had chosen this resort for its discretion, a place to indulge unsavoury pursuits without security. Taking him out had been easy.

Leaving was supposed to be just as simple. Callan moved through deserted corridors and shadowed pathways, already replaying Hathaway's last moments in his mind. He allowed a flicker of triumph, a rare indulgence.

He'd done well tonight.

He'd grown used to having every exit under control, to clearing jobs with minimal fuss. But that flash of self-satisfaction cost him. He heard footsteps—too late.

A blow to his ribs landed like a sledgehammer, driving the air from his lungs. He staggered, stunned. Another strike hit his jaw, snapping his head back. Pain flared white-hot. His body screamed at him to fight, but confusion dulled his reflexes.

Callan had run into someone his equal—or better.

"There's always a bigger bully," his stepdad used to say before boxing class.

Before he could register the ambush, his hands were zip-tied and a bag pulled over his head. When the bag came off, the air smelled of oil and dust. A warehouse, maybe. His arms burned from being bound for so long.

Unmasked men circled him, tattoos marking their arms and necks. Their collective presence radiated menace.

You're fucked if they let you see their faces. Every crime drama he'd ever watched had promised him that.

One of them, taller and broader than the rest, stepped forward. He said nothing, but his fists clenched in readiness.

Callan's head pounded, but he forced a lopsided grin. He was furious with himself. He had lost focus. But fear only made him defiant.

"Oh, thank God," he drawled, wincing at the pain in his temple. "I thought someone had kidnapped me. But this? This is clearly just a very aggressive job interview."

Silence.

He rolled his shoulders, testing the cuffs.

A muscle twitched in the leader's jaw. The rest stood like statues.

One of the masked men exhaled sharply. Maybe laughter. Maybe contempt.

The leader tensed—then held back, as a slow, mocking clap echoed behind Callan. A man in a tailored suit stepped into view, leaning against a rusted beam like he'd been waiting for his cue. "Gentlemen," the newcomer said, words laced with amusement. "Let's not break our guest before we've had a chat."

Reluctantly, the lead thug stepped back. Callan sensed the seething frustration. But this suited man had the power here.

He chuckled, stepping closer. "Mr. McWard. May I call you Callan?" he said, almost fondly. "This is indeed a job interview... of sorts."

***

A shrill meow cut through the memory like a blade.

He wasn't bound to a chair or choking on warehouse dust. He was in his bougie condo in downtown Miami. Right now, a very agitated feline wanted some grub.

His body still buzzed with the aftershock of the recollection, a stark reminder that losing control had nearly cost him before. But that time, it had worked out.

He couldn't count on it working again—not with a potential viral video or a detective's curiosity threatening to unravel everything he'd built. But no need to overreact.

CHAPTER 15

Callan stood in the dim glow of his condo, ribs aching, patience frayed. The city buzzed beyond the glass like a reminder he hadn't made peace with anything.

Tricia's number sat on the counter, taunting him.

He could ignore it. He should. But the memory of her laughter—and the chaos it promised—was already pulling him in.

He picked up his phone and dialled. Not texted like a sane person. Dialled.

Something about this whole mess made him revert to old habits.

He told himself not to call. Then called anyway.

The phone rang once. Twice. Then— "Hello?"

A pause. Callan cringed. "Oh, good. You still answer calls. I was worried I'd have to send a carrier pigeon."

Silence, then Tricia's amused voice. "Wow. Do I need to crank my rotary phone first, or are we skipping straight to Morse code?"

Callan chuckled. "Depends. Do you even know what Morse is? I could just show up and stare through your office window, Detective."

"Tempting, but you promised no stalking, remember? Also, I don't open the door for strange men lurking in the bushes."

"Phew. Guess I'm glad to be a regular man with a phone, then."

She sighed, clearly amused. "To what do I owe the pleasure, Callan? Couldn't handle leaving me hanging?"

He leaned against the counter, fingers drumming on the cool marble. "Figured I'd check in. You were looking for me."

"Ah. So, David told you."

"He did."

"And now you're... what? Returning the favour?"

Callan watched the city lights flicker. "Something like that. Besides, I'm old-fashioned. When a detective hunts me down, I prefer a conversation over cryptic texts."

Tricia hummed. "So, if I'd just sent 'We need to talk' at 2 AM, that wouldn't have done it for you?"

"Not unless you threw in an ominous ellipsis. Gotta sell the suspense."

"Noted."

He smirked, but his grip on the phone tightened. Flirting aside, she wasn't just making small talk. And he wanted to know why.

"So," he said, voice low, steady, "what's on your mind, Detective?"

A beat. Barely there. But he caught it. He was holding his breath.

"We should hang out," she said.

Callan exhaled slowly, buying time. The smirk stayed, but something coiled tight in his chest. That wasn't a cop move.

"Have you ever been to Java Junction?" he asked.

A pause. Then—

"I'm off around eight."

The line went dead.

Callan stared at the phone, then tossed it onto the counter. Beckett, curled up on a nearby chair, flicked an ear but didn't bother looking up.

What the hell does she want? I'm playing with fire. So why am I this eager?

He fed Beckett, then hit the shower—dismissing his second most reckless decision of the week.

Chapter 16

The humid night air was invigorating, the city humming around him in its usual rhythm—cars idling at red lights, distant sirens wailing, the faint murmur of evening conversations drifting from sidewalk patios. Normally, this noise usually faded into the background. Just another layer of static.

Tonight, though, it felt heavier. Maybe it was the ache in his ribs. Or maybe it was the fact that Tricia Langley had just invited herself into his life.

He kept his pace easy, hands in his jacket pockets, cutting through side streets. Java Junction. Wasn't far—ten minutes at most.

He passed a row of shuttered boutiques, their window displays frozen in perfection—designer handbags aligned in symmetrical rows, mannequins posed like they had somewhere better to be. The kind of places built for people with too much money and not enough self-awareness.

Ellen would love this, he thought, eyeing a jewellery store.

Tricia.

He hadn't been able to get a read on her yet. And Lord, he'd tried. She was the kind of woman who stayed in your head, whether you wanted her there or not.

He wasn't stupid enough to think this was a social call. She was a detective. Detectives didn't track you down unless they had a reason. She was looking for something.

The question was—what? And how much did she already know?

Ridiculous question, really. He was careful. *Meticulous*. His last job had been in Miami. No names. No ties. No fingerprints. And no evidence pointing back to Callan McWard.

He stopped at a crosswalk. A group of college kids stumbled past, laughing, wrapped around each other with that easy drunken intimacy that only youth allows.

The closer he got to Java Junction, the sharper his focus became. This was not a conversation he could afford to stumble through. Tricia was sharp. Too sharp. The kind of woman who noticed details you didn't realise you'd left behind.

The neon sign of the café came into view, casting a warm glow onto the sidewalk. Through the glass, the place was nearly empty—just a couple of stragglers nursing drinks.

And there she was. Corner table, facing the door. Casual. Composed. Shorter than him by a few inches, curvy in a way that suggested strength, not softness. Her blonde hair framed her sharp features, and her green eyes flicked over something on her phone. A half-finished espresso sat in front of her, lipstick smudged on the rim. Casual outfit—jeans, a flowy blue top. Civilian, not cop.

A choice. A calculated one?

Callan exhaled, ribs protesting. He squared his shoulders and stepped inside. The bell above the door chimed.

"Half-sweet mocha, whole milk, no whip," came Wanda's voice, without so much as a glance.

Callan laughed, stepping up to the counter. "Miss me?"

Wanda finally looked up, her eyes as unimpressed as ever. "I'd move mountains for you, hun."

"Charming as always."

"I'm a woman of consistency," she said, starting on his drink. She glanced toward the corner table. "That one of yours?"

He followed her gaze. "Yeah. What do you think?

Wanda didn't even blink. "She seems too smart for you, hotshot."

"Jealousy doesn't suit you."

Wanda returned to her espresso machine with a dismissive flick of her wrist. "Lord help that poor woman."

Callan grabbed his drink and crossed the café.

Tricia looked up, her smile warm but quiet. It wasn't the cocky confidence from their first meeting. It wasn't weakness either. Just... real.

"Hey, you," she said.

Callan slid into the seat across from her. "Hay is for horses." Another one of his stepdad's favourites.

She chuckled, but it didn't last. Her gaze slipped past him. Checking exits? Listening for backup?

"I, uh..." she sighed. "I wanted to apologize. For Dwayne."

Callan raised an eyebrow, took a slow sip. "Why? You didn't throw the punch."

"No, but I brought him. And... according to his ex-wife, he's a territorial asshole when he drinks."

Callan watched her. "How do you know his ex-wife?"

"Lydia and my ex are cousins. Anyway, I didn't think he'd—" She broke off. "I should've stopped him."

Callan's voice was quiet. "Didn't seem like you tried that hard."

She blinked. "Excuse me?"

"You know what I'm saying, Detective."

Her lips parted—ready to protest—but she stopped. Closed them again. "You think I planned that?"

"You brought him."

She leaned back. "Okay. You're not wrong. But I didn't expect you to actually..." She trailed off. "Never mind."

He waited.

Tricia stared into her cup. "I'm not great at this. The connection thing. I tend to... assess people. See how useful they'll be."

She looked up.

"It's not because I don't care. It's because I *do*. That's the problem."

Callan didn't speak. Just listened.

"You scare the shit out of me," she said. "But I think I like that. Danger makes people honest."

He took a slow sip of coffee. "Dangerous? No. Just... comfortable when things go sideways."

"That's what worries me."

She paused.

"You fight like someone who's been trained."

There it was, the unspoken truth hanging in the air.

He didn't flinch. "My stepdad was big on boxing. Wanted me to be the next Arturo Gatti."

"I don't know who that is." A pause. "I have something else to say. And it's weirding me out, so don't laugh."

"I make no promises."

She looked him dead in the eye. "I wanted to say thank you. No one's ever stood up for me like that before. All the men in my life lately? Toxic assholes."

He gave a soft chuckle. "I wasn't standing up for *you*. I was standing up for *me*."

"Still," she continued. "What got me wasn't the fight. It was the calm. Like you've done it a hundred times. And walked away clean. That's what you are, right? Controlled. Precise. Always have a plan." A pause. "Makes me wonder what would happen if someone ever took that away."

Callan tilted his head. "That a warning, Detective?"

"A compliment. Mostly."

Another pause.

"There's something else. Someone filmed the fight."

Callan didn't move. "Imagine how fat and slow we must look on TikTok."

Tricia smiled slightly. "You don't have to worry about that."

He studied her. "No?"

She didn't look smug. If anything, she looked... sheepish. "Ellen and I sweet-talked the kid into deleting it."

A real laugh escaped him. Ribs protested.

Tricia groaned. "Yeah. Genius move. Ellen promised a blowjob, I think."

Callan arched a brow.

She held up her hands. "I just watched."

Another long sip. He let the warmth settle.

"Best news I've heard all day," he said.

"Don't thank me. Thank your pal, Ellen—the reformed slut gaslit that poor student."

They locked eyes. Still studying each other. Still circling.

Then Tricia leaned forward, her voice low. "I've had a really long week," she said. "And I'd rather not go home alone tonight. You interested?"

Callan blinked. Direct. No games.

He shouldn't say yes. She was a cop. A threat.

But that thrill? That edge? He liked it.

He took another sip. "And you think I can solve that problem?"

"I think you're convenient," she said. "And you turn me on like crazy."

Callan chuckled. "And romantic, too."

"Oh, fuck off. You're looking for the love of your life. Come on!"

It was like she'd read his diary. He set down the cup, leaned forward slightly. "Well, Tricia, if you're looking for a mistake…" His smile curled. "You just found one."

Her grin was slow. Dangerous. "Good."

As they stepped into the oppressive Miami night, Diego's words echoed in his head. *This is how they get in. Through the cracks.*

Callan exhaled. He wasn't slipping. He was surrendering. And he knew the cost.

CHAPTER 17

Tricia was snoring.

Not the delicate, barely-there kind that some women made—the kind men lied about and called cute. No, this was real, unfiltered, borderline obnoxious snoring. The kind that came from needs being met, from deep exhaustion and full-on drooling sleep.

Callan lay beside her, one arm folded behind his head, staring at the ceiling.

Well. That happened.

The sheets were a mess. One of Tricia's legs was tangled in them, and her arm flung across his chest like she'd claimed territory in her sleep. Her body radiated warmth, and her breathing was steady, despite the snoring.

For all her sharp edges, her quick wit, and the way she had walked out the café earlier with that tight, controlled energy—she was out cold. Undone.

It wasn't that he'd never had women stay the night—he had. But they were usually the kind who understood the rules. The kind who left before morning. The kind who didn't stumble into what could be considered adorable territory.

And yet, here was Detective Tricia Langley, passed the fuck out in his bed, mouth open, breathing like a freight train.

A subtle smirk tugged at Callan's lips as he turned his head, studying her. She looked younger like this. Unguarded. Nothing about her now suggested the sharp detective who had been analyzing him hours earlier. No suspicion. No tension. Just sleep.

Completely at ease. He should get up. Maybe shower. Maybe clean up. Instead, he stayed where he was— watching, listening, amused.

The woman he'd been nervous about meeting for coffee was now snoring against his chest.

Callan was still smirking when a sudden thud landed at the foot of the bed—Beckett had arrived. The massive Norwegian Forest cat had finally mustered the interest to investigate the intruder in his domain. His tail flicked once, slow and deliberate, as he surveyed the scene.

Callan glanced down at him, whispering, "The hunter has caught the scent of its prey."

Beckett, naturally, ignored him. With the casual audacity only a cat could possess, he strutted up the bed, his giant paws sinking into the mattress as he approached Tricia's snoring form. He stopped just shy of her arm, head low, ears flicking—debating whether she deserved to exist in his space.

Callan sighed. "What are you going to do, old man?"

Beckett lunged forward and bit Tricia's arm.

She jerked awake with a sharp inhale, flailing as she yelped. "Ow! What the—?"

She blinked sleepily, caught between the remnants of a dream and the very real sting on her arm.

Beckett, mission accomplished, bolted off the bed like a furry little assassin. His claws scrambled against the hardwood as he vanished down the hall—leaving behind nothing but shock, betrayal, and Callan trying very hard not to laugh.

Tricia blinked, looking between Callan and the doorway where Beckett had disappeared. "Did... did your cat just attack me and run?"

Callan, still fighting amusement, reached over and inspected her arm. No blood. Just the faint impression of sharp little teeth. "He's a killer."

Tricia gawked at him. "Your cat just committed a hit-and-run."

Callan chuckled. "Beckett operates on pure spite. He'll hold a grudge now."

Tricia groaned, dropping her head back against the pillow. "Your cat is a first-rate asshole."

Callan chuckled, taking a sip of water from the glass on his nightstand. "You get used to it."

"Debatable," she muttered, rubbing her arm. She rolled over and pulled the covers over her head. Callan tugged the sheets back.

"Since you're awake," he murmured, leaning down to press his lips against hers.

***

Callan stood in the entryway of his condo, arms crossed, watching as Tricia pulled on her jacket. She moved with measured grace. No rush, no stiffness—just a woman getting dressed after a casual night with a man she barely knew.

He noticed she didn't have her cuffs or service pistol. Off duty. A compliment? It shouldn't have felt weird. He'd had casual flings before. But none that left him feeling... anchored.

Something about seeing Tricia slip out so casually made him realise he wasn't sure he wanted her to. She huffed, running her hand through her hair in the mirror. Still wearing the T-shirt she borrowed from him, her own top stuffed into her handbag. "Well. That was unexpected."

Callan tilted his head, smirking. "The part where Beckett tried to assassinate you, or the part where you fell asleep mid-snore?"

She narrowed her eyes. "I do *not* snore."

"Tricia. You sounded like a chainsaw with intimacy issues."

She barked a laugh, rolling her eyes. "Oh, okay, well, this was fun. Never doing it again."

"Uh-huh." He didn't move from his spot, watching her adjust her coat collar. It was a normal moment, and that was what unsettled him. It shouldn't *feel* normal.

She glanced at the door. "All right, then." No awkwardness. No hesitant glances. Just a clean, casual exit.

And somehow, that made it worse.

He stepped aside, opening the door. "Stride of pride?" he asked dryly.

She grinned as she stepped past him. "Damn right."

He was already closing the door when—

"Shit."

Callan stopped. Door still half-open, he saw her patting her pockets with a sigh. "I left my keys."

Of course she did.

He shook his head. "This is the worst walk of shame I've ever seen."

"It's only shameful if you make it weird," she shot back, breezing past him like she owned the place. She grabbed her keys off the counter, fingers pausing for just a second—like she was committing the layout to memory.

Then she was all smirk and stride again. "Okay, *now* I'm leaving." She gave him a crooked grin as she passed. "I always find what I'm looking for. Eventually."

Callan gestured to the door. "Sure you got everything this time?"

"Unless your cat swiped something, yeah." She lingered just a second longer than necessary, then tucked her keys into her pocket. "I'll see you around, Callan."

He nodded. She turned and walked out. This time, he shut the door behind her.

Silence.

Callan let out a slow breath, rolling his shoulders. Too easy. Too normal. It was just sex. Just another night. She hadn't made it weird. Hadn't treated him like anything special.

So why was he standing there like an idiot, staring at the closed door?

A heavy thump landed on the counter behind him.

The massive furry blob sat there, tail flicking lazily, golden-green eyes locked on Callan like he was judging every single life choice he'd ever made.

Callan muttered, "Don't start."

Beckett stared harder.

Message received, the cat stretched, flicked his tail once more, then hopped down and trotted toward the bedroom. Judgement delivered.

Callan sighed, rubbing a hand over his jaw. This was nothing. Just another morning. No different from any other.

He made his way to the bathroom. And there it was.

A single silver earring sitting on the sink. He stared at it. Too long. Too aware.

If it was just sex, why did her earring feel like a relic?

She could've stayed. That's what scared him. Attachment meant expectations. Expectations meant he couldn't do what he needed to survive.

He picked it up and shoved it into the drawer. Shut it like he could erase the morning in one motion.

He turned on the shower, letting the water drown out everything else.

Time to forget about it. He was back to work on Monday. But before he pulled the target package, he wanted to find out who Dwayne was.

***

By the time Callan had dressed, finished half his coffee, and shooed Beckett off the counter, he was booting up the laptop—the unmarked one running a custom OS most people would never see.

A few keystrokes later, he was bouncing through a secure VPN across multiple countries.

Welcome back, Lucian. The alias wasn't real. But to the right people? It might as well be. Callan bypassed the usual interface and dove to a deeper layer—into an encrypted database used by assassins, fixers, and information brokers. He typed in the name Dwayne Callister.

A hit.

Data scrolled fast—black-market repositories, law enforcement leaks, deep web intel circles.

Five possibles. He skimmed. Eyes narrowed on the last entry.

No official records past 2018. Flagged file.

Real name: Redacted

Military: redacted—except for Special Ops.

Callan blinked. Fucking figures.

It got worse. Redacted missions. Jiu-jitsu champ. Counterintelligence.

Prague. Berlin. Toronto.

Status: Alive.

Location: Unknown.

One grainy photo. But definitely Dwayne.

Callan leaned back, breathing deep. "Fuck me. I'm lucky to be alive."

Men like Dwayne weren't just dangerous. They were *hardened*. Unpredictable. Ghosts made of scars.

He sipped his coffee, thinking how often he'd dodged death. It wasn't just luck. Skill and caution mattered. Still, all it took was a half-second slip, and he'd be a memory.

More digging showed Dwayne in commercial real estate now. Three kids. Wife named Lydia. Tricia's story checked out.

But men like Dwayne didn't forget.

Callan closed the search window. Not relevant yet.

He had other priorities—a contract to review, logistics to plan, and a life to compartmentalize before it unravelled at the seams.

Encrypted inbox. New contract. No sender. Just coordinates, a profile, standard kill parameters.

Name: Lois Grafton.

Hawk-faced in her mugshot. Ex-cult. Kidnapped and tortured a girl with her husband, flipped for a reduced sentence. He got shanked. She walked free.

Callan raised an eyebrow. Request came from Diego—his handler. Rare. Odd. New York City. Plane ride. Plan.

He chuckled, startling Beckett. "Sorry, old boy."

He scanned more. Trash target. Still—something felt off. His brain shifted into gear. Timing. Strategy. Execution.

Heading to the bedroom, he caught it again.

Her perfume. Faint. Still there. Her heat. Her breath.

His fingers tensed. A smile pulled—then faded.
No time for distractions. No time for fantasies.

Chapter 18

Callan held the phone to his ear, half-listening as he scanned the sea of people going about their lives at Miami International Airport.

"Vegas?" Isabelle's voice rang with bright exasperation. "You *hate* Vegas. It's, like... the spiritual opposite of you."

"Yeah, well, it's convenient," he said, rolling his shoulder to ease a lingering ache—a reminder of earlier scuffles.

Not entirely a lie. Vegas was a revolving door of tourists, high-rollers, and people pretending to be someone else for a weekend. Perfect for disappearing. He'd flown in under one identity and would fly out under another—this time to Pittsburgh—before picking up a rental car for the drive into New York. No direct flights that tied him to his final destination.

His handler's network took care of the logistics: Fake passports, cover stories, seedy rental shops with knowing winks. Callan just followed the script, moving like a shadow.

"You ever think about a trip that isn't *work*-related?" Isabelle forged on, oblivious to his silence. "Something to actually feed your soul? There's this place in Sedona—"

"I'm not really the 'group meditation and vegan brunch' type."

"That's exactly why you need it!" she pressed. "You're trapped in this weird, closed-off energy field. A few days with a shaman would change your life."

"Or I'd punch the shaman and get banned from Sedona."

She gasped. "That's so unenlightened. Have you even tried breathwork? Cacao ceremonies?"

Callan sighed. "I eat chocolate. Does that count?"

"Ugh, Callan." She made a sound like physical pain. "Fine, ignore my wisdom. But seriously... maybe do something that doesn't involve a body count?"

He almost laughed. *Almost.* Isabelle had touched on a double entendre without realising.

"Just don't disappear on me, okay?" Her voice softened, concern creeping in.

Callan exhaled, rubbing the growing knot of tension at his neck. "I won't."

A lie, because he always did.

There was a pause before Isabelle cleared her throat. "I ran into Maggie's sister again."

Callan's grip tightened on the phone. A flicker of memory: Kevin clawing at his neck, realization coming too late. He shoved it down.

Guilt twisted in his gut. Isabelle didn't know he was behind Kevin's death—had no clue Kevin's last moments were anything but random. Kevin had deserved it—sure—but part of Callan still bristled at how much he'd savoured the kill.

"Some things don't have answers," he said quietly.

"I guess," Isabelle murmured. "But they should."

He didn't respond.

"Anyway," she went on, cheer forced now, "I should let you go before you miss your flight. Not that I know where you're *really* going."

"Vegas," Callan repeated, smirking a little. "My spiritual opposite."

"And yet, somehow, still full of people exactly like you." Her tone warmed. "Talk soon, Callan."

He hesitated, love for her hovering on the tip of his tongue, unspoken. "Yeah. Sure."

And then—*Tricia.* Isabelle's voice had nudged something. The memory rose unbidden: Tangled sheets, the soft snore, warmth he hadn't expected to miss.

She hung up. Callan stood at the terminal entrance for a second longer, then popped the SIM card from his phone and flicked it into a nearby trash bin. The soft plink against crumpled coffee cups sealed it: Another identity gone. A clean break—the only kind that mattered.

Shifting his bag, he clenched his sore shoulder again. Too many close calls lately. But no time to dwell.

He had a flight to catch. From Pittsburgh, he'd drive a rental car into NYC. Another job. No more distractions.

***

Callan pulled up to The Lexington Grand, easing the rental into the valet lane. The gold-lettered sign promised luxury, but the place exuded corporate blandness—an illusion for business travellers and weekend tourists.

He rolled down the window as the valet, a wiry kid named Ricky, stepped up.

"Checking in, Mr. *Bill Smith*?" the kid read off the slip, snorting. "Man, that's gotta be fake."

Callan smirked, passing him the keys. "What gave it away?"

"Too few syllables."

Callan grabbed his duffel and stepped onto the sidewalk. He headed toward the entrance—then paused. Something across the street caught his eye.

A cramped storefront wedged between a deli and a pawnshop, its window crammed with antiques, trinkets, and handmade jewellery. Isabelle's words nagged at him. Something about feeding his soul.

Utter nonsense.

He turned back toward the hotel, shutting down the persistent pull in his chest.

Time to work.

***

Lois Grafton lived in Brooklyn.

Not the gentrified, overpriced-loft Brooklyn—the old Brooklyn, where minding your own business wasn't apathy; it was survival. She didn't hide who she was or what she had done.

That, more than anything, infuriated Callan.

Her name was public record. Her crimes were all over the internet—five minutes and a Google search away. Yet here she was, walking free. A twisted plea deal, a mockery of justice. Her ex-husband got gutted in a prison shower. She got a rent-controlled brownstone, likely funded by whatever blood money she stashed before her arrest.

She had a security system. Rudimentary, according to the file. But it was the invisible barrier of fear that kept neighbours from asking questions. She wasn't worried about revenge. But her neighbours knew.

Callan saw it in their body language—how they crossed the street when she walked by, how doors shut a bit faster, how the barista at the corner café kept things short and polite.

In a city full of monsters, she was something worse.

Untouchable.

But not to him.

From his parked car half a block down, Callan watched her brownstone. Lights on. Curtains drawn. The street was quiet but not deserted— enough passing traffic to blend in, not enough to complicate things.

He'd been watching for a couple of days. No visitors. No real movement except the occasional shadow behind the curtains. Lois was comfortable. Too comfortable. And that made him uneasy.

He started the engine and pulled away slowly. As he drove past her home, a twitch of movement caught his eye—just a flicker behind the curtain. Too fast to clock. He slowed, watching.

Nothing now. Maybe a shadow. Maybe not.

He'd be back later—once the city's shadows deepened and people stopped pretending to care.

According to Diego's dossier, Lois had a habit: She hit a grimy dive bar most nights to play video lottery terminals, returning around closing time.

That gave him a window.

CHAPTER 19

Hours later, the brownstone looked the same—silent and undisturbed. Yet, the air felt heavier now, like the world was holding its breath.

Callan approached on foot, moving like he belonged. Measured pace. A shadow among shadows. He passed the row of brownstones, then doubled back once he was sure no one was watching.

The security system was easy. He tapped into the external control box under the eaves, spliced the signal line, and looped the feed. A soft click confirmed the bypass. The lock, though—top-of-the-line, reinforced—took minutes to pick. Longer than he liked.

He slipped inside, pulling on a balaclava as he shut the door behind him.

Dark, stagnant air. The house reeked of old carpet, rancid sweat, and neglect. He stood still, letting his eyes adjust. Listening. Fridge hum. Distant city rumble. A leaky faucet dripping.

Less than an hour before Lois would return. Enough to scope the place, choose his spot, and wait.

Then—A floorboard creaked from the back of the house.

A voice called out warbly and unsteady, "Lois? You're back early."

He froze—but only for a breath. His body was already shifting, adapting.

What the fuck?

The dossier hadn't mentioned anyone else. No roommates. No visitors. A variable he hadn't accounted for.

"Lois?"

He moved toward the voice, quiet as a breath. Rounded a corner.

An old man sat slouched in a recliner--late sixties, maybe older. Thinning hair, stained undershirt, sagging sweatpants. He looked soft. Faded. His eyes squinted up.

"Who the hell—"

Callan was behind him in a flash, arm locked around his throat. The man struggled weakly, then went limp.

He pulled out his work phone, snapped a photo, and sent it.

A buzz: *Harold Finch. Registered sex offender. Ten years for child exploitation. Out early on good behaviour. Cult ties. In the dossier.*

A chill ran up his spine. How the hell had he missed this? He crouched. Studied the man's slack face. A cockroach in human skin. Finch stirred. Groaned.

Callan zip-tied his wrists tight. Finch blinked up, confused.

"Who are you?" he slurred.

"I'm here for Lois. You were in the wrong place, Harold."

Callan patted him down—flip phone, some crumpled bills, tattered license matching the brownstone's address. He'd wasted precious time tonight—thinking of Tricia, of distractions.

Finch blinked again. "Please. I didn't see your face. I can keep quiet."

Technically true. But Harold was a predator. Parole hadn't reformed him. And Callan didn't leave loose ends.

He drew his Walther P22. Screwed on the suppressor.

"Please…"

He hesitated for less than a second.

Phfft.

The bullet punched into Finch's forehead. Head jerked. Body slumped.

No grim satisfaction. Just a necessary equation. *All pays the same*, he thought, but the joke landed flat. Then—keys jangled at the front door.

Shit

"Harold, I won big tonight and bought us Chinese food," came Lois's voice.

He hadn't relocked the front door.

She moved through the house, casual. Keys, rustling bags, fridge clunk.

Noise. Good.

He moved fast but silent, using her movement to mask his own. He slid into the shadows of the hall between the front and back of the house. Waited. Listened. Then pivoted into the kitchen.

Not a tired old woman.

A demon. Holding a shotgun.

No thought. Just movement. He dropped low.

Boom. The shotgun blast shredded the air where his torso had been. Drywall exploded. Cabinets rattled.

He rolled behind the island. Lois racked another shell.

Where the fuck had she been hiding that?

Still no panic. But this was a mess.

One shotgun. Twelve feet. Limited cover. Compromised weapon at range.

She moved with purpose. No fear. No hesitation. "You think I wouldn't be ready?" she spat—nothing like her tone with Harold. This was feral.

Another blind shot.

Boom.

Splinters sliced his arm. Close.

She moved in.

He surged to meet her. Forward. Fast.

Everything slowed.

Her pupils—blown wide. Powder burns on her hands. Her stance too aggressive. Too sure of herself.

He crashed into her hard. They hit the floor. The shotgun skittered.

She clawed at his face. He drove his elbow into her throat.

A choked gasp. A second strike. She gagged, still fighting.

Her knee found his already tender ribs. Pain bloomed white-hot. His grip slipped.

She rolled free. One arm swung wildly.

He barely dodged, but a miss is a miss.

His left hand clamped onto her wrist as he pressed the Walther under her chin. She grinned. "Do it, cunt. You're not the first. They all think they're the last." She laughed.

So, he pulled the trigger.

Phfft.

She stiffened, grin still frozen. Then crumpled.

Blood pooled, thick and dark.

He exhaled. Slow. Controlled.

Shit.

Ribs throbbed. Arms burned. But he was alive.

And she wasn't.

He listened.

No sirens. Yet. He scanned the room. Clean. Shells loaded by the quartermaster. No prints. But still a mess.

Dead cultist in the kitchen. Shotgun blast through the wall. Time was ticking. He looked down at her twisted face. Still grinning.

It stirred something. Fear? Respect? He couldn't afford to know.

Out the back. He crossed the kitchen. Silence. Listened again. Nothing. He slipped out the door. Three strides to the back gate—and ran straight into a kid.

Shit.

Teenager in a hoodie. Maybe sixteen? Eyes wide.

He saw too much.

The kid sucked in a breath. About to shout—

Callan yanked him into the yard. Seconds mattered. He needed to get on the move.

He ducked behind the kid and choked him out.

Ten seconds.

The kid sagged in his arms

Puerto Rican or Dominican. Cheap earbuds. Smelled like weed. No threat.

He hadn't seen Callan's face—thanks to the mask.

He let him drop gently. Alive.

This time, he exited smarter. A clear alley.

Sirens now. Distant. But moving.

He sprinted south—opposite the noise. Slipped into another alley. Tore off the mask. Slowed. Breathed.

A clusterfuck of a night. But he wasn't caught. Not yet.

He emerged onto the street, hoodie zipped, pace casual.

Just another ghost in the city that never sleeps.

Chapter 20

Callan tipped the cab driver and eased out onto the sidewalk. His ribs still ached from the earlier scuffle—every step a reminder he wasn't twenty-five anymore.

A dive bar loomed ahead, the kind that had never passed a health inspection. A flickering neon sign promised *Cold Beer,* barely piercing the film of dust on the window.

A man stood outside, smoking. Dark-skinned, broad-shouldered, posture relaxed but deliberate. He locked eyes with Callan, exhaled a slow stream of smoke, and flicked the butt into the gutter. "Lucian," he said.

Rough voice. East London accent, if Callan had to guess.

Callan didn't flinch at the alias—just noted the test. "Yes."

The man studied him a moment, then turned and pushed open the bar door. "Come," he grunted.

Callan followed.

The bar smelled of stale beer, cheap whiskey, and too many college parties. Sweat and weed clung to the walls. Lighting was low—more necessity than ambiance. A jukebox in the corner played a blues track so worn it sounded underwater.

A handful of patrons hunched over drinks, heads down. Privacy wasn't just expected here—it was enforced.

Callan trailed the man across the sticky floors. The bartender glanced up, then back to an ancient TV. They slipped past a narrow hallway into the kitchen. The air shifted, from sour to hot grease and raw meat. A cook in a stained apron chopped onions like a machine. Steam hissed from a pot. Metal clanged somewhere beyond.

They weaved through the cramped space to a walk-in freezer. The Brit turned, drew a 1911 pistol from a pancake holster, and pointed at a face scanner beside the door.

"Red is dead," Callan said. The scanner beeped green. ID confirmed.

Inside, metal shelves lined with frozen meat hummed under the compressor. The man reached behind one shelf, pressed something, and a faint click echoed. A panel at the back of the freezer swung open, revealing a dim corridor. He stepped through.

Callan hesitated a beat, eyeing the frozen slabs of meat, then followed. The door shut behind them with a solid *thunk*.

The passage was narrow—bare concrete—cold, damp, and utilitarian. Overhead lights buzzed softly, casting long shadows. Then the air changed.

Gone was the musty chill of the freezer. Replaced by a crisp, filtered sterility. Clinical. Reassuring. This wasn't a hideout—it was a top-tier medical facility.

At the end of the passage, the man tapped a panel. A soft hiss, then a reinforced door slid open. Inside were pristine floors, white walls, surgical lights. Stainless steel tables arranged with the precision of a morgue. Some held tools. Others nothing.

Callan's eyes shifted to an operating station with an adjustable surgical chair. Nearby, a rolling cart held scalpels, syringes, bone saws—all perfectly arranged. Cold. professional. Diego's signature.

A woman in scrubs adjusted an IV without looking up. Across the room, a man in a lab coat flipped through a digital chart, expression unreadable.

Callan finally broke the silence. "This is one hell of a setup for a bar with piss-stained floors."

His guide stepped aside.

From an adjoining room, a silver-haired man in his fifties emerged. Tailored suit. Calm authority.

"Lucian," he said smoothly. "Welcome. Let's begin."

Callan settled onto the medical bed. The doctor got to work: Antiseptic on cuts, pressure on bruised ribs. Nothing life-threatening, just cleanup. Patch and prep.

Once done, the nurse led him down a short hall to a plain room with a shower. "There's soap, towels, everything you need inside," she said in a clipped New York accent.

Callan didn't argue. He stripped off his bloodstained shirt and stepped under the hot spray, letting the water erase the night. This wasn't comfort. It was routine. Maintenance.

Diego's philosophy was simple: Fix the damage, erase the traces, keep the asset running.

Callan ran a hand through his hair, watching the water swirl red, then clear. When he stepped out, he dried off quickly and dressed in clean, functional clothes: Black slacks, a dark grey T-shirt, lightweight hoodie. As he exited, the nurse gave him a once-over and nodded.

The ride back to the hotel was silent. City lights blurred past, neon and shadow. His body ached deep—bone-tired— but it was a familiar exhaustion. The aftermath of a job. A fight. Survival.

He checked his burner. No messages. Good.

When the cab pulled up to his hotel, he paid and stepped out without looking back. The lobby was empty. The concierge didn't glance up.

Back in his room, Callan dropped the hoodie onto a chair and collapsed onto the bed, not bothering with the covers.

His flight was tomorrow evening.

For now, he'd rest.

Chapter 21

Callan eased the car between a dented sedan with mismatched doors and a grille-less minivan in the lot of EZ Auto Rentals. The place looked even sketchier in the daylight—a tired front for a business that had long since stopped pretending to care. A sun-bleached sign over the door read *EZ Auto Rentals–Best Rates, No Questions.* In Callan's experience, that meant: *Return it with bullet holes—just pay cash.*

He killed the engine, stretched his sore shoulder, and stepped out. As expected, the guy behind the front desk had a greasy ponytail, stained tank top, and skin untouched by sunlight since the MTV era. He barely looked up from his phone. "You returning?"

"No, came back to visit." Callan tossed the keys on the counter.

Ponytail Guy blinked, unimpressed. "You fill the tank?"

"Yeah."

"Full?"

"Yeah."

"Full full?"

Callan stared at him.

Ponytail Guy leaned over and eyed the keys like they might bite. "Lemme check the car."

Callan tapped his fingers as the guy shuffled outside, clearly dragging it out, looking for mystery scratches, invisible dents, or bad vibes he could upcharge. After a slow lap, he meandered back in, still chewing a toothpick.

"Looks fine," he said, like it physically pained him to say it.

Callan nodded, exchanged a few deadpan pleasantries, and left. It was a short walk to the airport shuttle.

***

Pittsburgh International Airport was easy enough to navigate. Callan stood in the security line, bored and phone-less after ditching the burner last night.

Security was a breeze. Make TSA's job easy, they make your life easy. Start yelling, and you're asking for a colonoscopy with a flashlight.

He'd barely settled into his aisle seat on the flight to Miami when someone lost a battle with their stomach. A still-drunk frat boy—red-faced, reeking of last night's tequila—was hunched over, retching onto the aisle floor like his body had finally rejected every bad decision he'd ever made.

Callan watched the mess spread. It felt about right—like the Grafton job. He closed his eyes and slept through the flight.

***

Callan's passage through Miami International blurred past on autopilot. Taxi line, curb, back seat. No chatty driver, no talk radio—just the steady hum of tires on asphalt and the city lights slipping by.

He rested his head against the window. His body ached in that deep, post-job kind of way—bone-tired and familiar.

The job hadn't gone clean, but he wasn't burned. No orders to leave town. No loose ends, or at least none that mattered. Still, something clung to him—an itch he couldn't scratch. Maybe it was just the ribs.

Didn't matter. He needed a shower, a real bed, and a few hours pretending to be just another guy with a mortgage and an overpriced coffee habit.

When the cab pulled up to his building, Callan left without waiting for change and stepped into the crisp night air. The city felt still. Most found that unsettling. He found it calming. Fewer variables.

The elevator was empty. His muscles protested as he reached his floor. Then something felt off.

The condo was dark. Too dark. And silent.

He flipped on a light. Nothing out of place—everything as he'd left it. Pristine. Minimal.

Except for Beckett.

The massive Norwegian Forest cat usually greeted him within seconds, all attitude and silent demands. But tonight? Nothing.

"Beckett?" Callan called, frowning.

Silence.

His gaze swept the room. Empty. Then something caught his eye. The hallway closet—slightly ajar, a sliver of shadow showing through.

He eased it open.

Beckett was curled on a pile of winter coats in the back, green-gold eyes blinking slowly, head tucked. Just... hiding.

Callan crouched. "Why're you hiding, boyo?"

The cat shifted but didn't move toward him. No tail flick. No meow. Just a tired blink.

Callan reached in, scooped him up. Beckett didn't resist, just let himself be carried to the couch, heavier than usual.

He swapped SIM cards in his phone. It lit up instantly—messages, notifications. One from Lucy, his cat sitter. Six-foot wrestler on a scholarship, a rich Midwestern ranch kid, lived a few doors down. Not the usual cat person, but dead serious about the gig.

Lucy: Hey,—Beckett wasn't eating much while u were gone. Nothing major, but he seemed off. Hope your trip went well! :)

Callan scratched Beckett behind the ears. "You mad at me, old man?"

A weak purr. No movement.

"You picking up my bad habits, huh?" he murmured. "We both suck at asking for help."

Beckett flicked an ear but stayed quiet.

Callan got up, opened a can of food. The familiar clatter usually brought Beckett trotting over. Not tonight.

Beckett glanced at the sound. That was it.

Eventually, he dragged himself over, took a few slow, mechanical bites, then wandered back to Callans' side and curled up again.

"All right. We'll keep an eye on you," Callan said quietly, hand on soft fur.

***

His phone buzzed. *Isabelle: Are you alive?*

Then, sometime later. *I'm assuming yes, since I haven't had a vision of you in the afterlife. But, like... text back, asshole.*

Callan smirked.

Callan: Barely. Woke up in Vegas married to a woman named Destiny. It's unclear if she's a stripper or a financial analyst.

Instantly, Isabelle: God, I hope she's real. And I hope she takes you for everything. Call me later, loser.

Same old Isabelle.

Ellen: Oh, don't worry about me. I'm FINE. Just sitting here, reflecting on my life and the fact that I NEARLY DIED, but it's cool, Callan. I don't need a text back. I'll just be here. Probably needing therapy, but it's fine. It's FINE.

Callan exhaled.

Callan: You? Therapy? That poor bastard has no idea what's coming.

Ellen: LMAO you're deflecting, but okay, I'll allow it. You owe me dinner.

Callan: Fine. Pick a place with "deconstructed" food again and I'm walking into traffic.

Ellen: Fair. Italian?

Callan: Done.

Settled. Then came Tricia.

Tricia: Heard you were back. Not sure if I should say "welcome home" or "good luck."

No demand. Just presence.

Callan: Why not both?

No reply.

He set the phone down. Beckett stirred, paws heavy across his thigh like an anchor. Buzz.

Tricia: Hey you.

Callan: Hey back.

Typing. Gone. Back again.

Callan: Spit it out, lol.

Silence. Then--

Tricia: I miss you.

His breath hitched. "Jesus Christ."

He didn't reply.

The phone sat untouched for a full minute.

Three.

Buzz.

Tricia: Sorry, that was stupid. Pretend I didn't send it.

The first message had been a whisper.

This one—a retreat.

He was starting to recognize the pattern.

CHAPTER 22

Three simple words. They felt strange. Foreign. Like something borrowed, not earned. He should have seen it coming. Should've known things with Tricia weren't finished. Should he have deflected, made a joke—just like always?

But this time, he didn't.

He sat there, phone in hand, his mind blank, voice silent. That didn't happen often. Beside him, Beckett shifted, letting out a rumbling sigh—sensing the weight of Callan's hesitation.

He let out a slow breath. Fingers hovered over the screen. Every instinct said: Wait. Calculate. Disengage. Instead, in a rare moment of tired vulnerability, he chose truth.

Callan: I miss you too.

He hit send before he could overthink it. Something tightened in his chest, then eased.

A beat later, he typed again. *Callan: Dinner this week?*

The chat bubble appeared, vanished, came back.

Tricia: Yeah. I'd like that.

Callan stared at the message, something unspoken settling beneath the ache in his ribs. For once, he didn't want to run from it. He stood and headed for the bedroom, Beckett followed, silent and steady—like a witness to something neither of them would say aloud.

Chapter 23

The mattress curved to his body like a lover, exhaustion dragging him under the second his eyes closed. At first, there was nothing—just the heavy, blissful pull of sleep.

But then, as too often happened lately, a thought of Diego slipped through—and the past clawed its way back in.

***

Twenty years earlier...

His wrists ached from the cuffs, raw and bruised where metal bit into skin. His shoulders burned from hours—maybe days—of restraint. His ribs pulsed with the dull throb of too many hits.

But Callan stayed silent.

A single bulb flickered above, casting warped shadows across damp concrete walls. Somewhere, water dripped. The air was cold. Stale with blood and sweat.

Across from him sat the man in the suit—calm, composed, patient.

Men like that never rushed. They waited until they were sure.

"You're a blunt instrument," the man said, tone mild. "Precise, yes. But still a tool. Tools don't decide. They serve."

Callan said nothing.

The man sighed, almost disappointed. "You killed Grant Hathaway."

No flinch. No denial. That name wasn't public. Which meant this wasn't intimidation. It was leverage.

"You thought he was just another Wall Street parasite. But Hathaway didn't just steal from rich men. He stole from the cartel."

So that was it.

"You killed him before we got our money back. Before we could ask the right questions."

Callan shifted against his restraints, the cuffs biting deeper. "So, you're pissed I was faster?"

A sharp jab to the kidneys from behind sent fire through his spine. His knees buckled, but he didn't cry out.

The man stood, adjusted his cuffs, then turned toward the shadows. "You should be dead," said Diego.

Callan met his gaze. Pulse steady. Calculating.

"But I don't waste good talent," Diego continued.

Ah, Callan thought. Not an interrogation. A test.

Diego had been sent to recover the money—and kill Hathaway. Callan had gotten there first. Instead of being angry, Diego was impressed.

That was why Callan was still breathing.

"You're disciplined. Smooth. Calm."

Callan licked the blood from his lip. "You offering a performance review?"

A twitch of a smirk. "I'm offering a career."

The room stilled. A beat passed.

"You work alone because you don't trust anyone. That's not always bad. But it makes you predictable."

Callan arched a brow. "So, you're here to fix me?"

"No. I'm here to make you better."

Callan didn't blink.

"You can say no," Diego said. "I'll even let you walk out of here. But you and I both know you won't get far. There's always someone out there who'll find you more useful dead than alive."

A slow exhale.

"Or... you work with me."

The weight of the offer settled between them. Callan's ribs ached. His head spun. But one thing was clear. He looked Diego in the eye.

"Where do we start?"

Diego smirked. "Good choice." He stood.

And just like that, the memory dissolved.

***

Callan's eyes snapped open. His breath was steady, but his chest was tight, muscles coiled from something long past.

Twenty years. And still, Diego's voice echoed in his head.

Beside him, Beckett stirred, flicking his tail in sleepy irritation.

Chapter 24

Callan smiled as he watched the small twitches of Beckett's paws, his whiskers flicking like he was chasing a mouse—or maybe just a rogue dust bunny. Not exactly the most ambitious hunter. Callan let his hand rest on the cat's back, feeling the steady rise and fall of his breath. It was as good a reason as any to stay in bed. A perfectly valid excuse.

He sank deeper into the pillow, eyes fixed on the ceiling. Nothing pressing. No job. No obligations. Just silence settling over the apartment, like a wool blanket, thick and heavy weight, making movement feel unnecessary.

Still, that nagging unease lingered—ever since his last conversation with Isabelle. He hadn't reached out. Neither had she. Maybe that was for the best, but it left a small, unshakeable itch at the back of his skull. Or maybe it was his ribs, still sore from New York.

Beckett let out a tiny, startled chirp in his sleep, one leg kicking out. Callan huffed a silent laugh and rubbed his face, like he could scrub away the thought.

"You got it, bud."

Eventually, he sat up. Just for a beat. Then pushed himself to his feet.

Beckett blinked awake, stretched out like a spoiled prince, then hopped down after him, tail held high.

In the kitchen, Callan flipped on the coffeemaker out of habit. As it gurgled, he leaned against the counter and let his gaze drift across the room.

The dream about Diego wasn't new. It had surfaced before—once with rage. Now it felt distant. Like watching an old, grainy film reel through someone else's eyes.

But something still felt off. A subtle itch beneath the morning routine. The coffeemaker gurgled, its hum mingling with his slow, deliberate breaths. Callan exhaled and rolled his shoulders, trying to shrug it off. Maybe it was nothing. Or maybe it was everything—too many quiet days, too much time to think. He poured a mug, added a splash of cream, and watched the swirl dissolve.

Beckett leapt onto the counter, stretched, then collapsed next to the mug, tail flicking. His unblinking golden-green eyes studied Callan, with that unnerving feline judgement.

Callan scratched behind his ears. "Don't look at me like that. I'm fine."

Beckett blinked once. Unimpressed. Then, without warning, swiped a paw and knocked the mug off the counter.

Crash. Ceramic shards. Spreading coffee.

"The fuck?" he muttered.

Beckett let out a sharp, high-pitched meow—absurd coming from something his size.

Callan sighed and dragged a hand through his hair.

"I fucked up in New York. All because I've been preoccupied. With Tricia," he admitted softly.

The cat flicked his tail. *Finally, he gets it.*

Callan crouched to clean up, grabbing paper towels, his movements slow and distracted. The words had slipped out too easily.

New York. Tricia.

He hadn't let himself to dwell on it—what it meant, what it said about him. About how easy it had been to play at normal. That terrified him.

You are unattached... Diego's voice again. His subconscious, reminding him what he had to lose?

He should've been sharper. More in control. But he'd let himself get soft. Comfortable. His grip tightened on the paper towel.

That wasn't who he was.

And yet... the quiet mornings, the easy rhythm, the mundane rituals—they'd fit him more naturally than he liked to admit. Maybe that was the worst part.

He'd always believed he was built for something else. That normal wasn't an option. But New York had proven him wrong.

Beckett let out a grumpy little meow, dragging him back.

"Yeah," Callan said, tossing the towels into the trash. "I know." He braced both hands on the counter. Exhaled.

This wasn't a crisis. Just a reckoning. Slipping into normalcy didn't mean he belonged there.

It just meant he'd lost focus.

CHAPTER 25

With his grip adjusted on the dumbbells, Callan cranked out the money reps. Breath steady, settling into a rhythm. His ribs still ached from New York—deep, pulsing reminders of his own mistakes—but he wasn't about to let that slow him down.

Light workout today. Nothing fancy. Dumbbell squats, just enough to keep the blood moving. Short, controlled bursts. Power through, then recover. No ego lifts, no reckless reps. Discipline wasn't just about knowing when to hit—it was knowing when *not* to.

The gym was quiet at this hour. A few early risers scattered across machines, the low hum of treadmills filling the space. No posturing. No noise. Just people getting their work in.

Racking his dumbbells, he moved to the rower. A light endurance session. The resistance felt good. Controlled. He focused on the movement—legs, core, pull. Fluid. Efficient. Not just exercise— *maintenance.* His body was a machine. Machines needed upkeep.

The rower next to him wasn't empty.

A man, mid-fifties, maybe early sixties, moved with patient precision. Wiry build, deep tan, the kind of body you only got from a life spent outdoors.

After a few minutes, the man glanced over. "You train regular?" he asked, barely winded.

Callan smirked. "Only when I have to."

The man chuckled. "Same. My knees hate running, so here I am." Another stroke. Deliberate. "You from around here?"

"Moved down a while ago," Callan said, keeping his breath even.

"Yeah? What brought you to Miami?"

He exhaled. Could've said business. Weather. Could've said nothing. Instead, he went with the truth.

"Fishing."

The man lit up. "Now *that's* a damn good reason. Name's Mel."

"Callan." A nod. "Been looking into charters," Callan added. "Something out of Biscayne."

Mel's eyes sharpened. "My boy runs a boat down there. Deep-sea. Serious gear. No bachelor-party bullshit. He takes people who actually want to catch something."

Callan arched a brow. "Danny, right?"

Mel blinked, then grinned. "Yeah. You heard of him?"

"Was already on my list."

Mel looked him over with a little more respect. "Then you'll get along just fine. Tell him I sent you. He'll knock a hundred off if you don't puke or embarrass yourself."

"I'll try not to ruin the family name."

Mel chuckled and rowed on, like the conversation had never happened.

Callan left the gym twenty minutes later, already pulling up the charter's info again. It wasn't really coincidence. Biscayne Bay was Tricia's turf. The fishing was excellent—sport-level, some deep-sea excursions. He'd done his research.

Fishing made sense. The patience. The silence. The stillness before the fight. No distractions. No noise. Just the waiting.

And when the moment came? You either set the hook, or you lost the fish.

Simple.

He called the number. Booked a trip for the following morning.

***

Callan was up before the sun. The city hadn't quite woken. Streets damp with humidity, streetlights flickering against asphalt. Miami was different before dawn—briefly quiet before the chaos of the day. He liked it.

Dressed in a fitted long-sleeve fishing shirt, lightweight cargo shorts, and his well-worn cap, he tossed a small duffel bag into the passenger seat of his Mazda. Sunscreen. Sunglasses. Phone. Wallet. Essentials.

The drive to Biscayne Bay Marina was smooth. Sparse traffic. The kind that made the city feel hollow and open. As he pulled into the lot, the scent of saltwater hit—crisp and clean, mixed with diesel and bait.

The marina was already alive with early risers—fishermen loading gear, deckhands prepping lines. No loud voices. Just the rhythm of the early hours and people who *worked*.

He spotted Mel easily, standing at a slip, talking to a younger man—Danny, no doubt. Mel waved him over, grin already in place. "Figured you weren't the type to flake."

"Not my style," Callan said, stepping onto the dock. "Besides—you've got my credit card info."

The younger man turned. Mid-thirties, stocky. Built like someone who moved heavy things for a living. His handshake was strong, but he didn't overdo it. Callan respected that.

"You must be Callan," he said. "I'm Danny. My old man says you know what you're doing."

"We'll see."

Danny grinned. "Hope you're not a freshwater guy. We're going deep. Good report on some Mahi running offshore."

Perfect.

Callan stepped onto the boat, inhaling deeply—salt, fuel, and the faint metallic scent of wet line and tackle. It smelled like every good morning on the water. The boat was clean, well-kept. Thirty-two feet. Twin outboards. Solid rig. Danny untied the dock lines. Mel settled into a seat near the helm.

"You need anything before we head out?" Danny asked.

Callan shook his head. "I'm good."

Danny nodded. "Then let's go catch something."

The engines rumbled to life—a deep, steady hum that vibrated through Callan's chest. As they pulled away from the dock, the city shrank behind them—skyline dissolving into the horizon.

Callan leaned on the rail, eyes on the fading land.

He'd forgotten how easy it was to breathe out here.

CHAPTER 26

The boat cut through the water like a blade, the early morning sun just starting to burn off the mist that clung to the surface. The scent of salt and fuel filled the air, mingling with the rhythmic slap of waves against the hull. Callan stood near the stern, hands loose at his sides, body relaxed in a way it hadn't been in weeks.

Danny steered them toward deeper water, past the last markers of civilization, until nothing remained but sky and sea. The Miami skyline had long since vanished behind them. Just the three of them now—Danny at the helm, Mel setting up the rigs, and Callan sinking into the boat's slow, hypnotic rhythm.

It had been a while since he'd done this. Too long.

The radio crackled with weather updates, but otherwise... Callan appreciated that. No forced small talk. No filler. Just the hum of the engines and the cry of a gull overhead.

"All right, this is the spot," Danny said, cutting the engines.

The sudden quiet was jarring, but Callan welcomed it. The ocean stretched in all directions—pure, endless blue.

The boat eased into a slow troll. Lines set. Baits running just beneath the surface. Callan leaned on the rail, one hand resting on a rod, the other gripping a bottle of water. Danny adjusted the spread. Mel watched the teasers skim across the water, eyes sharp for movement.

Trolling was patience. Discipline. Not the quick, brutal strikes of freshwater fishing. It was a slow game.

"You ever troll for big game?" Mel asked, breaking the comfortable silence.

Callan smirked. "I've worked with bait before."

Mel let out a dry chuckle. "Yeah, but the fish ain't usually the ones getting hooked, huh, ladies' man?"

He winked.

Callan's smile didn't fade, but something in his chest pulled tight. No one had ever called him out quite like that—so casually, so easily.

He didn't confirm or deny. Just drank his water and let it pass.

Mel didn't press. Neither did Danny.

That's the thing about the ocean. It made people observant, but it didn't demand answers.

So they trolled.

Minutes stretched. The hum of the engines faded into the backdrop. Lures danced behind the boat, teasing the surface, waiting for something fast, hungry, and mean.

Then—a reel screamed. Callan's reflexes kicked in instantly, but Danny was already on the move. "Fish on!"

The line cut hard to starboard, the rod bending deep.

Callan grabbed it, planted his feet, and the fight began. The Mahi ran fast—flashes of gold and green beneath the surface, thrashing to shake free.

"Keep it tight!" Danny called.

Callan didn't need coaching. He let it run, then cranked in short, controlled bursts. The fish dove, twisted, fought like hell.

But Callan didn't lose fights.

A few minutes later, the Mahi was on the deck, flopping wildly until Danny skillfully handled it.

Callan exhaled. Shoulders loose. Forearms burning. Fingers tingling. It felt good.

Mel gave the fish a nod. "That's a nice one. Hell of a fight, huh?"

Callan smirked. "Not bad."

Mel eyed him. "Still nothing like a *real* fight."

The smirk stayed, but something in Callan twisted again.

This was supposed to be an escape. But Mel had a way of looking through the surface.

Before he could dwell on it, Danny cut in. "Wait—hold up."

One of the baits skipped weirdly. Off pattern. Hit, maybe.

Then—another reel screeched.

Danny's eyes widened. "That's a big one."

The line peeled off, screaming, slicing the ocean clean.

Mel shot forward. "That's a damn marlin!"

Callan barely had time to react before Mel took the rod, locking in.

And just like that—the fight was on.

The marlin cut across the surface like a torpedo, then exploded into the air in a violent breach, its body twisting, glinting silver-blue in the sun.

Callan's pulse kicked up.

The fish crashed down, sending up a wall of spray. The reel spun wildly, the drag whining wildly under the strain.

Mel gritted his teeth, muscles taut, hands steady.

Callan watched.

He'd seen men fight before—real fights. Watched them grind past pain, past sense, refusing to break.

That's what this was. Not just a fish.

A *war*.

Danny kept the boat angled right, calling adjustments while Mel worked the rod like a weapon. The fish dove, surged, twisted. But Mel held.

Minutes stretched. Callan's hand clenched on the rail. He wasn't watching the fish anymore.

He was watching *Mel*.

The way he moved. The discipline in his hands. The set of his shoulders. Those weren't fisherman's hands—not just. Not entirely.

That kind of control didn't come from weekends on the water. This was muscle memory born elsewhere.

The marlin surged again—one last, wild thrash. And Callan felt the pull deep in his chest.

Some fights weren't about strength. Some were about will. And right now, Callan wasn't sure who wanted it more.

Mel won. Dragged the marlin close. Danny moved fast—deft hands, clean work. The fish secured.

Mel slumped back, laughing through gritted teeth, hands shaking.

Danny clapped him on the back. "Hell of a fight, old man."

Mel didn't answer. Just grinned, satisfied.

Callan couldn't remember what that felt like. He just watched.

CHAPTER 27

The dock was alive with movement as they eased the boat into its slip, the familiar groan of weathered wood underfoot as Callan stepped onto the dock. The midday sun hung high, throwing sharp reflections off the water, and the air was thick with salt and the scent of fresh catch being gutted along the marina.

Danny tossed the mooring line over a cleat, securing the boat with practiced ease. "Not a bad haul," he said, eyeing the mahi in the cooler. "Damn good fish."

Callan smirked. "I do what I can."

"That marlin put up a hell of a fight." Mel let out a satisfied grunt, rolling his shoulders as he stepped onto the dock. His face was flushed from the sun, but he looked more alive than Callan had ever seen him.

Danny shot his father a look. "And you're lucky your damn heart didn't give out in the middle of it."

Mel chuckled but didn't argue.

Callan grabbed the cooler, lifting it with one hand. "Where are we taking this?"

Danny nodded toward the row of seaside restaurants lining the marina, all of them built for fishermen looking to turn their morning work into an afternoon meal. "There's a spot up ahead. They'll fillet it fresh, do it up however you want."

Callan followed the two of them down the dock, weaving through locals and tourists alike. Seagulls hovered overhead, eyeing the buckets of fish scraps being dumped into the water by deckhands who moved with the quiet efficiency of men who had done this a thousand times.

The restaurant Danny led them to was tucked into the corner of the marina—a weathered, open-air joint with a thatched roof and the kind of plastic chairs that had seen decades of sun and salt. A chalkboard sign out front read, *WE COOK YOUR CATCH,* in bold, sun-faded letters.

Inside, the air was cooler, shaded from the heat of the afternoon. A ceiling fan spun lazily overhead as the scent of lime and fresh seafood drifted through the space. A man in a white apron—knife already in hand—gave them a nod from behind the counter.

Danny leaned in. "Sushi and ceviche?"

Callan nodded. "Works for me."

The chef lifted the lid of the cooler, inspecting the mahi with a practiced eye. "Good catch. You want the whole thing done up, or you keeping some?"

Callan thought for a second. "Keep the fillets we don't use."

The chef nodded, already setting to work.

Mel eased into a chair, groaning slightly as he stretched out his back. "Damn fish nearly killed me."

Callan laughed "You held your own."

Mel shot him a look, the corner of his mouth twitching. "You didn't think I could?"

Callan shrugged, playing it casual. "I've seen men younger than you drop after half that fight."

Mel didn't answer right away. Just took a slow sip of the beer Danny had set in front of him. "Yeah, well. I've had my fair share of fights."

The way he said it was too smooth. Too knowing.

Callan let it sit for a second. Then, "What kind of fights?"

Mel's gaze flicked up to meet his. And for the first time since they'd met, something in the old man's eyes shifted—just a fraction. He offered a dangerous smile "The kind that remind you there are monsters out there masked as men."

Callan took a slow sip of his own beer, his grip on the bottle light but steady.

Danny, completely oblivious to whatever was happening between them, pulled his phone from his pocket and started scrolling. "You two wanna stop eye-fucking each other and enjoy the damn fish?"

Mel chuckled. Callan just shook his head.

A few minutes later, the chef returned with a platter—half sushi, half ceviche. The chef neatly arranged the thin slices of mahi over rice. The ceviche, fresh and citrusy, was served alongside tostadas, the sharp scent of lime cutting through the air.

Callan popped a piece of sushi into his mouth, the clean taste of fresh fish and wasabi hitting just right.

Mel took a bite of the ceviche, nodding in approval. "Now this is how you end a trip."

Danny raised his beer. "To good fishing."

Mel clinked his bottle against Danny's, then Callan's. "And good company."

Callan met his gaze. Smirked. "Most of it, anyway."

Mel let out a sharp laugh. "You're all right, Callan."

"You too, Mel." But Callan was still turning over that look. That knowing look.

Like maybe, just maybe, Mel knew exactly who he was.

CHAPTER 28

The car's air conditioning was barely holding on as it idled in the parking lot. Florida was a furnace today. The scent of salt and sunscreen still clung to Callan's skin, and his arms had turned a deeper shade beneath the sun. The back of his neck burned with the slow, dull sting of a sunburn he hadn't felt settling in.

His body felt heavy in a good way—the slow, hazy weight of a man who'd spent all day in the sun, a beer in hand, his belly now full of fresh fish. A rare moment of stillness. The afterglow of a good time.

He set his hands on the wheel, eyes drifting across the marina. Boats bobbed in their slips, the last light of day sinking behind them. Water lapped gently against the docks. A gull cried in the distance. All of it soft. All of it quiet.

For a moment, he just sat there, letting it be what it was. Then he blinked, sighed, and reached for his phone. First time he'd turned it on all day.

The screen lit up. Missed calls. Emails. Junk. He ignored all of it—except one message.

Ellen: Did you die, or did you just forget I exist? Because either way, rude.

A grin tugged at the corner of his mouth. He rubbed his jaw, picturing her mock outrage, the sharp edge under it that said *I noticed*. He typed, slow and easy: *Neither. Just went fishing.*

The dots appeared almost instantly. *Ellen: Fishing? Like. With a pole? Outdoors? In the sun??*

She knew he fished. He'd talked about it with David's friends before. But this wasn't about the facts.

Callan: Yes, Ellen. Fishing. Outdoors. In the sun.

A pause. *Ellen: Are you being held hostage?*

Callan: No.

Ellen: Blink twice if you need rescue.

He chuckled, fingers stretching out over the steering wheel before tapping again. *I had ceviche and a beer. I'm fine.*

Ellen: HAD. CEVICHE. AND A BEER. WHO EVEN ARE YOU?

His grin faded. The day settled over him again—warmth in his skin, the low hum of alcohol in his blood. He felt unguarded in a way he couldn't name.

He typed: *Just needed a break.*

Another pause.

Ellen: Yeah. I get that. All right. But just so we're clear when you say fishing, we're talking about actual fish, right? Not some sad euphemism for how long it's been since you got laid?

Callan: Strictly fish. I even had a pole.

Ellen: That's good. Hate to think of you out there fumbling with your equipment.

He laughed. Quiet and short, the kind that stayed in his chest.

Then silence. The car dark, the dashboard glowing softly. The engine the only sound. Until...

Ellen: You want company?

He stared at the words for a second longer than he needed to. Then typed: *Yeah.*

Ellen: Your place. I'll be there around 7.

He tossed the phone onto the passenger seat and pulled out of the lot, the marina slipping behind him.

CHAPTER 29

He barely had time to push himself off the couch before the door swung open.

Ellen stepped inside like she just got home from college. No knock. No pause. It was part of her charm—or maybe just a deeply ingrained lack of boundaries. Either way, Callan didn't bother calling her out on it.

She kicked off her sandals by the door, one hand raking through the loose waves of her honey-blonde hair, the other clutching a bottle of overpriced wine. Her skin had that "just back from the beauty parlour" glow. Callan knew it was just genetics. Some people aged. Ellen didn't.

He hadn't really noticed before but, seeing her now, it made sense why she'd been a model once. Bright, sharp blue eyes, delicate features, legs that went on forever. She'd even popped up in a couple of music videos back in college—not that she ever brought it up. Callan only knew because David had once joked about marrying a woman who'd slow-danced on a rooftop with some washed-up alt-rock singer.

Ellen turned heads without trying. Never chased attention. Never had to.

And yet, she was just... Ellen. Sharp-tongued, fast-talking, and too nosy for her own good. The only person who'd ever kept up with David—and somehow, over the years, she'd become Callan's friend, too.

She lifted the wine. "You drinking, or was that beer a one-time lapse in judgement?"

Callan smirked. "I'll have a glass."

Ellen grinned. "Good. I'd hate to drink this whole thing myself."

She moved through his kitchen like she owned it, digging out the corkscrew with a practiced hand. There was an ease to her movements. Not just comfort—intention.

She poured them each a glass and slid his across the counter. "So, tell me," she said, raising hers. "Was it actually a good day, or are we drinking because it wasn't?"

Callan took a slow sip. The wine was sharp, cool. "It was a good day."

She gave him a look. Then a small, satisfied smile. "Huh. I'll drink to that."

The bottle was empty before he realised. Ellen set it down with a thud, leaned against the counter, and watched him. "You know what we should do?"

Callan sighed. "You're gonna tell me anyway."

"We should go out."

"Ellen."

"Oh, come on. You ate fish, sat in the sun—you're practically a whole new man. Let's keep the momentum going."

"Eating someone else's cooking doesn't make me a new man."

"No, but it gives me hope for you." She stretched, catlike. "Besides, I'm starving. And my husband's out of town, which means you're officially in charge of dinner."

"We literally just drank a bottle of wine."

"Exactly. Time for carbs."

Callan groaned. "If we go out, you're gonna pick some bougie place where they charge forty bucks for a salad."

Ellen gasped. "I do not *always* pick bougie places."

He just looked at her.

"Okay, fine. I have taste. Not my fault. I used to be famous."

"You were in two music videos."

"Three." She grinned. "It's worse than you thought."

He was already grabbing his keys. "This is why David drinks."

"Exactly. And since he's not here, *you* get to suffer."

***

The restaurant was exactly what Callan expected—low lighting, velvet seats, the kind of place that called appetizers "small plates" and added edible flowers to everything.

Inside, the air was just as humid as outside. Ellen leaned against the bar like she was born there, charming the bartender in minutes.

Callan surveyed the place—a little fancy, but the drinks looked decent. And he *was* hungry. "This place smells like truffle oil," he muttered, flipping the menu.

Ellen barely glanced up. "Because they have truffle fries. Which we're getting. I need to pee."

Callan smirked. "Go on, old lady. I'll try not to get lost without you."

She pointed at him as she walked off. "You're lucky you're cute."

He shook his head, watching her disappear into the crowd.

And just like that, the quiet returned. Callan sat with his drink, the clink of ice, the hum of conversations, the faint pulse of music. That was Ellen—she blew in, filled the space, and left it echoing when she walked away.

The bartender grinned. "Nice pull, bro."

Callan blinked. "What?"

The guy nodded toward the hallway. "She's a knockout."

Callan huffed a laugh. "She's married."

The bartender shrugged. "Yeah? Still."

Callan tipped back his glass. "She's my friend. Her husband's my friend."

"Fair enough." The bartender wiped down the counter, still grinning.

Callan just shook his head, letting the taste of the drink linger. It wasn't the first time someone had made that assumption. Wouldn't be the last. Ellen was hard to miss.

But his mind drifted elsewhere. To Tricia. She always showed up in these in-between spaces—quiet, unguarded moments. Not like a memory, exactly. More like an ache.

He remembered the way she used to rest her hand on his knee mid-conversation, like it was just the natural place to be. The way she'd look at him across the table and already know what joke he was about to make. The way she made everything feel a little sharp, a little brighter—like he was always one step away from tipping into something dangerous.

It had been a long time since he'd felt anything like that.

Maybe that was for the best.

He took another sip, letting the warmth of the liquor smooth over the edges.

Ellen slid back onto the barstool beside him like she'd never left. "Crisis averted. What 'd I miss?"

Callan lifted his glass. "Just me contemplating my tragic love life."

She snorted. "You're a man whore; what's tragic about that?"

He laughed—and whatever ghost of Tricia had crept in, it faded under the glow of the bar lights and Ellen's playful grin.

Chapter 30

The restaurant hummed with low conversation, and the glow of candle-light reflected off their wineglasses. Their meals had been ordered. Now there was only time to fill.

Callan swirled the last sip of his Negroni, warmth settling into his limbs. He wasn't drunk, just loose. Comfortable. A little more inclined to let things slip.

He set the glass down, tilting his head. "So, how do you know Tricia?"

Ellen blinked. Her fingers, which had been idly tapping the stem of her glass, stilled. She took a swallow of wine before answering. "That's random."

"Maybe. But you knew her. I just never asked how."

She leaned back, drumming her fingers now against the table. "We went to high school and college together. Same sorority, just two bimbos from Florida." She smirked, though it didn't quite reach her eyes. "She was way more of a troublemaker than me."

"I find that hard to believe."

"Oh, please. She had a fake ID before any of us. Knew every bouncer in town. Always got away with shit I'd be grounded a month for." Ellen shook her head. "She was sharp. Too smart for half the guys she dated. And she had the thing—made you feel like you were the only person in the room when she talked to you."

Callan nodded, eyes on his glass. "Yeah. I know."

The memory came like a muscle reflex. Her voice in his apartment. The door closing. The silver earring still tucked in a drawer. He shoved the thought back down.

Ellen studied him for a second, unreadable. Then she leaned forward, propping her chin on her hand. "Why'd you ask?"

Callan considered the question. What he was really asking. Because he never talked about Tricia. Not to anyone. Not even to himself, if he could help it. That he'd mentioned her now—casually, like it didn't mean anything—was already a slip.

He thought about lying. Thought about dodging the truth with something half-clever. But instead, he just smirked. "No reason."

Ellen narrowed her eyes, swirling her wine. Then she said, "Oh, fuck off, Callan. I know you two hooked up."

He stifled a laugh. "Is that so?"

"I wasn't born yesterday. I saw the way she looked at you. And I know you. No way you didn't at least try."

He let the silence stretch. He could deny it. But tonight, he didn't feel like pretending.

He tipped his glass. "Yeah," he said quietly. "We did."

"She never told me."

Callan blinked. "What? You totally mind-fucked me, Ellen."

"She never told me you two had a thing," she clarified. "Did she matter to you?" Her voice was gentler, but the question landed hard.

Did she matter?

Of course she did. But saying it out loud felt like peeling open a wound that had already scarred over. "Yes and no."

Something flickered across Ellen's face—tightness in her jaw, the subtle press of her lips like she was biting something back. Callan didn't miss it. Maybe it was nothing. Or maybe it was more.

"Huh," she murmured, taking another sip of wine.

She stared at the candle for a long beat, nails tapping against her glass—rhythmic, restrained.

"Say what's on your mind," Callan said, watching her carefully.

Ellen let out a small laugh that didn't quite reach her ice-blue eyes. "Nope." She looked at him, gaze sharper now, but something else flickered beneath it. She held his eyes for a long moment before letting out a breath and shaking her head.

"You're impossible," she muttered. She raised her glass, clinking it gently against his, this time no teasing. "I hope you know what you're getting into."

"Because with her," Ellen added, "it was never just a fling. Not for anyone." The weight of it settled between them.

Callan didn't press. He knew better.

Then, as the server passed by and topped off her glass, Ellen spoke again—softer, slower, like the words had been waiting. "Tricia... she's the kind of woman who knows precisely what people want from her. And she's smart enough to make them think they've got it."

Callan met her gaze. "That manipulation?"

"I don't think she sees it that way. I think she sees it as survival." Ellen swirled her wine. "She was always two things at once. Charming and cold. Warm and cutting. The kind of person who'll hold your hand just long enough to see what you'll do when she lets go."

He didn't respond. He didn't have to. He knew exactly what she meant.

"She's dangerous, Callan," Ellen said finally. Not cruel. Not dramatic. Just honest. "Not because she means to be. But because she's always had to be."

They sat in silence.

Then Ellen offered a tight smile. "But hey," she added, raising her glass again. "At least you're consistent."

Callan clinked his glass against hers. "I try."

The rest of the night eased out in softer tones. Lighter conversation, easy laughter. But underneath it all, her words stayed with him.

She's always had to be.

He'd known that already. He just hadn't let himself say it out loud.

CHAPTER 31

It was the kind of slow wake-up that came with just enough of a hangover to be annoying but not enough to count as a problem. His mouth was dry, his head heavy—but the real weight wasn't the gin. It was the conversation with Ellen. About Tricia.

Beckett flicked his tail from the chair across the room, half awake and already judging. Like he knew Callan was about to do something stupid.

"Not a word," Callan muttered, shoving the blanket off.

By the time he had coffee in hand, the dull ache in his skull was fading. But the question wasn't.

Ellen knew Tricia. Ellen also didn't throw out warnings lightly.

Which meant Callan had to know.

He sat down at the kitchen counter and flipped open his work laptop. This was the secure machine. The one inside Diego's network. The one that didn't just look things up—it found them. Last time he'd used it, it had been for Dwayne.

His fingers hovered over the keyboard.

He should walk away. He should.

Instead, he typed it.

Langley, Tricia.

A second passed. Then another.

Then—

SEARCH RESTRICTED. LAW ENFORCEMENT QUERIES REQUIRE APPROVAL. ALERT LOGGED. REVIEW IN PROGRESS.

Callan didn't react. At least not in any way that mattered.

But inside, something coiled tight.

Oopsy daisy.

His jaw clenched as the weight of it settled. Diego's team just saw that. The Archive wasn't Google. It wasn't some backdoor hacker forum. It was monitored. Secure. Every query went somewhere. Every search left a trail.

And apparently, law enforcement lookups triggered an automatic internal review. It took all of thirty seconds. A flashing icon. A message appearing in the screen's corner.

REQUEST FOR SEARCH CLARIFICATION.

He opened it, already knowing it wouldn't be good. It was an automated form—standard protocol for flagged searches. Cold. Impersonal. Designed to expose any hint of weakness.

• Reason for inquiry?

• Is this request related to an active contract?

• Has your security been compromised?

• Do you suspect law enforcement is aware of your activities?

• Do you require immediate extraction?

• Is this request for personal reasons?

Callan exhaled through his nose. Shit. That last question. Callan sighed, then typed, *Yes.*

NEW MESSAGE FROM: OPERATIONS REVIEW.

Callan clicked it open, keeping his breath steady.

"Your request will be reviewed. Flagged searches require manual clearance. Review complete."

"WARNING: Personnel should avoid engaging in unnecessary interactions with law enforcement. Fraternization presents an inherent security risk and may compromise operational integrity. Continued inquiries of this nature will require further oversight."

"Information Request pending."

Callan stared at the screen.

Message received. Loud and clear.

CHAPTER 32

The phone vibrated against the counter, the screen lighting up with *Tricia Langley*. He stared at it for half a second before picking up. "Yeah."

"Wow. No fake greeting? Not even a 'Hey, Tricia, great to hear from you'?" Something was different in her tone—still playful, but with an edge underneath.

Callan smirked, rubbing his temple. "Didn't realise we were at the stage where I needed to sweet-talk you over the phone."

"Always a good habit to have." Her voice light. Teasing. But something was off.

Callan exhaled. "What's up?"

A brief pause. "Come have a beer with me."

He frowned slightly. "You're so forward. That an order?"

"Would it work if it was?"

"Doubt it."

Tricia laughed. It sounded like a bell. "I'm out in Homestead. There's a bar here I like. Not fancy, just beer, wings, and people who mind their own business."

Callan arched a brow. "Homestead? You move?"

"Nah, just wanted some space from the city." Another pause. "And I figured you might too."

There it was again—that something in her voice.

Callan leaned against the counter, glancing toward the dimly lit living room. Beckett flicked his tail in his sleep. Outside, the city lights bled into the sky, turning the night hazy.

He considered saying no. Should say no.

But Tricia had that effect. Showing up just enough to remind him that she existed and leaving just as fast.

And if Ellen's words were still ringing in his head, maybe that was reason enough to say yes.

"Text me the address."

Another pause. She spoke with a cocky clip in her voice. "Knew you'd say yes."

***

The elevator doors slid open with a soft chime, spilling cool underground air into the stillness. Concrete. Motor oil. Faint cigar smoke lingered from some other resident's bad habits.

Callan stepped toward his section, passing the labelled reserved spots.

The previous owners of his condo, a retired couple from Montreal, had owned three parking spaces, because why the hell not? They'd only needed one, but they kept the extras, "Just in case." Callan got them in the sale.

His 2023 Mazda CX-5 sat closest to the elevator. Blacked-out trim. Tinted windows. Low-profile. Forgettable. A workhorse, meant for errands, long drives, blending in.

Next to it, the 2009 Porsche 911 Turbo, a relic from another version of himself. Guards Red. Six-speed manual. Unapologetic. He didn't drive it much, but it stayed because he liked the feel of something he actually had to control.

And then, the Triumph Street Triple RS. Matte black. Sleek. The closest thing to real freedom he ever allowed himself. The bike was a problem-solver, a way to cut through traffic, disappear, feel something other than calculation for a while.

Tonight, though?

Not the bike. Too far of a ride. The Mazda felt... off.

That left the Porsche.

Callan slid into the driver's seat, the leather cool beneath him, the soft glow of the instrument panel flickering to life. He adjusted the mirror, studied his reflection for a beat longer than necessary.

Homestead was a ride, but not a complicated one. Miami faded into the rearview, streetlights stretching thinner until only the open road remained. Wide stretches of land, citrus groves, and patches of Everglades swallowing the dark.

***

The place was easy to find but, in the end, Tricia's choice of location wasn't surprising.

Because it was a cop bar.

Not the kind that advertised itself as one. No precinct flags. No framed department plaques. But Callan knew the signs.

The parking lot spoke first. The clustered motorcycles near the entrance. Not a deterrent, just a statement.

The beat-up pickups belonged to men who put bodies in the ground but not in a metaphorical sense.

The unmarked Crown Vics and Explorers tucked into corners of the lot weren't rentals.

The atmosphere inside did the rest.

The hum of conversation didn't stop, but it shifted—a second-long hitch in the air as eyes flicked toward him. Not suspicion exactly. Just cold observation. Callan wasn't a cop, and everyone knew it.

The bar itself was worn in. Dark wood, scarred from decades of boots and whiskey spills. A dartboard in the back, a jukebox frozen in time, a bartender who knew every name in the room—except his.

At the bar, a pair of older guys—former military, if he had to guess—drank in comfortable silence.

Near the dartboard, a sharp-eyed,woman. early forties, tattoo peeking from under rolled-up sleeves, nursed a beer, listening without inserting herself.

Cops. Detectives. Maybe a few feds.

And they all knew he wasn't one of them.

Callan let them clock him, but didn't give them a reason to keep looking.

His eyes flicked across the room and landed on Tricia.

She was waiting,

A beer in front of her. Untouched.

Callan didn't hesitate. He crossed the room, eyes on her, aware of the others but ignoring them. He pulled out the chair opposite Tricia and sat, fingers drumming against the table, before meeting her gaze.

"You drinking, or just trying to look friendly?"

Tricia smirked, finally reaching for her beer.

Her nails tapped against the bottle in a small, deliberate gesture.

"I was waiting for you."

Callan leaned back, tilting his head. "That so?"

She took a slow sip. Set the bottle down.

"Yeah."

Callan watched her peel the label from the beer with surgical preci-sion, each curl of paper deliberate.

"You call it your place," he said. "But you sit with your back to the wall..."

She didn't flinch. Just smiled, low and unbothered.

"Habit."

Callan tilted his head. "Control."

Tricia's smile widened, but it didn't reach her eyes.

"Semantics."

She finally took another sip, then set the bottle down and folded her hands around it. Her nails were neat, short, practical—but painted dark. A detail most people wouldn't notice. But Tricia made sure you did.

"You always read people this hard?" she asked.

"Only when they ask me out to bars an hour outside the city for no reason."

She laughed—soft, short. "You think there's no reason?"

"I think there's always a reason with you."

She met his gaze, level and unwavering.

"Good. That means you're paying attention."

A beat.

Then she leaned toward him, just enough to draw his focus.

"You want to know why I picked this place?"

Callan gave the barest nod.

"Because I can see the exits. No one asks questions here. If I needed to vanish, three people in this room would help me without a second thought."

She paused. "And because you wouldn't pick it."

Callan sat back. Let the silence stretch.

She watched him, waiting.

"So, what's the play?" he asked. "You lure me into your little fortress and see what I'll say when I'm off balance?"

"No," she said, voice low now. "I just wanted to see if you'd come."

That landed differently.

For a moment, the armour cracked—not gone, just shifted.

But then it was back. Her posture eased. The smirk returned, cool and practiced. "And hey," she added, raising her beer, "you did."

Callan clinked his bottle lightly against hers. The sound was soft, but final.

They drank in silence, surrounded by low conversation, the hum of bad country music, and the watchful gaze of people who didn't forget faces. And Callan couldn't help but wonder: If Tricia had a Safehouse, a panic room, a last place on earth—this would be it?

And she'd let him inside. That wasn't nothing. But it wasn't everything either.

He should have walked away a drink ago.

But here he was. Watching her scratch meaning out of a beer label.

CHAPTER 33

Callan had felt a physical attraction to Tricia from the moment he met her. Sharp, confident, a woman who turned heads without trying—but tonight? Tonight, she wasn't just attractive.

She was dangerous.

Her blonde hair was loose, a little messy, like she'd run her fingers through it one too many times. Jean shorts, ankle boots she couldn't play cop in, and a fitted black tank top that left just enough skin showing to keep things interesting.

But more importantly, it was how she sat.

Back against the chair, legs stretched out, unbothered, waiting. That slow, unreadable smile curving her lips. A look that wasn't just confidence—it was deliberate. Like she was testing something.

Finally, he smirked. "So, was this beer invitation just an excuse to get me alone? Because if it was, you could've just said so."

Tricia scoffed, rolling her eyes, but he caught the flicker of amusement in them. "Right. Nothing says romance like a cop bar and questionable lighting."

Callan leaned back, stretching one arm lazily over the backrest of his chair. "Could've fooled me. You're dressed like you were planning to ruin someone's night."

Tricia took a slow sip of her beer, lips wrapping around the bottle in a way that wasn't accidental. "Maybe I am."

She let that hang between them for a beat, then tilted her head.

"Didn't say it had to be yours, though."

Callan laughed, shaking his head. "Cold, Langley. Real cold."

Before she could fire back, the waitress appeared. A little older than Tricia—forties, lean muscle, sharp eyes. She wore a flowy white top that highlighted a certain strength that came from throwing assholes out of bars for a living. No name tag, unsurprising because she worked out in the sticks at a cop hangout. Everyone knew her name.

Right now, she focused on Callan. Sizing him up. And then, just to test the waters—"You want another?"

Her question was aimed at Tricia. But the waitress wasn't looking at her.

Callan grinned, saying nothing. He didn't have to, because Tricia's fingers tightened around her beer bottle.

Subtle. Too subtle for most people to notice.

Callan noticed.

He just wasn't sure what it meant yet.

Tricia shifted in her seat. Nothing big. Just enough that her body angled closer to Callan's.

Just enough to close the space between them.

A move that told Casey exactly what she needed to know.

Mine.

Tricia nodded at Casey without looking at her. "And get him one too."

Callan raised a brow. "Ordering for me now?"

Tricia tilted her head, still watching him. "You'd only complain if I didn't."

Casey let out a soft chuckle, but something about it was different. Lower. Sharper. Like she felt the shift in the air. Like she wasn't entirely sure she minded it. "Oh, I like him," Casey said, still watching Callan, her grin curling slow.

Tricia's hand stopped tapping against her beer.

Callan took a sip, grinning against the rim of his bottle. This was getting interesting.

Casey noticed. And she liked the game. Her gaze flicked back to Tricia, amused. A silent challenge.

For a second, Callan could have sworn he felt the temperature drop.

Tricia's green eyes snapped up—sharp, direct.

The look wasn't hostile.

But it was a warning.

Casey held her gaze for just a beat longer, then smiled, as if she were impressed. And just like that, she walked off.

Tricia didn't look away.

Callan exhaled through his nose as he picked up his beer. "Something on your mind?"

Tricia took another slow sip, deliberate, letting the silence do the talking.

Then, finally, she leaned forward, elbows on the table, closing the distance just a fraction more.

"She's got a type," Tricia murmured, tilting her bottle toward where Casey had disappeared. "And I don't like when people think they can take things that aren't theirs."

Callan didn't move. Didn't speak. Just let the weight of that hit.

Tricia leaned back, looking far too pleased with herself, like she hadn't just declared war over a beer.

Then she laughed. "What are we drinking to?"

Callan raised his bottle, mirroring her easy posture.

"Bad ideas."

Tricia clinked her bottle against his. "Fitting."

And just like that, the tension shifted.

Possession acknowledged. Territory marked.

Casey reappeared, grinning like she hadn't forgotten. "Another round?"

Callan had been expecting it. She wasn't the type to let things sit unfinished—especially not after Tricia had all but snarled at her earlier.

Tricia didn't hesitate. "Yes."

Callan shook his head. "I'm good."

Tricia's brow lifted in challenge. "Seriously? You're cutting yourself off already?"

Callan exhaled through his nose as he leaned back in his chair. "I drove a heat-score car to a cop bar, Langley. One's my limit tonight."

Tricia's lips parted, just enough for Callan to know she hadn't clocked that detail before.

Casey, however, had. Her gaze flicked to him, sharp, assessing. "Oh?"

Callan shrugged. "Porsche. Guards red. Thought I'd go all-in."

Casey let out a short, amused laugh, shaking her head. "Jesus. You really are ballsy."

Tricia's expression shifted. Something flashing behind her eyes. Like she hadn't realised how reckless it was until just now.

"You're an idiot," she muttered.

Callan grinned. "You invited me."

Tricia just shrugged.

Instead, she turned back to Casey. "Fine. Just me, then."

Casey returned a moment later, setting Tricia's drink down. "Here you go."

Tricia lifted it in a silent toast, her eyes locked on Callan's.

She took a slow sip.

Then casually finished the beer in one go, banged the bottle down and hopped off her chair. "Okay, hotshot. Take me for a ride."

Callan didn't miss the eyes tracking them. Tricia had asked. He was saying yes.

Chapter 34

Tricia wasn't acting the way she had when they first met—sweet, affable, always the sharpest person in the room. This was something different. Reckless. Impulsive.

The only other time she'd been this forward? The night they fucked.

No hesitation. No second-guessing. She'd made up her mind and acted on it.

And right now?

She had that same look, which meant one of two things: She was either drunk enough to be making bad decisions—which didn't seem likely, given she was only a few beers in—or she wanted something from him.

Callan dragged his tongue across the edge of his teeth, considering that.

Just as he opened his mouth to say something, he felt it.

The shift.

Not overt. Not aggressive. Just... a change.

Two older guys at the bar, men who had been quiet all night, drinking like it was a ritual, had stopped talking.

They weren't staring, not exactly.

But they sure as hell were watching.

Callan knew that look.

The slow, weighted once-over. The kind men gave when they disapproved but didn't want to say it out loud.

They weren't looking at Tricia.

They were looking at *him*.

Cops. Old-school. The kind with their own internal rulebook. And apparently, him walking out of here with Tricia didn't fall under "acceptable behaviour."

Could he ignore it? Hell, he probably should.

But this wasn't *his* bar. It was Tricia's. Her space.

And whether she realised it or not, she was drawing a line in the sand by leaving with him.

She didn't seem to notice. Or maybe she just didn't care.

She raised a brow, waiting. Waiting to see if he'd back down.

Callan smirked.

Like hell.

He stood up, easy, stretching his arms like he had all the time in the world.

"You sure you can handle that?" His tone was light, casual—just loud enough for anyone still watching to hear.

Tricia grinned. "You're the one who's supposed to impress *me*, remember?"

The tension shifted. Not completely, but enough. Enough that Callan felt it—the unspoken acknowledgment between him and the old-timers.

They didn't like it. But they weren't going to stop it, either.

He tipped his head toward the door.

"All right, Langley. Let's go."

Tricia was already walking out before he finished speaking.

And Callan had a feeling that the real fun hadn't even started yet.

CHAPTER 35

The Porsche 911 Turbo snarled as Callan shifted gears, the twin-turbo flat-six engine roaring to life as they shot down the moonlit highway. The city lights blurred in the rearview mirror, swallowed by the dark stretch of open road ahead.

Tricia leaned back in the passenger seat, the wind from the cracked window teasing strands of her blonde hair loose. She looked over at him, eyes gleaming with something that was amusement or challenge.

"That's it?" she taunted, voice dripping with mock disappointment. "I thought a man with a car like this would know how to really drive."

Callan caught the taunt but didn't take the bait. His hands rested lightly on the wheel—relaxed, but in complete control. The Porsche could go faster, much faster, but he wasn't in the habit of making mistakes. That kind of button-pushing was a distraction—dangerous, if it came from anyone, much less from an attractive detective.

Still, something in her expression as she said it, the way she'd been acting all night, was different. Pushing buttons just to see what happened. Testing boundaries. Callan wasn't sure if she was chasing the thrill or chasing something else. With Tricia, it hooked something deeper. A challenge to the part of him that prided itself on control, now itching to prove he still had it.

Tricia shifted, stretching out her legs, her movements unhurried. Calculated. "You seem like a guy who loves control, but I have to wonder, do you ever just let go?"

Callan flicked his eyes toward her, then back to the road. "Control is how you stay alive."

"Yeah?" She laughed softly, like that answer amused her. Like it confirmed something she'd already decided about him. Her world thrived on risk. His recoiled from it.

He hated how close she got with a single question.

Callan exhaled, tightening his grip just on the wheel. He'd never been the type to show off. Speed wasn't the thrill he chased. Precision was. The absolute marriage of man and machine moving as one.

Tricia was watching him, waiting, pushing just enough. And whether or not he admitted it, her challenge stirred something deep inside him.

He shifted into a higher gear.

The Porsche surged forward like a living thing, tires gripping the asphalt as the speedometer climbed. The engine's growl deepened, the whole car vibrating with restrained violence. Streetlights flashed past like gunfire, the wind slicing through the open window in a low, hungry whistle.

Tricia laughed, a sharp, delighted sound, fingers curling against the edge of her seat. "That's more like it."

Callan didn't respond, focused now.

The road ahead curved, and instinct took over. He eased into the turn, not braking—never braking—but feathering the throttle just enough to shift the car's weight, guiding it through the bend with a practiced ease most drivers could never dream of.

***

It came back to him in flashes—Diego's voice, sharp and merciless. "Again."

The training ground had been an abandoned airstrip outside Bogotá, heat rippling off the pavement, the thick scent of burned rubber and gasoline in the air. The cars weren't luxury machines like the Porsche—no, Diego's team had trained him in control, not comfort. Beaten-up sedans, reinforced SUVs, vehicles that could take a hit and keep going.

"You're fighting the car, Callan," Diego had growled, arms crossed as Callan wrestled a battered Audi through a high-speed corner. "You don't fight it. You feel it. You let it tell you what it needs."

The next run, he'd listened. He'd felt the car instead of forcing it, learning the delicate balance between power and restraint. Learning how to make a machine an extension of himself.

And now, all these years later, it was instinct.

***

Callan snapped back to the present as the Porsche shot out of the curve onto a long, empty straightaway. He pushed harder, the RPMs climbing, the road blurring beneath them.

Tricia turned to him, grinning, breath uneven. "Shit. You can drive."

Callan allowed himself a grin. "Thought you already knew that."

She bit her lower lip, then exhaled, shaking her head. "I thought I knew. Now I'm sure."

He should have slowed down then. Should have eased off the gas.

But then, red and blue lights exploded in the rearview mirror.

A siren wailed to life.

Callan's jaw tightened. "Fuuuuuuck." He was already calculating next steps—license, registration, badge checks, questions. Tricia? She was smiling like the game hadn't even started yet.

She didn't just invite chaos. She flirted with it.

Tricia twisted in her seat, glancing back at the flashing lights behind them. Instead of looking concerned, she grinned.

"Pull over," she said.

Callan sighed through his nose but didn't argue. He let off the throttle, the Porsche growling in protest as he guided it onto the shoulder.

The cop car rolled up behind them, engine idling. A long, tense pause followed before the officer stepped out.

Tricia turned to Callan, her expression the perfect blend of amusement and mischief. "Relax. I've got this."

Before he could stop her, she was already rolling down the window, flashing her badge with the effortless authority that made Callan wonder just how many times she'd done this before.

The cop hesitated, his stance shifting. "Detective?" The shift was instant. Flirt to detective in a single breath. He'd seen assassins with less control.

"Yep," Tricia said, all business now. "Just stretching the legs in my friend's car. We were talking shop, got a little carried away." She flashed an easy smile. "You know how it is."

The officer's eyes flicked between them, then back at the Porsche. His jaw shifted, just slightly, a flicker of something Callan couldn't quite read.

A long pause.

"Keep it under the limit, Detective."

Callan didn't miss the way the officer took one last glance at him before walking away. The moment the patrol car pulled away, Tricia burst into laughter.

"Jesus," Callan muttered, shaking his head.

She grinned at him, still catching her breath. "That was fun."

Callan glanced at her, then back at the road.

Maybe it was.

Tricia was still grinning, her blonde hair tousled from the rush of speed, the chase, the escape. She turned to him, eyes flickering with something that wasn't quite satisfaction—something more.

"About a mile up, there's a county road," she said. "Take it north."

Callan flicked an eyebrow at her. "You giving me a scenic tour now?"

She smirked. "You'll like this road. Trust me."

He didn't trust people. That was a rule. But he trusted himself, and right now, his instincts told him to follow her lead.

With a smooth shift of the gear lever, he pulled back onto the highway, keeping the speed just civilized enough to avoid any more interruptions. A mile later, just as promised, the county road appeared on the right, a narrow strip of blacktop cutting into the dark countryside, disappearing into the trees.

Callan took the turn without hesitation.

The road was different, no streetlights, just the pale wash of moonlight filtering through the branches. It was tighter, winding, a road that demanded attention. The kind of road that separated real drivers from amateurs.

Tricia sat back in her seat, watching him with something close to curiosity. "Ever get tired of playing it safe?"

Callan smirked. "That what you think I'm doing?"

"You tell me," she shot back.

Callan exhaled through his nose, then downshifted. The Porsche lunged forward, a predator uncaged.

The tight curve ahead came fast, but Callan had already seen it, already felt it before it arrived. A slight flick of the wheel, a controlled throttle tap, and the Porsche glided through the bend with surgical precision.

Tricia let out a low moan. Not fear. Admiration.

He pushed harder. The road twisted unpredictably through long sweeps followed by sharp switchbacks, demanding both power and precision. Callan's hands moved on instinct, guiding the car, making microscopic adjustments before the road even asked for them.

Something inside him felt alive.

Diego's voice echoed in his head again. "If you want to win, Callan, stop thinking about the car. Think about the road. The car already knows what to do."

The next turn came sharp and fast. Callan didn't brake. The Porsche hugged the bend perfectly, tires barely whispering against the pavement as he shot out onto a long straightaway.

Tricia let out a short laugh, shaking her head. "Goddamn."

Callan finally glanced at her. "Satisfied?"

She was still catching her breath, but her smirk was back, slow and knowing.

"Not yet," Tricia murmured, her voice lower now, something richer behind it. She glanced at him, eyes flicking to the deserted road ahead, then back to him. "Pull over."

Callan didn't hesitate. He eased off the gas, guiding the Porsche onto the gravel shoulder. The engine rumbled in the quiet, heat still radiating off the hood, the car thrumming with the aftershocks of speed.

Tricia shifted in her seat, her hair tumbling over one shoulder as she turned toward him. There was a weight to the moment, not hesitation, not uncertainty, just electricity. A charged silence stretching between them like a drawn wire.

Callan tilted his head slightly, watching her. "You always celebrate reckless decisions like this?"

Her smirk deepened. "Only when they're worth it," she said, her fingers already tracing the line of his jaw, sliding lower. Deliberate. Teasing. Taking.

Callan exhaled slowly, letting himself sink into it. He wasn't the type to lose control, but Tricia had a way of testing his edges, pushing just enough to see if he'd push back.

And right now? He didn't want to push back.

She moved closer, her breath hot against his neck, her lips grazing just beneath his jaw. Her voice was barely above a whisper. "Relax."

The word was a challenge, not a suggestion.

Then she was on him fast, unhesitating, hungry. Her hands worked their way down, and he groaned as she unzipped his pants, her fingers cool against his heated skin.

Her lips closed around him, not tentative—claiming. The first contact was a jolt of heat, sharp and electric. Callan gasped, his head snapping back against the headrest, the leather creaking with the force of it. His fingers found her hair, but not to guide her—just to hold on.

She didn't ease in. She took.

Steady, hungry, merciless in her rhythm. The slick drag of her tongue, the deliberate pressure, the way she hollowed her cheeks—it was brutal in its precision, like she was proving a point.

He groaned, low and wrecked, as she grazed his most sensitive spot with a calculated flick, then did it again, harder. His hips jerked, involuntary. Tricia didn't slow. She kept going, dragging another sound from him—raw, helpless, hers.

She wasn't asking. And Callan didn't want her to.

The night wrapped around them, the only sounds the fading hum of the Porsche's engine and the quiet, deliberate movements of Tricia's mouth. She took her time—not just giving, but owning, controlling, savouring. The hunger in her touch wasn't just about him. It was about control. About reminding him who was setting the rules tonight.

He wasn't sure if it was the thrill or losing control that left his hands shaking. Maybe both. Maybe that was the point.

CHAPTER 36

The air between them crackled, thick with the aftermath of what had just happened. Callan leaned back against the driver's seat, dragging a hand through his hair. His pulse had steadied, but the energy lingered—coiled tight beneath his skin.

Tricia watched him, moonlight cutting across her smirk like a blade.

Callan let the silence breathe before tilting his head, matching her look. "So," he murmured, voice still rough. "Your place?"

Tricia didn't answer right away. She let the moment hang like she was weighing a bet. Calculating. Unrushed. And just when he thought she might lean in—

She smiled. Slow. Amused.

"Tempting," she said, her voice husky, still warm from before. "But I think I'm heading back to the bar."

Callan's brow ticked up. "The bar?"

"Yeah," she said easily. "I've got friends to catch up with. And besides..." She tilted her head. "Wouldn't want you to get the wrong idea."

Callan huffed a dry laugh. But the way she said it—like this was just a game she controlled—settled wrong in his chest.

"And what idea is that?" he asked, voice easy, unreadable.

"That I'm easy."

Her tone was light. Final.

Callan held her gaze. Didn't blink. "I never thought that."

Something flickered behind her eyes. No softness—satisfaction.

"Good," she said, brushing her hands against her thighs. "Then you won't mind dropping me off."

He exhaled through his nose. Amused. Impressed. Maybe a little wrecked. He didn't argue. Just turned the key, the Porsche growling to life.

The drive back was quiet.

Not awkward—just weighted. A silence that said something happened here, even if no one wanted to name it.

Streetlights pulsed across the dash. Tricia watched him from the passenger seat, her face unreadable.

By the time they reached the bar, she turned toward him, hand brushing his arm. Brief. Casual. Like it meant nothing.

"Thanks for the ride," she murmured. "And for... everything."

He looked at her. Really paid attention.

Then she kissed him—soft, final—and slipped out of the car.

"Goodnight, Callan."

The door shut. No glance back.

Callan sat still, engine idling, headlights washing over the now-empty sidewalk.

He should've felt satisfied.

He didn't.

She didn't just leave—she took something with her. Something he hadn't meant to give.

And he couldn't stop wondering if she'd done it all on purpose.

He shifted into gear, the Porsche easing back into the road.

The city swallowed him whole, and he felt like he was being hunted.

CHAPTER 37

The sea stretched to the horizon, the sky a perfect blue. They had weather that made the world beyond the horizon feel irrelevant. And the steady roll of the ocean beneath them, the pull of the fishing lines, the crack of beer cans opening—this was the exact combination that settled Callan's mind.

It had been a couple of days since he'd seen Tricia. She wasn't lingering in his thoughts, but she hadn't left them either.

Mel and Danny had been suitable company, the type that understood when to talk and when to let silence do the work.

But all good things ended. As they pulled into the marina, the sun hung low in the sky, its golden light cutting sharp against the rippling water. Danny eased the boat into its slip with practiced precision, the engine's low hum fading into the dockside noise of clinking masts and distant conversation.

Callan stepped onto the dock, rolling his shoulders, feeling the weight of a long, satisfying day settle into his muscles.

Then his phone powered on. A vibration rattled against his palm as the screen flooded with notifications. Callan exhaled, already knowing this was going to ruin his good mood.

One missed call from David.

A text from Ellen—before David's call.

Sixteen messages and four missed calls from Tricia.

His jaw ticked. That's... a lot.

Mel, finishing up with the ropes, caught the look on his face. "Bad news?"

Callan was already scrolling through the messages. "Not sure yet."

Ellen's text was short, sent earlier in the day: *Call me when you get this.*

David's missed call had come in about an hour later. David wasn't the type to not leave voicemail.

Then there was Tricia. Her messages weren't frantic, but they were insistent. The first had come in the night before.

Tricia: Need to chat when you get a chance.

Then, hours later: *Callan, I need to talk to you. It's important. Where the hell are you? I swear to God, if you're ignoring me...*

The rest blurred together. Variations of *call me* and *we need to talk*, the most recent from just before he'd turned his phone on.

Tricia: Fuck you, Callan!

Callan locked the screen and shoved the phone into his pocket, exhaling slow.

Jesus Christ.

Whatever this was, it wasn't good.

Mel eyed him from the dock. "You need to take that?"

"Yeah." Callan nodded toward Danny. "You good handling the rest?"

Danny waved him off. "Go. You look like you just realised you left the stove on."

Callan smirked, but it didn't quite reach his eyes. He stepped off the dock, his mind already shifting gears. Fishing was over. Reality was waiting.

Sliding into the Mazda, he shut the door but didn't start the engine. He just sat there, staring at the phone in his hand, debating.

He could call Ellen. He could call Tricia.

But David's missed call felt like the most immediate threat.

He tapped the screen, bringing the phone to his ear. It rang twice before David answered.

"Where the hell have you been?" David's voice was sharp, edged with something Callan wasn't used to hearing from him. Panic.

"Out on the water," Callan said evenly. "What's up?"

A bitter laugh crackled through the receiver. "Oh, I don't know, Callan. Maybe the fact that my wife has been fucking someone behind my back?"

Callan's grip tightened. "There's no way…"

"Don't you patronize me, Callan," David snapped. "Ellen. My wife. The one I've been married to for ten goddamn years. The one I trusted. She's cheating on me, the bitch."

Callan let the words settle, his mind switching gears. David wasn't the type to jump to conclusions. If he was saying this, it might be real.

"How do you know?" Callan's voice stayed calm, measured.

"Because I fucking caught her, or near enough to it!" David spat. "Came home early last night, and she was acting weird. Nervous. So, I checked her phone while she was in the shower." A sharp breath. "There were texts. Not a lot, but enough."

Callan exhaled slowly. "Enough?"

David let out a bitter laugh. "Yeah. Not explicit, nothing I could use as hard proof, but definitely not innocent. Late-night messages. Some asshole calling her baby, saying he missed her. She didn't respond much, but she sure as hell wasn't shutting it down either."

Callan frowned. "That's not exactly concrete."

David scoffed. "Oh, come on, Callan. She's been going out all the time. Late nights, last-minute plans. Always some excuse. And when I ask her? She gets defensive. Says I'm being paranoid." His voice dropped lower, raw. "I know my wife. And I know when I'm being lied to."

Callan stayed quiet. David was spiralling, fast.

"I'm sure there's some explanation."

"I'm a fucking attorney, Callan. I read liars for a living." David was raging now.

Then Callan's phone buzzed—another call, flashing Ellen.

"Fuck, Dave, I'm getting pulled over. I'll call you back." Callan ended the call before David could protest. Then he immediately answered Ellen.

"Ellen," Callan said, voice low, wary. "What the hell is going on?"

A pause. Then a sigh. "I need a favour."

Callan pinched the bridge of his nose. "Ellen—"

"Listen, I just—" She cut herself off, then softened her tone. "I need you to tell David we were together last night."

Callan's stomach sank. "Ellen."

"I just need an excuse, Callan. That's all. David's losing his mind, and I need something to buy time."

He exhaled, staring at his own reflection in the rearview mirror. His jaw was tight, his pulse ticking steadily beneath his skin.

"Ellen, if you're lying to me—"

"I just need a cover. Please."

Callan's fingers tightened around the phone.

"Fuck, Ellen. Fuck you." His voice was low, but the anger was there. "How could you?"

Her pause stretched on longer than it should. "I'll explain everything tonight," she whispered. "I just need David to calm down."

Callan closed his eyes, gripping the steering wheel hard enough to make the leather creak.

"Please, Callan."

The way she said it—soft, pleading, wrapping around him like a trap—made something cold settle in his gut.

Ellen had always been quick. Sharp. Charming.

But now, for the first time, Callan wasn't sure if he was talking to someone scrambling for cover—

Or someone who'd just started playing her hand.

He sat in the car, the salt of the ocean still in his hair, and realised the day had curdled. There was no peace to return to. Only reckoning.

Tricia's phone rang and rang before she answered. "Hello?"

Silence. Then her voice, low and flat.

"You're avoiding me."

Callan rubbed his eyes. "Busy week."

"Busy," she repeated, voice sharpening. "Right. Is that what you call it? Busy?" A pause. "Or just done with me now that you got what you wanted?"

Callan's eyes narrowed. He stayed silent.

Tricia's voice shifted silk over barbed wire. "Thought you could use me, then disappear? Treat me like some slut?" Her breath hitched, like she was on the edge of laughing or screaming. "You're not special, Callan. You're just a coward with a hard-on and a dead phone."

"Tricia," he said evenly, "stop."

"No." Her voice cracked like glass. "You think I don't see it? The way you look through people. The way you looked at me. Like I'm a tool. Something to be managed."

"Babe." He blurted it out despite himself. "I was fishing with Mel and Danny today."

"Oh." she snapped. "But you couldn't be bothered to tell me." Her voice dropped to a whisper. "I shouldn't have to beg for your attention."

Silence.

Tricia breathed in shakily. "You made me feel like I mattered. And now you want to pretend none of it happened." Her voice sharpened again, cutting and raw. "You're a bastard, Callan."

Click.

Callan sat still, the phone warm in his hand, her words hanging in the air like smoke. He could handle surveillance. He could handle corpses. But this? This was personal. And personal was messy.

CHAPTER 38

The phone buzzed again before he even had time to process the last call. *Tricia Langley.* He stared at the screen. Pulse steady. Mind already shifting gears. She was calling back. That wasn't a mistake. That wasn't heat-of-the-moment anger—this was calculated.

Callan let it ring once. Twice. Then answered. "Tricia," he said, voice carefully neutral.

He heard her shaky breath on the other end. Then—"I'm sorry."

Callan didn't respond. Let the silence stretch, let her sit in it, feel the weight of it.

"Callan, I didn't mean that," she continued, her voice softer now, stripped of the venom. "I just... I lost my temper. It's been a long week, and I..." She trailed off, like she was grasping for the right words.

Callan exhaled slowly, leaning his elbow against the console. *Let's see where you're going with this, Langley.* Because this wasn't about him not answering his phone. It was about her history.

People who'd been abandoned clung too hard, too fast. And when that grip slipped? They either crumbled... or retaliated.

He didn't know yet which one Tricia was built for.

"That wasn't fair to you," she admitted, voice tight. "You didn't deserve that."

He let the silence settle before speaking.

"What's really going on, Tricia?"

A small laugh, hollow and self-deprecating. "Would you believe me if I said work?"

"Try me."

She sighed—a sound that said she wasn't sure how much to give him.

"

"We lost a CI yesterday. One I'd been working for months."

Callan didn't respond right away. Because that tracked. A confidential informant flipping on the wrong person could go sideways fast. Those who believed police protection would keep them safe found themselves in a dumpster before sunrise.

"Shit," he said finally.

"Yeah." Her voice dropped. "And it wasn't clean, Callan. Execution-style. We didn't even find the body—his *kid* did. Seven years old."

Callan felt something in his chest tighten. He wasn't sentimental about dead men. But a kid finding the body? That hit different.

"I'm sorry," he said. And for once, he meant it.

"Yeah, well." Tricia let out a bitter chuckle. "It gets better. He was feeding me intel on dirty cops working with the cartel. And now he's dead. And guess who looks like they fucked up?"

Callan already knew.

"Internal Affairs breathing down your neck?"

"Like a goddamn hurricane," she muttered. "I'm telling you, Callan, the whole thing stinks. This wasn't some random hit. This was a cleanup job. And now I've got half the precinct looking at me like I'm the leak."

Callan frowned, rolling that over in his head.

A corruption case, a dead CI, and a tight-lipped department? Yeah. That would do it. IA wouldn't be the only ones watching—her own people would be colder than concrete.

"That why you've been so on edge?" he asked, keeping his voice level.

"Part of it."

Silence again. Then she sighed, and her voice softened, just enough to make him question if it was real or rehearsed.

"Callan, I shouldn't have snapped at you like that. I just... I needed to feel like I had some kind of control over *something*."

Control.

That word lingered between them.

Because that was the truth of it. This wasn't an apology. It was a reset. She was walking it back, realigning the board. And it was working.

Callan wasn't naïve. He knew manipulation when he saw it. Hell, he lived it.

But Tricia wasn't sloppy. She was *good*.

And this?

This wasn't someone cleaning up a mess. This was someone who knew the mess, and how to fix it.

Callan had seen cleaner cover stories in cartel dossiers.

It tracked. The story had all the right beats.

But she was a detective. And detectives knew how to spin a narrative.

"You know," Callan said, tone dry, "if you'd just led with that..."

"Yeah, well." He could hear her smirk. "I never claimed to be great at this whole communication thing."

"No shit."

She let out a soft laugh. "You forgive me?"

That was the question, wasn't it? Did he? "I don't hold grudges, Tricia."

Not a yes. Not a no.

She heard it. Of course she did.

"Good," she said. Then, softer, "Callan?"

"Yeah."

"... Are you going to leave me now?"

CHAPTER 39

The sofa wasn't going to run away from home, but Callan wasn't taking any chances. With one arm draped over the back, his eyes half-lidded, he let the evening settle around him. The soft glow of the city lights bled in through the windows, casting long shadows across the room—and for once, the stillness wasn't unwelcome.

Beckett was curled against his side, warm and grounding. The cat had been unusually needy tonight—not that Callan minded. Normally, Beckett kept his affection measured, doled out in rare, begrudging moments. But tonight, he was stretched across Callan's ribs, purring like a damn engine, head tucked into the crook of his arm.

Callan ran a slow hand down Beckett's back, feeling the rhythmic rise and fall of his breathing. "What's got into you?" he murmured, scratching the sweet spot just behind Beckett's ear. The cat let out a low, satisfied rumble but didn't move. Callan smirked, shaking his head. Maybe Beckett could tell he needed this. Needed something *simple* for once.

His phone sat face down on the coffee table, blissfully silent. No new messages. No missed calls. Tricia hadn't texted—not since the vague promise that she'd let him know when and where she needed him.

That was fine. Better, even.

Callan wasn't in a hurry to dive headfirst into whatever web she was spinning. He wasn't sure if he'd step in at all.

His fingers idly traced circles against Beckett's fur as his mind drifted. He should've been enjoying the peace. Should've been sinking into the quiet. Instead, his thoughts twisted, circling back to the last time he let himself believe in the illusion of stillness.

He exhaled, long and slow, dragging a hand over his face.

Tonight, though, there was no one to interrupt. No phone call dragging him back in. Just him, the quiet hum of the city, and a cat who—for reasons unknown—had decided Callan was the only thing in the world worth sticking close to.

Callan let the silence stretch, Beckett's weight grounding him in the present. He should've stayed like that, let the moment linger.

But of course, he didn't.

His work laptop was on the island, closed but not forgotten. The secure one, the one he wasn't supposed to use for personal matters. The one that had nearly gotten him flagged for searching Tricia's name.

Slowly, he eased Beckett off his chest. The cat made a small, irritated sound before resettling in the warm spot he left behind. Callan didn't bother apologizing—Beckett would get over it.

He flipped open the laptop. The screen glowed to life, prompting him for his credentials. A gauntlet of encrypted logins, firewalls, identity checks.

The Archive wasn't a place you just checked into. It was a vault—and it only opened if you knew *exactly* how to ask.

Callan navigated through the layers of security until he reached the job board.

A list of active contracts loaded: Southeast U.S., Central America, the occasional high-risk European job.

But one stood out. *Winnipeg, Manitoba. Canada.*

Callan frowned. "Ewww. Surveillance." He rarely took surveillance gigs. They were tedious, time-consuming, low-paying. Surveillance wasn't action. It was waiting. Watching. Sitting in cars for hours, eating cold takeout, pissing in bottles, and hoping something interesting happened.

Low effort. Lower reward.

Callan had spent years refining his skills to avoid exactly this kind of thing. But still--this one was different. Because it was in Winnipeg.

He didn't know why he clicked it. Instinct, maybe. Curiosity. Or something closer to fate. The file loaded. Target: Pending. Contract: Pending Approval. Low risk. Low exposure. Long-term surveillance. No immediate action required. Just observation.

He drummed his fingers against the counter.

He could ignore it. Let someone else take it.

But then... there was Isabelle.

Callan wasn't sentimental. He didn't check in on people just because. But he hadn't seen his sister in years.

His finger hovered over the "Request Assignment" button. A surveillance job in Winnipeg wasn't worth his time. But Isabelle was.

Request submitted. Pending approval.

Request approved.

Callan blinked as the green light flashed. Fast. *Too* fast.

Surveillance jobs usually took time to process—low risk, low urgency. But this? Approved instantly.

The contract details refreshed. Two-week minimum. Subject: Unnamed male, mid-40s. Possible human trafficking.

So, at least he might run into some heavy types—cartel, bikers, gangs.

"I mean," he muttered, "it could get exciting."

And it was Winnipeg. He couldn't remember the last time he missed anyone. But right now?

He leaned back, staring at the screen. Fingers drummed lightly against the counter. He'd been feeling squirrelly for a while now. Maybe a road trip was exactly what he needed.

He texted Tricia.

Callan: Heading out of town for work. Few days.

He didn't elaborate. He didn't need to. Three dots appeared. Then disappeared. Then reappeared. *Tricia: Where?*

Callan debated ignoring it, but that would just invite more texts. Better to give just enough. *Callan: Winnipeg.*

More dots. *Tricia: Since when do you work in Canada?*

Callan: Since five minutes ago.

The dots lingered... then vanished. No response.

Fine by him.

Next, he pulled up his cat sitter's contact.

Callan: You free for a few days? Last-minute trip. Beckett needs supervision.

Lucy: You've got some timing, man. But yeah, I can do it. How long we talking?

Callan: A week. Maybe more. I'll leave extra supplies.

Lucy: No problem. Your spoiled son will be in good hands.

Callan: Appreciate it. Key's in the usual spot.

Lucy: Got it. Safe travels.

Callan set his phone down and exhaled.

Winnipeg. A random surveillance job. An immediate approval. Too convenient. But the decision was already made. He was going.

He sighed, rubbing his jaw as he scrolled through his contacts. Might as well give her a heads-up. He tapped Isabelle's name and brought the phone to his ear.

It rang. And rang.

Then—voicemail.

He exhaled through his nose. Not surprising. Isabelle wasn't the type to hover over her phone.

The beep sounded.

"Hey, sis. What are you up to this weekend?" A pause. "Call me back when you get this."

He ended the call and set the phone down and returned to the couch, sat down.

Beckett, still curled beside him, flicked his tail once, then settled again. Sound asleep.

CHAPTER 40

The steady churn of Miami International Airport always made Callan feel at ease. His pace was unhurried but efficient. The early morning crowd was the usual blend of red-eyed business travelers, parents wrangling overtired kids, and over-packed tourists already regretting their choices.

He moved through it without issue, carry-on slung over one shoulder, personal phone in his pocket. No aliases. No disguises. This job didn't require any of that.

Low risk. Low effort. Surveillance was boring as hell, but it paid the bills.

A toddler wailed near security. A couple argued in whispers over a carry-on. Callan took it all in without reacting—like a ghost sliding through the living.

He was flying under his own name today. Rare. Felt weird. But not wrong. The risk was minimal, and the job was only half the reason he was going.

He hadn't been to Canada in years—not since a job in Toronto, almost a decade ago. But Winnipeg? That was different.

That was Isabelle.

He checked the time. Thirty minutes to boarding. Just enough time for a coffee and a quiet moment to remind himself that this was just another job.

Still, something nagged at him. Not the work. The job was clear-cut. Observe, report, get paid. It was everything around the job that tugged at him.

Isabelle hadn't called back. And Tricia? Barely a reaction. Her text had been short and clipped: *Got it. Be safe.*

No questions. No complaints. Too easy.

Callan exhaled, pushing those thoughts aside as he stepped into line at a kiosk. Four days. Maybe five. In and out. No complications.

Hopefully the universe got the memo.

He waited near the kiosk pickup counter, hands in his pockets. The air smelled like burnt espresso and overpriced pastries. Conversations murmured around him, blending into the tinny crackle of overhead announcements—gate changes, final boarding, the endless rhythm of transit.

His phone buzzed.

Isabelle.

Callan smirked, swiping to answer. "Hey, sis."

"Callan!" Isabelle's voice came through bright, warm, unfiltered. "I just got your message. Are you actually coming to Winnipeg?"

"Yeah. Heading there now. Should land by noon."

"Oh my God, this is amazing! Why didn't you tell me sooner? I would've made actual plans!"

Callan chuckled, shaking his head. "Figured I'd surprise you."

"Well, colour me surprised. This is perfect. Where are you staying?"

"Downtown. The Radisson."

Isabelle made a noise of disapproval. "Come on, a hotel? You should stay with me."

"I already booked it."

"So? Cancel it. I've got a guest room. Well, technically, it's my office-slash-reading nook, but it has a bed and actual furniture. It's not fancy, but it beats a soulless hotel room."

Callan hesitated. He hadn't even considered staying with her. "Didn't want to impose."

"You're not imposing, Callan. We haven't seen each other in forever. And if I leave it up to you, I'll get a rushed dinner and a vague promise to meet for coffee before you disappear again."

He winced slightly. Not unfair.

"You really want me to stay?"

"Obviously. You're going to be here for a few days; we should actually catch up."

Callan exhaled. "All right. I'll stay with you."

"Good. And don't make dinner plans—I've got something in mind. No weird health food, I promise."

Callan huffed a quiet laugh. "That remains to be seen."

"You'll survive."

Her excitement came through in every word, and something about it twisted in his chest—not unpleasant, just... unfamiliar. The same quiet ache that made him take the job in the first place.

He had questioned the wisdom of all of this. Now, hearing her voice? He was questioning it more.

Her enthusiasm filled him with the kind of anxiety he hadn't felt in decades—not danger-anxiety. Something worse. The kind that came with expectations.

He was already pushing the limits of human interaction.

This might be a step—or ten—too far.

CHAPTER 41

Winnipeg had always struck Callan as a city that balanced its historical roots with a vibrant cultural scene. The iconic BMO building at Portage and Main stood as a testament to early 20th-century architecture, its neoclassical design a reminder of the city's rich past. Not far from there, The Forks offered a lively convergence point where the Assiniboine and Red Rivers met, serving as a hub for markets, eateries, and community events.

Callan's last visit had been for a concert—The Small Glories, that folk duo with harmonies that got under your skin. Good music. Honest lyrics. A reminder that this city knew how to feel.

Now, as he navigated the familiar streets, the blend of old and new stirred a sense of anticipation in him. The memory of strangling a priest who'd groomed the wrong woman's child surfaced without warning in a place that didn't feel violent at all. It made him grin. Nostalgia, Callan-style.

Isabelle's battered Subaru rattled through the streets of Winnipeg, the soft hum of the engine barely covering the silence between them.

Callan sat in the passenger seat, relaxed. Somehow still trusting his sister behind the wheel despite the missing glasses and her casual relationship with traffic laws.

They'd covered the basics—his flight, delays, airline food—when he finally asked, "So... when'd you actually move into the city?"

Isabelle kept her eyes on the road, her fingers tapping lightly against the wheel. "Couple of years now. The place I was renting, at West Hawk Lake, got sold out from under me. Bit of a bummer, but I guess it was time."

"That sucks. I know you loved it out there."

"I did," Isabelle admitted, a wistful smile tugging at her lips. "It was peaceful. But y'know, I always knew it was gonna be temporary. The owner cashed in while the market was hot, and I wasn't about to fight it."

Callan nodded as she flicked on the signal and turned onto a quieter street.

"So, how's city life treating you?"

She laughed. "Different. But I can walk to a decent coffee shop in under five minutes now, so... trade-offs, right?"

Callan smirked. "Depends how good the coffee is."

"Oh, it's solid. I have standards. I'd rather live in a tent than suffer through bad coffee every morning."

Callan chuckled, shaking his head. "Guess it worked out, then."

She glanced at him, mock-offended. "It's not so bad. I found a little house in Wolseley with cheap rent, decent landlord, lots of trees. It's kind of got that small-town feel, which helps."

"You? In Wolseley? Hippie central? That tracks."

"What's that supposed to mean?" Isabelle shot him a playful glare before rolling to a stop at a red light.

Callan smirked. "You, in a neighbourhood known for hippies, tree-huggers, and artists? Feels pretty on-brand."

She gasped theatrically. "Excuse me! I am a responsible, grounded adult."

Callan snorted. "Uh-huh. How many crystals in your house right now?"

"Rude," she huffed. "Only like... seven."

He shook his head. "Yeah, totally grounded."

***

They pulled into the driveway of a squat one-storey tucked between two tall elms. The porch light flickered like a candle about to give up. Wind chimes, chipped planters, and what looked like a stolen patio chair gave the place a lopsided charm.

Callan stared at it for a moment. "Looks nice."

Isabelle grinned, unclipping her seatbelt. "Welcome to my humble little corner of Winnipeg."

Inside was chaos, as expected. Incense hung heavy, the couch sagged, and mismatched lamps and pillows adorned the room. Half-finished projects, half-loved memories, and forgotten things filled the space. Isabelle's mess spoke volumes. A coffee table bore years of wear and tear, a tarot deck lay beside a dying candle. In the kitchen, dried herbs hung from a rack near the stove, and a tiny ceramic owl watched the sink. Mismatched cabinets made Callan's eyes water.

He dropped his bag by the door. The disorder made his palms sweat. But this was Belle. Of course it was. "So, Belle," he said, letting the old nickname slip like it had never left. "What's for dinner?"

Isabelle turned, brows up. "Belle? Wow. You are softening."

He leaned on the kitchen doorframe, watching her rummage in the fridge. "Don't get used to it."

She tossed a head of kale onto the counter with dramatic flair. "Chickpea stew. Surprise."

Callan's smirk faded. "Jesus Christ."

She laughed. "Relax, tough guy. I was messing with you. I wouldn't do that to you on your first night. We're going out. Dinner club."

"Dinner *club*?"

"Yeah. Weekly thing. We rotate restaurants. Low-key, good food, good people."

Callan folded his arms. "And tonight?"

"Ukrainian. Best pierogies and borscht in the city. You'll live."

He gave her a look. "Not sure beet soup qualifies as living."

"Trust me; you're gonna love it."

She nudged him toward the hallway. "But if you insist on being a buzzkill, at least unpack first."

"I need an hour. Work stuff."

She sighed. "Fine. I'll go vibe alone."

***

The guest room was cozy in the way small, quiet rooms often are. The quilt on the bed looked handmade. The bookshelves were stuffed with old novels, plant-care guides, and a couple of journals that screamed *please don't read me.*

Callan dropped his laptop bag, opened it, and booted up.

"Here you go," Isabelle said, gesturing around the room. "It's not a five-star hotel, but it's cozy."

"It's good. Thanks."

Isabelle sighed. "I'll go put on some music so you don't get too sucked into whatever mystery you're solving."

Callan waited until Isabelle disappeared down the hall before pulling out his work laptop. He powered it on, then grabbed his burner phone and used it as a hotspot. The familiar hum of the machine booting up filled the small room as he leaned forward, settling into a familiar mindset.

Hotspot active. VPN live. Encrypted network online.

The system hummed. *New file available.* He clicked it.

POI: Trent Ziggler.

Location: 274 Barrow Street, Winnipeg, MB.

A name, finally. Until now, this had been a faceless job. Just another line in a spreadsheet.

But names changed things. Names meant direction. Names meant it was time.

Chapter 42

The Ukrainian restaurant was small but packed, the air thick with the scent of garlic, dill, and slow-simmered broth. Embroidered tapestries lined the walls, along with old black-and-white family photos and a few faded newspaper clippings in Cyrillic script. It had the charm of a place that had been around forever—slow, unfussy, everything made from scratch.

Callan sat at a long communal table, surrounded by a lively dozen—Isabelle's so-called dinner club. He hadn't expected the group to be this big or eclectic.

On one end, two guys in Patagonia vests and dress shirts were deep in conversation about something finance related. Across from them, two women in flowing skirts and layers of beaded necklaces were passionately discussing their favourite mushroom-foraging spots. A quiet couple in their fifties shared a plate of dumplings nearby, and beside them, a wiry man in his sixties had the deep tan of someone who spent half the year somewhere tropical.

To Callan's left sat Claire—twenty-eight, maybe thirty—radiating influencer energy. Sleek blonde hair, flawless makeup, fitted black turtleneck. Delicate gold jewellery and nails that clicked lightly against her glass.

To his right, in stark contrast, was a grandmotherly woman with short silver hair and kind, smiling eyes. She wore a hand-knit cardigan over a floral dress and smelled faintly of citronella. A woven bracelet hugged her wrist like something a teenager might wear. But she carried the quiet authority of someone people listened to.

"Okay, Callan," Claire said, turning toward him with the practiced charm of someone used to being the centre of attention. "You've been a mystery all night. Isabelle barely told us anything about you. Spill."

Callan felt the table shift toward him, a dozen pairs of eyes flicking his way. The room suddenly felt louder—cutlery clinking, laughter swelling, a little too close to his ears. He gave Claire a small, practiced smile. The same one he used at networking events when he'd rather be anywhere else.

"Not much to tell," he said, casual. "Just work, mostly."

He was vague in order to dodge follow-ups, but he could feel the interest lingering. Waiting. His fingers curled around his glass, anchoring himself. He glanced toward Isabelle, hoping for a redirect, but she was busy pouring more wine.

"I'm pretty boring," he added with a shrug. "I live in Miami, spend too much time in the office. That's about it."

A beat of silence followed—a palpable opening where someone could press him. His pulse quickened. He kept his posture relaxed, the trick being to stay just unremarkable enough: Not evasive, not too available.

Claire tilted her head, clearly tempted to double down. But a joke cracked at the far end of the table, dragging her attention away.

Beside him, the older woman chuckled. Her eyes twinkled as she gently scolded, "Oh, leave him be, Claire. Not everyone needs to be an open book."

Callan exhaled slowly. The knot in his chest loosened just a little.

Still, the questions kept coming. Not aggressively, but Callan felt it: curiosity.

Eric, the friendly marketing guy, leaned in. "So, Callan," he said with a smile, "what's it like growing up with Isabelle? She's basically everyone's favourite person here."

"Was she always this cool?" one of the finance guys added, grinning. "Or was she, like, secretly a total nerd?"

Isabelle gasped in mock offence. "How *dare* you."

Callan smirked, lifting his glass. "Let's just say she was always the free spirit. More into collecting rocks and rescuing stray animals than worrying about schoolwork."

Claire laughed. "Oh my God, you still do that."

"I don't have any animals *right now*," Isabelle said.

Which, Callan thought, was not obvious based on how her house smelled. Still, he smiled, and the table laughed with her. The attention lingered on him a little longer—more questions, more warmth. Not interrogation, not performance. Just... curiosity.

It felt strange.

They liked Isabelle, so they wanted to like him too. That was all. But it was unfamiliar. It wasn't guarded. It wasn't strategic. It wasn't a dance toward leverage. It had been a long time since he'd sat at a table like that.

At some point, the woman beside him turned again, her gaze soft but sharp. "You're quiet, but you take everything in."

Callan raised a brow. "That a bad thing?"

She smiled. "Not at all. Just means you're careful."

Dinner wrapped up lazily, the plates nearly licked clean, conversation winding down into that easy post-meal lull. Claire, ever the social spark plug, clapped her hands together. "All right, people. We can't just call it a night. Who's coming out for drinks?"

The finance guys perked up. One of them—Greg or Graham, Callan hadn't been paying attention—grinned. "Depends where we're going."

"There's a lounge a few blocks from here," Claire said, pulling out her phone. "Live music, solid cocktails. Not too loud."

The mushroom foragers begged off—early hike. The older couple smiled but shook their heads. A few others hesitated, weighing comfort against curiosity.

Then Claire turned her attention to Isabelle, resting her chin on her hand. "Belle, you never come out. Come on, just one drink."

Isabelle gave an exaggerated groan, but Callan saw the flicker of hesitation in her eyes. She wanted to say yes.

Claire, sensing weakness, doubled down. "You used to be the life of the party. Don't tell me you've gone full settled-down adult on us."

"I'm not *that* settled," Isabelle scoffed.

"Prove it."

Isabelle looked to Callan, maybe looking for an out. Instead, he smirked. "I'm in if you are."

Her eyes narrowed, amused. "You just want to watch me make a fool of myself."

"Obviously," he said.

She rolled her eyes. "Fine. One drink."

The table cheered.

Claire, victorious, stood up, clapping her hands. "Yes! All right, let's go."

They spilled out into the warm night, Callan shoving his hands in his pockets as the group set off down the sidewalk. He glanced at Isabelle out the corner of his eye. She didn't get to do this kind of thing much, he could tell.

Callan was craving a halfway decent Negroni. That was reason enough.

But as the bar's neon sign flickered in the distance, another name echoed in the back of his mind— *Trent Ziggler.*

Another world. Waiting right outside the door.

Chapter 43

Claire made the walk to the bar feel like an event. She hyped up the place the entire way—claimed it had the best cocktails in the city, the perfect blend of upscale and laid-back, and (her words, not Callan's) "a perfect ratio of people you'd flirt with versus people you'd just steal outfit ideas from."

Callan half-listened, hands in his pockets, focused on the shifting group dynamics.

Claire and Isabelle gravitated toward each other, their conversation easy, their laughter frequent. Isabelle always had a way of drawing people in—making them feel like they belonged—but with Claire, it felt like they were already old friends catching up.

And then there was Greg. Or maybe Graham. Callan still wasn't sure, but whatever his name was, he was sticking close to Isabelle. And, to Callan's mild surprise, she didn't seem to mind.

Greg was smooth, in the way people get after growing into their looks—finance guy, effortless charm, rolled-up sleeves just so, highlighting the watch and forearms. A confident smile. The complete package.

"You know," Greg said, leaning slightly toward Isabelle as they walked, "I've been to, like, five of these dinner clubs now, and somehow, I've never seen you come out after."

Isabelle laughed, her smile genuine. "Guess I'm unpredictable."

Greg smirked. "I like that. A little mystery is always good."

Callan watched his stepsister, the same way you'd watch someone poking a tiger with a stick. She was clearly interested—and not bothering to hide it.

Greg clocked it too.

"You live in Wolseley, right?" he asked. "I used to live there. Great neighbourhood. A little... artsy, but in a good way."

Callan watched Isabelle tilt her head, amused. "Wow, a finance guy who survived Wolseley? What was that like?"

Greg chuckled. "Hey, I appreciate character. Plus, I'm all about supporting local businesses. If the coffee's good, I don't care how many crystal shops are next door."

Claire snorted. "Yeah, sure, Greg. You totally seem like the oat-milk-latte and a tarot-reading type."

Greg was undeterred. "I like to keep an open mind. Maybe you could show me your favourite spots sometime?"

Isabelle actually considered it. "Yeah," she said, with a small smile. "Maybe."

Greg's grin widened.

***

The bar was tucked into a historic brick building, marked only by a sleek black awning and a discreet brass plaque marking. No neon. No gimmicks. The kind of place that didn't need to advertise.

As they approached, the doorman gave them a once-over, his expression unreadable behind dark sunglasses, despite the fact it was well past sunset. Callan clocked the earpiece, the tailored jacket—subtle markers that said this wasn't just a bar. It was a business on the surface, but there were deeper currents. He'd been around long enough to recognize the signs.

Didn't matter. He wasn't working tonight.

Inside, the place was low-lit and plush. Velvet seating, dark wood, gold accents. A long marble counter stretched across one wall, manned by bartenders in crisp shirts with quiet confidence, mixing drinks with the kind of precision you paid too much for and didn't regret.

The crowd was polished. Professionals, creatives, a few who looked like they carried untraceable cash and didn't bother with receipts. Nobody was flashing anything overtly illegal, but Callan would bet good money that not every conversation in those corner booths was about mergers and acquisitions.

"Tell me this isn't the coolest bar," Claire said, twirling toward Isabelle, who was already scanning the menu. "Like, best vibe, best cocktails. It's my favourite spot."

Isabelle laughed, nudging her playfully. "You say that about every bar."

"Because I have great taste," Claire shot back.

Callan smirked, leaning against the bar, taking it all in. The music was low and smooth. candles flickered on the tables. The place was polished but not stiff. He could admit it—it had charm.

Greg sidled up to Isabelle again. "So," he said, elbow on the bar, "better than your usual dinner club spots?"

Isabelle tilted her head. "It's different. But I like it."

Greg grinned. "Let me buy you a drink. You a whiskey girl?"

She hesitated, then smiled. "Depends on the whiskey."

Greg lit up. "All right, I'm choosing. No objections?"

"If I hate it," she said, "you owe me two drinks."

"Deal."

Callan just shook his head as Greg flagged down the bartender. Isabelle seemed entertained. Not overplaying it, not shutting it down. Callan couldn't tell whether she was into Greg or just enjoying being wanted. Either way, he wasn't going to play overprotective brother.

Instead, his gaze drifted. Faces, voices, body language. Habit more than anything.

The older guys sipping whiskey in the corner? Not just finance. Not just government. Something in between. The way they subtly prioritized certain customers. The guy near the door, sipping but scanning.

This place? Guys like Callan fit in here more than people like Claire did.

The thought made him laugh.

***

The night unfolded effortlessly. The cocktails were exactly what Claire had promised—carefully curated, balanced, dangerously smooth. Callan stuck to two, enjoying the slow burn of a Negroni. The crowd buzzed with energy, music humming just under the conversation.

Claire floated between the groups, absolutely in her element. The finance guys got louder. Others broke off into clusters. Callan listened without needing to join in.

Across the bar, Isabelle and Greg had settled into their own little bubble. She leaned in, laughing softly, tracing her glass with one finger. Greg murmured something, and she hesitated before nodding. He touched the small of her back as they stood.

Moments later, she was at Callan's side, looking like a kid confessing to a broken window. "Hey," she whispered. "Greg asked me to go back to his place for a bit." She grimaced. "But I feel really bad leaving you."

He placed a hand on her shoulder. "I hope you have fun. Truly. I hope he puts your back out."

She squinted at him, trying to read if he meant it. Then she laughed, eyes lighting up. "God, you're such an asshole. Love you."

"Love you three," he said. A nod to her dad.

She wiped at the corner of her eye. "I hope Greg has protection," she muttered, tapping her cheek like a Rhodes Scholar deep in thought.

"Jesus," Callan groaned. "Leave before you make this weird."

She grinned, turned, and disappeared into the night with Greg.

She deserved this. Something easy. Something light. If Greg was all that, great.

Callan finished his drink, already thinking about the breakfast she'd promised earlier. He was just about to consider heading out himself when a voice slid into his ear like a key in a lock.

"So, now that your sister's ditched you..." Claire appeared at his side like she'd always been there. "What do you say we get out of here?"

Callan turned, eyebrow raised.

Claire's smirk was pure mischief. "Come on," she said. "Live a little."

He tilted his empty glass. "That depends. Where exactly are we going?"

"That's the fun part," she said, leaning in. "You'll have to trust me."

He let the moment stretch. Then, with a soft clink, set the glass down.

"Well," he said, standing, "guess we'll find out."

Claire grinned. "That's the spirit."

CHAPTER 44

Stepping out of the bar with Claire at his side filled Callan with some feeling he couldn't name. Maybe pride? Maybe something less useful. He filed it away under things to unpack later. The night air was crisp, cutting through the warm haze of alcohol in his system. The street still buzzed—clusters of people spilling from nearby lounges, the hum of passing cars mixing with laughter and late-night conversation.

Claire walked with easy confidence, heels clicking against the pavement, her hair catching the glow of the streetlights.

"All right, mysterious man," she mused, slipping her phone into her purse. "I've decided we're going somewhere a little more fun. Less velvet, more energy."

Callan smirked. "What, that place wasn't fun enough for you?"

She shot him a look—teasing, sharp-edged. "I'm doing you a favour. You look like you need to loosen up."

He chuckled quietly. "Lead the way, then."

As they walked, Callan's eyes swept the street—his instincts doing what they always did. Nothing pinged. Just people heading home, others lingering outside in lazy clusters. Normal city noise.

But then—

A glance.

A man leaning casually against a lamppost, cigarette glowing faintly in the dark. Not doing anything suspicious. Just watching. Not staring. Not obvious. But... watching.

Callan's gaze passed over him without stopping. His mind didn't flag it as a problem—just a guy, a cigarette, a city night.

Claire nudged him. "You zoning out on me already?"

He shook off the thought. "Just taking in the sights."

She grabbed his hand, grinning. "Try to keep up, Miami."

They cut down a side street where neon lights bled into the pavement. Another bar, this one louder, rougher around the edges. The kind of place you drank in, not just posed with your drink at.

Claire slipped through the crowd like she belonged there—because she did—and flagged down the bartender like a pro. She turned, full attention on Callan.

"So," she said, elbow on the counter, "how much of the brooding mystery guy thing is real?"

Callan huffed a quiet laugh. "I didn't realise I was putting on a show."

Claire smirked. "You might not think you are but, trust me; you've got a vibe." She leaned in, her voice dropping a shade. "Dangerous."

He sipped his drink, eyes on her. *You have no idea*, he thought. But what he said was, "That why you dragged me out? Recon for Isabelle?"

She shrugged. "Maybe. Or maybe I'm just curious."

"And what exactly are you so curious about?"

Claire tapped her glass. "For starters? How the hell you two turned out so different. She's all sunshine and trees, and you're…" She waved a hand at him. "All clouds and shadows."

Callan found that vaguely insulting but let it slide with a dry chuckle. "Different lives. That's all."

"Mhm." Claire studied him for a beat longer, then switched gears. "So, why Miami?"

He rolled the glass between his palms. "I like fishing. And the beach."

Claire smirked. "That's the most non-answer answer I've ever heard."

Callan exhaled through his nose, amused. "You always this persistent?"

"Only when I want to be."

The drinks came and went. Claire had a way of keeping things light while still digging under the surface—playful, sharp, always a step ahead. Callan gave her enough just to keep her interested.

At some point, her hand brushed his—light and teasing. He didn't pull away.

"You don't let people in easily, do you?" she asked, her voice softer now.

"That your official assessment?"

Claire grinned. "Something like that." With a glint in her eye, she continued. "You know I'm not going to sleep with you, right? No matter how mysterious you are."

"Cheque please," Callan half shouted, glancing around theatrically.

Claire laughed, full and unfiltered. "God, you're such a guy."

"I prefer *man of mystery*," he said.

She leaned closer, grinning, "You know what your problem is?"

"It's cute you think there's only one."

Claire tapped his arm. "You think being emotionally unavailable is a personality trait."

He shrugged. "It's efficient."

Claire shook her head, laughing. "Come on, Miami. Let's get out of here before I psychoanalyse you for sport."

"Too late."

They walked a block in comfortable silence, the city humming around them. At the corner, Claire slowed. "All right," she said, letting go of his arm. "This is me."

"You heading back alone?"

Claire gave him a look. "Relax, I've done this before. Besides, I've got mace, keys, and killer instincts."

Callan scanned the street anyway.

Claire grinned. "I'll text Isabelle. Let her know you were almost charming."

He gave her a look. "Almost?"

"Don't push it."

She leaned in and kissed his cheek—light, confident, nothing owed. "Night, Miami."

"Night, Claire."

She turned and walked into the glow of the streetlamps. Heels tapping on concrete.

Callan watched her go, hands in his pockets. Then he turned, heading the other way.

No rush.

Just the long, familiar dark waiting at the end.

CHAPTER 45

Finding Trent Ziggler wasn't difficult.

Callan hadn't even settled into his rental car before he had eyes on the guy. Mid-thirties, a little on the doughy side, with the look of someone who spent most of his waking hours behind a desk. Ordinary, forgettable. The kind of man who could disappear in a crowd. Which, Callan figured, was probably an asset in his line of work.

Trent worked at an insurance company in an unremarkable office building near the edge of downtown Winnipeg. Callan parked across the street in a nondescript sedan and watched him arrive at exactly 8:04 AM—coffee in hand, wearing a wrinkled button-down and a tie that didn't quite match. The guy looked like someone who'd settled into routine a little too comfortably. Which, as far as Callan was concerned, was the first red flag.

For hours, Callan watched. Trent went in. Stayed in. Didn't reappear until his lunch break, which he spent at a café two doors down, eating a ham and cheese sandwich and scrolling his phone like a man without a secret in the world. Then, just as predictably, he returned to the beige-lit abyss and didn't reemerge until 5:00PM sharp.

Callan tapped his fingers on the centre console. If there was something interesting about Trent Ziggler, it wasn't immediately apparent.

His habits were predictable. His movement routine. No suspicious meetings. No late-night drives. The guy was boring.

But at least it gave Callan an excuse to get out of Isabelle's cluttered abode. A few days there had his skin crawling. He also missed Beckett—his big boy was probably sprawled in the sunlight of Lucy's east-facing balcony, living his best life. Callan smiled faintly at the thought.

By early evening, it was clear that Trent was as thrilling as a bowl of plain oatmeal. He drove home to a quiet residential street with well-kept hedges and a golden retriever that practically wagged itself to death when he walked through the door.

Nothing about the man screamed "person of interest." But someone had paid for eyes on Trent Ziggler. Which meant something had to be there. It just hadn't surfaced yet.

That was a problem for tomorrow.

Tonight, Callan had dinner plans.

***

Isabelle was already at home when Callan walked in. With her feet tucked beneath her, she sat curled on the couch in an oversized hoodie and leggings. The smell of fresh coffee and something sweetly sour hung in the air.

She glanced up and grinned. "Oh, look who finally decided to show up. Did you get lost?"

Callan smirked, dropping his bag by the door. "Busy day. You survive your night out?"

Isabelle let out a dreamy sigh, positively glowing. "More than survived. Thrived."

Callan arched a brow. "That good, huh?"

"Oh, Greg is amazing," she gushed, grabbing her mug. "Like, not just the sex—though, yes—but seriously, Callan. He listens when I talk. Do you know how rare that is?"

She barely paused for breath. "I told him about that time in grade eight when I cut my bangs with kitchen scissors, and he actually asked what I was trying to prove. Like, not in a judgy way—he was curious. Who does that?"

Callan hid a grin as he headed into the kitchen. "Yeah, shocking. You babble on and on."

"I'm serious!" she called after him. "He's so easy to talk to. Funny, but not in that 'I'm trying too hard' way. I wasn't expecting much, but we talked until like... five in the morning."

Callan returned to the living room with a glass of water, leaning against the arm of the couch. "Talking, huh?"

Isabelle rolled her eyes. "Oh, shut up. Mostly talking. And then I crashed at his place."

"So, you like him?"

She bit her lip, and for a second, Callan saw the shy teenager he used to know—the one who overthought everything. "I think I do," she said quietly. Then she brightened again. "And he texted me this morning. No dumb three-day wait. He wants to see me again."

Callan nodded. "Congratulations. You found one of the good ones."

Perfect. The more she fixated on Greg, the more distracted she'd be from Callan's actual work.

"I know, right?" She beamed. "It's just nice. No games. No wondering where I stand. He's just... honest about liking me."

Callan studied her, feeling a quiet sense of relief. Isabelle had always put everyone else first. She deserved something that wasn't complicated.

Then she narrowed her eyes. "What about you? You didn't just go straight home last night, either."

He exhaled, shaking his head. "Had drinks with Claire."

Isabelle gasped, sitting bolt upright. "Claire? You?"

He shrugged, smirking. "We talked. Got along. One thing led to another."

She smacked his arm. "I knew she was into you! Oh my God, Callan!"

"Relax," he said. "It wasn't a big deal."

"Not a big deal? She's going to be so smug about this. Claire lives to win."

"I'm aware."

"Did you get her number?"

"Yeah."

"And?"

"And what?"

She groaned. "Are you going to see her again?"

Callan smirked, deliberately withholding. "We'll see."

"Ugh. Fine. Keep your secrets."

He took another sip of water. Isabelle, still buzzing, launched back into gushing about Greg, and Callan let her. He nodded in the right places, occasionally grunted, and let her fill the spaces with her joy. For a moment, sitting there, Callan felt like maybe he was getting the hang of this *normal life* thing. Domesticity. Familiar voices. Safe places.

The thought unsettled him.

He'd built his entire life avoiding this kind of stillness. Its comfort was starting to feel like a warning.

CHAPTER 46

Callan perched at the small desk in his guest room like a hotel night auditor, fingers moving steadily over the keyboard as he updated his report on Trent Ziggler. The past few days had been uneventful—if anything, they'd only confirmed what he already suspected.

Trent lived a life so routine it could've been clockwork. Work at the insurance firm from 8:30 to 5:00. Lunch at the same café every other day. Occasional phone calls that didn't last more than a few minutes. His evenings were predictable too—home by 5:30, dog walked by 6:00, lights out by 11:00.

There was no hint of anything shady. No secret meetings, no visitors beyond the usual Amazon deliveries. No odd detours on his way home.

But tonight was Friday. Time to see if Trent had another side to him.

Callan finished his report update, keeping the tone neutral. No conclusions yet—just facts. He closed his laptop, stretching his arms overhead, and checked his phone.

Nothing urgent. Claire had sent a message that morning—light, teasing, but not fishing for anything. They'd exchanged a couple of texts since the other night, but neither had pushed to meet up again. It had been fun. Uncomplicated. That seemed to suit them both.

Tricia had responded only when Callan texted first. Her answer was clipped and pouty.

Isabelle, on the other hand, had been practically glowing every time he saw her. She and Greg had been out twice since their first night together, and she'd texted Callan after both, giddy with excitement. He was happy she was having a good time. Even happier because she was staying out of his business. Greg seemed solid, and Isabelle deserved someone who showed up for her.

The clock told him it was time to get ready.

He shut the laptop, grabbed his keys, and checked his gear. Time to see if Trent Ziggler's life had even a single interesting thread to it.

"Be safe," Isabelle called distractedly, still glued to her phone. Probably texting Greg.

Callan smirked. "I always am."

She waved a hand at him, and he let himself out, heading straight for his car. It didn't take long to get into position near Trent's workplace.

Callan parked a block down and waited, watching as Trent wrapped up his Friday at the insurance firm. Right on schedule—five o'clock sharp—he walked to his car and drove home.

But tonight, Callan was watching for anything different.

Trent pulled into his driveway at 5:25 and didn't leave the house for nearly two hours. Routine movements: lights flicked on in different rooms, the occasional silhouette pacing behind the blinds.

Then, at 7:15, Trent reappeared.

He was dressed more casually—jeans, a dark jacket. Nothing flashy. The kind of outfit that blended in.

"Finally," Callan muttered.

He started his engine, keeping a generous distance as he tailed Trent's car through the city. At first, the drive was uneventful—just steady movement through Winnipeg's Friday night traffic. Then Trent turned down a more industrial stretch of road.

Callan followed.

The area wasn't deserted, but it wasn't exactly lively, either. A mix of old warehouses and repurposed commercial buildings lined the street, most with faded signage or security gates rolled down over the entrances.

But one warehouse stood out.

It looked normal enough—large metal siding, a row of small windows near the top, nothing suspicious. But it had a doorman.

Callan parked down the block and watched.

The man at the door wasn't dressed like a bouncer, but he wasn't just some bored security guard either. Lean, alert, clearly checking everyone before letting them inside.

Trent pulled up, rolled down his window, and after a brief exchange, was waved through. He parked, got out of his car, and walked inside.

Callan narrowed his eyes.

A warehouse with a doorman? That wasn't normal.

His first instinct was to get closer, find a way inside—but patience was a virtue. Move too soon, and he'd tip his hand.

An hour passed.

People came and went. Mostly men, a few women. Not dressed for a club, not quite business either. The whole thing had the quiet feel of something low-key. Something not meant to draw attention.

Then, at 8:30, Trent reappeared.

And he wasn't alone.

Callan's jaw tensed as he watched Trent walk to his car with a girl. Young. Too young.

She couldn't have been more than sixteen.

His fingers tightened around the steering wheel.

She wasn't dressed like a party girl. No heavy makeup, no heels. Just... young. Her body language was stiff, uncomfortable. Trent didn't seem to notice—or care.

Callan didn't like it.

Didn't like how suddenly Trent had become interesting.

Didn't like what it implied. He took a steady breath, forcing himself to stay level.

He was getting paid to watch. Nothing more.

Still watching from his car, Callan pulled out the burner phone. His real one, tied to his identity, was safely back at Isabelle's. He tapped out a quick, urgent message.

Lucian: Trent just left a warehouse w/ underage girl. Something's off. Please advise.

The response came faster than expected.

D: Job amended. Intercept. Find out where she's going. No need to kill Trent, but we need a name. Drop-off location is the priority.

A second message followed.

D: If possible, impersonate. Get inside.

Callan exhaled slowly.

Well. That changed things.

No wet work—but finally, some action.

He'd expected surveillance, maybe light intervention. But this? A direct insertion. If he pulled it off, he'd get inside that warehouse. Maybe meet the buyer. Maybe more.

And if he didn't?

That wasn't an option.

Callan pocketed the burner and rolled his shoulders, forcing himself to relax as Trent walked the girl to his car. The kid looked nervous. Hands clasped tightly in front of her, shifting her weight from foot to foot.

Callan clenched his jaw but kept his hands steady on the wheel. No room for emotion now.

Patience. Timing. Precision.

Trent unlocked the passenger door. The girl hesitated, then climbed in. Trent followed. As soon as the engine started, Callan was already in motion.

He kept a safe distance, trailing them through the darkened streets of Winnipeg.

No hurry. No panic. Just a smooth, steady drive.

But Trent wasn't heading for a hotel. Or a club. Or anywhere public.

He was cutting toward a quieter part of town.

Callan's grip tightened on the wheel as they turned again, this time into a quiet residential street.

The opportunity was coming.

Then, in his rearview mirror, Callan caught movement. A black sedan two blocks back. Headlights steady. No lane changes.

Probably nothing.

But his gut said otherwise.

CHAPTER 47

Following Trent's car through the quiet Winnipeg streets, the night air was crisp, the roads mostly empty, just the occasional streetlight casting long shadows over the pavement.

Callan could feel the energy shifting inside him. His hands were steady on the wheel, his breathing even, but something coiled in his chest—dark and eager. He wanted this. The anticipation. The certainty of action. He had spent days watching, waiting, documenting.

But now? Now it was time to do something.

Then his work phone rang.

Callan reached for the phone, keeping one hand on the wheel as he answered. "Yeah."

A clipped, professional voice came through the speaker. Male. Corporate. Detached. One of the higher-ups—not Diego—just another "company" man.

"Your task just changed," the man said. No preamble. No pleasantries. "We have received intelligence that the RCMP is closing in on the target and his operation. Could be tonight, could be in a few days, but they're close."

Callan's jaw flexed. "And?"

"Abandon the project." No room for interpretation.

His fingers tapped against the steering wheel. He could still ice old Trent. One quick move before the RCMP got involved. Clean. Efficient. Germane.

Callan let out a slow breath, pushing down the urge clawing at his chest. He wanted to kill. Like a crackhead digging through the carpet for a penny rock.

Which made his answer feel… off. "Fine."

There was a brief pause. Then the voice returned, "Acknowledged."

The call disconnected.

The deal was done. The right choice. The smart choice.

Didn't mean he had to like it.

Callan tapped out a quick message on his burner phone, keeping one eye on Trent's taillights ahead.

L: Can I pull the girl out before the handoff?

A few seconds passed. Then his phone vibrated with the reply.

D: Confirm buyer's address first. Then do what you want with Trent. He's expendable.

Callan smirked, a flicker of satisfaction cutting through his frustration. *Expendable.* Interesting choice of words.

He flexed his fingers against the steering wheel, forcing his grip to stay loose. At least this gave him something. A reason to still be in play. The RCMP would get their bust, but by the time they did, the girl wouldn't be part of the evidence pile.

Trent's car took another turn, pulling away from the main roads and into a quieter neighbourhood. This wasn't a club, a warehouse, or a drop site—just somewhere meant to be discreet.

Callan's stomach twisted, a familiar heat settling into his limbs.

Fine. He'd confirm the address.

Then Trent was fair game.

Callan tailed Trent's car as it veered deeper into the residential streets. Modest houses lined the block—quiet, faintly lit, unremarkable. Trent finally pulled up to a weathered bungalow, windows dark, the lawn unkempt.

Callan's pulse slowed as his focus sharpened.

This was it.

He eased his car to the curb half a block away and killed the engine. From the glove compartment, he retrieved a black balaclava and a pair of thin leather gloves, sliding them on without hesitation. He pulled out the burner phone and quickly texted the address to the team.

No reply needed.

Callan stepped out and moved fast. Silent. Efficient.

Trent had barely finished shutting off his ignition when Callan yanked the driver's door open. Before Trent could even process what was happening, Callan dragged him from the car and slammed him against it.

Trent's eyes widened in shock. "Hey, what the—"

Callan's fist silenced him. The first punch broke his nose— blood sprayed across the sidewalk.

Trent struggled, but Callan was faster. Stronger. Filled with lethal calm. He drove a knee into Trent's ribs, then followed up with a brutal strike to the stomach.

Trent crumpled, gasping for air, but Callan wasn't done. He grabbed him by the collar and hauled him up just enough to whisper, low and cold,

"You don't ever touch kids."

The fear was so thick Callan could taste it.

"I don't touch them—"

Another punch. Then another.

By the time Callan let go, Trent was barely conscious. Blood dripped from his face. He moaned weakly as he slumped onto the pavement. Not dead, but close enough.

Callan had been reckless. But assault in Canada was a slap on the wrist. Murder was something else. This would have to do. Trent was in rough shape either way.

He stepped back, chest rising and falling as he fought the urge to finish him. Another scumbag in the ground. But not tonight.

Instead, he rounded the car and opened the passenger door. The girl inside recoiled, eyes wide and terrified. Callan lifted a hand slowly.

"I'm not here to hurt you," he said. "You're safe now."

She didn't move, but she didn't run.

Skinny. Terrified. Dark hair in a messy braid. Clothes plain. Sneakers worn nearly through.

The look in her eyes should have gutted him.

He'd dig into why it didn't—later.

She knew. She knew exactly how bad this could have been.

Callan's voice softened. "I'm going to take you to the police. You trust me?"

She didn't blink. "Are you one of them?"

"No."

That was all.

Her lip trembled, but she gave a small, sharp nod.

Callan reached in gently, helping her out and guiding her to his car. Once she was inside, seatbelt fastened, he cast one last glance back at Trent's broken body. No movement. No rise or fall of the chest.

Maybe he got the kill anyway.

He'd check the news in a few days.

"Is he dead," the girl asked, eyes fixed on the wreck on the pavement.

"More likely than not," Callan replied

"Good."

He climbed behind the wheel and pulled away. No hesitation. No second-guessing.

Ten minutes later, Callan pulled up outside the nearest police station, tucked into the edge of downtown. He killed the engine and turned to her.

"Walk inside," he instructed softly. "Tell them you need help. That's it."

She stared at him, eyes glistening. "You're not coming with me?"

He gave a faint, apologetic smile. "Can't. But you're safe now."

She nodded, swallowed hard. "I won't say anything about you. Thank you. You saved my life." She was crying—but didn't hug him.

That was for the best.

She slipped out of the car. He watched her hurry toward the door, disappear into the station. Only then did he let out a long breath and merge back into traffic.

"If the Mounties are close," he muttered, "they'll find Trent bleeding on the pavement by morning."

He paused. "If they're slow... well—someone else might get there first."

CHAPTER 48

Isabelle flitted around the kitchen, humming to herself as she prepped ingredients for what looked like another homemade masterpiece. Late afternoon light streamed through the window, casting warm streaks across the hardwood floor and making the whole house feel even more inviting.

"You want garlic in this, or are you still pretending you don't like it?" Isabelle teased, glancing over her shoulder.

Callan smirked, tapping his phone. "You know I don't pretend about food."

She chuckled, chopping herbs with practiced ease. "Fair enough."

Callan's eyes drifted toward the window, catching a glimpse of a silver sedan idling too long at the curb across the street. Nothing overt, but it wasn't a car he recognized. He filed it away—*not paranoia yet, but not nothing either.*

As they bantered, his attention flicked between their conversation and the steady buzz of his phone. Two separate text threads lit up—one with Tricia, the other with Claire.

Tricia: Still thinking about you... Call me later?

Claire: So, when's date two? Or are you too busy being mysterious again?

Callan sipped his coffee, thumbs working quickly.

Callan (to Tricia): Might have to check my calendar, but I'll make time for you.

Callan (to Claire): Mysterious is part of the charm, remember?

Both responses came fast.

Tricia: Don't make me wait too long. Feels like you're slipping away.

Claire: Maybe I like a little mystery. Just don't ghost me, Miami.

He smirked, enjoying the contrast. Claire's light, flirty tone was a pressure valve. Tricia's, though—it felt like a tightening noose. The "slipping away" wasn't innocent.

"Who's got you smirking like that?" Isabelle raised an eyebrow as slid a pan onto the stove.

"Work stuff," Callan lied smoothly, pocketing the phone.

Isabelle rolled her eyes. "Uh-huh. Sure."

Callan leaned back, stretching. "You making enough for Greg, or am I getting the full chef's special tonight?"

She grinned. "Just you. Greg's on a work thing."

Callan nodded, though his eyes drifted to the window again. The sedan was gone now. Or maybe it never mattered. Still, his gut said otherwise.

He let the conversation drift to safer ground—her garden, Greg, an upcoming art fair—while his phone sat face down beside his plate. But eventually, curiosity won out.

Callan (to Claire): What are you doing tonight?

Claire: Depends... are you about to make my night interesting?

Callan: Could be. I'm free after 7.

Claire: You mean actually low-key, or Callan-low-key, where you show up looking like you just stepped out of a noir movie?

Callan smirked.

Callan: Guess you'll have to find out.

Claire: Deal. I'll text you the spot. Wear something dangerously charming.

He locked the phone, still smiling. *Normalcy.* It had its charm—even when it was fleeting.

"You're awfully quiet over there," Isabelle said, plating something that smelled suspiciously like garlic had made it into the dish after all.

"Just making plans," Callan replied. "Keeping the calendar full."

She gave him that knowing big-sister look but let it slide.

He settled into the meal, letting the simple comfort of home-cooked food distract him —until his phone lit up again. He reached for it without urgency, but his jaw ticked as he read the texts.

Tricia: You're ignoring me again. Why are you always doing this to me? I need you.

Tricia: I feel you slipping away. Why won't you answer me? I need your attention.

Callan rubbed his jaw, the pressure building again.

Callan: Busy. Relax.

Tricia: You know I can't handle being ignored. It's killing me when you do this.

Then—

Tricia: No one understands you like I do. You're mine, and you need me. Don't forget that.

Callan exhaled, running a hand down his face. There it was—the push-pull. Not quite a threat. Not quite innocent. But heavy.

Callan: I'm out of town for work. You know that.

Tricia: "Work." You always choose everything over me.

Tricia: I'm the only one for you. Don't make me remind you.

Callan: I'll text you tomorrow.

No response. But the read receipt glared back at him, pulsing like a warning light.

He pocketed the phone and let the tension bleed out in increments. The night outside seemed still, calm—but the feeling of being watched no longer seemed so abstract.

CHAPTER 49

After dinner Callan and Isabelle sat at the kitchen table, basking in the silence that comes from delicious, nurturing food.

"You ever think about how fast it all went?" Isabelle asked.

Callan looked up. "What?"

"Our lives. How we ended up here. You with your disappearing acts. Me in therapy twice a week and still somehow screwing everything up."

Callan didn't answer. Just waited.

"I used to think you had it all figured out, you know?" she asked. "When we were younger. You were calm. Controlled. I thought that meant strong."

He gave a dry laugh. "It meant I didn't say things out loud."

She nodded like she already knew that.

"You've always had secrets, Cal. I stopped needing to know them a long time ago. But sometimes..." She looked at him now, eyes steady. "I just need to know if you're still in there."

"I'm here," he said.

"That's not what I mean."

"You mean, do I still feel anything?" he asked.

"Yeah."

He thought about lying. Instead, he gave her the closest thing to the truth he could offer. "Sometimes I do. Sometimes I don't."

She nodded again, her voice was softer now.

"I don't need to know what you've done. Just promise me you haven't lost yourself doing it."

He looked up at her. No judgement. No probing. Just space.

"I'm trying," he said.

"Good," she said. "Because I don't want to lose anyone else." She stood, pausing at the edge of the dining room. "I love you, you know. Even if I don't always understand you."

"Same." He raised a brow. "Why do you look like someone cancelled your favourite holiday?"

She didn't meet his eyes. Her voice barely made it out.

"I know you killed Kevin."

For a second, everything stilled.

Callan didn't blink. "Kevin?"

She nodded slowly, like the truth hurt to carry. "I read your journal. Years ago. I wasn't trying to snoop, but... I saw enough. I saw too much." Her head shook gently as tears crept out.

His expression didn't change, but something behind his eyes flickered—fear, or memory, or both. He sipped his tea. Said nothing.

"You tracked him. Waited. Then made it look like he disappeared."

"He killed Maggie," Callan said. It was all he could manage. "Walked out smiling. I fixed that."

Isabelle didn't answer right away. Just stared into her cup like the rest of the conversation might be written in the tea leaves. She looked at him, tired. Not angry. Just worn down by years of holding it in.

"You should've told me."

"What would it have changed?" he asked

"You don't get to decide that," she responded

"I did," he said. "You looked at me like I wasn't broken yet. I wanted to keep it that way."

She let out a breath and set the mug down. "Did it help?"

"No. But it didn't hurt."

Isabelle stood there for a while, then nodded. Just once. "She was a broken person with a genuine heart. She did what she did to support her family."

"I know, Isabelle."

"I told myself you did it for justice," Isabelle said. "That maybe you did it for me. Or for her."

"I didn't," Callan said. "I did it because someone had to."

"You mean someone had to kill him? Not arrest. Not expose. *Kill.*"

"You think he didn't deserve it?"

"Of course he did," she said. "But that's not the same thing."

A long pause.

"What you did wasn't justice, Cal. It was revenge. Don't pretend it was anything else."

Callan exhaled through his nose. "Fine. Maybe it was."

He looked down at his hands, fingers flexing of their own accord.

"And maybe I liked it. That part of me I try to bury? It liked the way he looked when he realised he wasn't walking away this time."

Isabelle didn't flinch. Just nodded, slowly. "At least you're honest about it." She looked away, her voice lower now. "But that's what scares me. That maybe you believe revenge is the same thing as making things right."

"You think I've lost the difference?"

"I think you're getting too good at pretending there isn't one."

She picked up her mug and left the room.

Callan stayed where he was. Let the silence settle. It was familiar. And deserved. Because she wasn't wrong. Every time he crossed the line, it got easier to forget it existed.

A few minutes later, he followed her to the kitchen.

"What now?" he asked her.

She didn't look at him when she answered. "Nothing. We move on."

Callan frowned. "That's it?"

"What do you want me to say? You can't undo it. You can't un-kill him. And I can't lose you too." She looked at him then, her eyes sharp but steady. "I lived with it for years already. You just didn't know I knew."

He nodded. That tracked. "I should've told you."

"Yeah. You should've."

Silence again. This one was less jagged than before.

"Does it change how you see me?" he asked.

"No," she said. "It just confirms what I already knew."

Callan exhaled through his nose. "Which is?"

"That you've always carried the weight for everyone else. Whether or not we wanted you to." She sipped her coffee, gave a small shrug. "It's not forgiveness. But I'm not kicking you out either."

"Progress."

She almost smiled. "Don't push it."

He eased down into the dining room chair closest to her, the tension in his chest loosening just a notch. She didn't forgive him. Not really. But she understood. And that was enough for now. "You gonna turn me in?"

Isabelle blinked, then laughed—soft and bitter.

"To who? The cops? Half of them would probably shake your hand."

She sipped her tea, then added, quieter "And even if I wanted to... I wouldn't. Not for this. I loved Maggie so much."

Callan studied her face, trying to read what she wasn't saying. But it was all there—grief, resentment, exhaustion.

And something else.

Something like loyalty.

CHAPTER 50

Isabelle and Callan both agreed they needed a little space. Callan's mind still reeled from the fact Isabelle had known about Kevin for years. He'd stopped journalling ages ago, once he realised his hobby-turned-career was going to stick. He was scared—but also relieved. He'd always kept secrets, but he'd wanted to tell Isabelle about Kevin. He couldn't have predicted she'd take it so well.

Callan took up Claire's offer for a second date. Her building was an older condo building that oozed old-world charm. The tepid Winnipeg night air was thick with the scent of blooming linden trees. True to form, he stepped out to open the passenger door for her. Claire arched a brow as she slid into the seat, clearly amused.

"Chivalry," she said as he closed the door. "Didn't think that still existed."

A ghost of a smile touched Callan's lips as he got behind the wheel. "I'm old-fashioned."

"No kidding," she teased, glancing at him sideways. "But in a good way."

They made easy, superfluous conversation as they drove, the warm, fragrant air drifting in through the open windows. But beneath it all, a subtle tension hummed. Callan found himself studying her—the way her hair caught the soft glow of the streetlights, the delicate curve of her collarbone. He was reminded now of how Beckett watched birds that landed on their patio.

By the time they were seated at the restaurant, he was enjoying her company more than he'd expected.

She sipped her wine, smiling over the rim of her glass. "You know," she said, "I can't remember the last time a guy opened the door for me. Or pulled out my chair."

Callan raised a brow, leaning back. "Low bar."

Claire laughed. "Seriously. Most guys my age just send a 'u up?' text and think they're smooth."

Callan chuckled, swirling his drink. "Yeah, I'm a bit out of that loop."

Claire tilted her head. "Can I ask how old you actually are?"

"Forty-six," Callan replied without missing a beat.

Claire blinked, then grinned. "Huh. You wear it well."

He gave a small smirk. "Appreciate it."

She leaned forward, resting her chin on her hand. "So does that mean you think this—" she gestured between them "—is weird?"

Callan paused. "I think a sixteen-year gap isn't nothing. But I don't live by conventional rules."

Understatement of the century.

Claire rolled her eyes, smiling. "Callan, are you a player? The strong, silent act gets me every time."

"I feel like it some days," he deadpanned, thinking of how Tricia had given him that same look not long ago.

She laughed, but there was a softness behind it. "Look, I'm not saying we're picking out curtains, but I don't think age is some insurmountable thing."

Callan nodded slowly, but the weight of the topic lingered longer than he liked. She seemed to want reassurance that what they had wasn't nothing.

With a smirk, he shifted gears. "So," he said lightly, "besides charming older men, what else do you get up to?"

Claire laughed, the awkwardness dissolving. "When I'm not working or saving you from boring dinners, I freelance. Marketing, mostly. Social media."

Callan raised a brow. "Influencer?"

"God, no," she said, laughing. "But I work with a few. Pays the bills."

Their conversation drifted—travel stories, favourite restaurants, lighthearted banter. By the time the cheque came, the chemistry between them was undeniable.

Claire set her fork down, grinning. "You know, this has been really nice."

Callan smiled, the easy kind he didn't give often. "Yeah," he admitted. "It has."

After dinner, Claire insisted on taking Callan to a favourite dessert spot—a tiny café close by with a worn brick façade, big bay windows, and string lights draped across the ceiling. It felt like a secret, even though half the city probably knew about it. The smell of fresh pastries and iced coffee hung in the air.

They found a corner booth, shared a slice of lemon tart, nursed their iced coffees.

Claire leaned back, that same curious glint in her eyes. "So... Isabelle," she said, her tone thoughtful. "You two seem close."

Callan shrugged. "We aren't, really. Not because she doesn't try. I'm just...hard to pin down."

Claire picked at the edge of the napkin. "She's kind of like the glue around here, you know? Everyone loves her."

"Yeah," Callan said quietly. "I get it."

"She makes people feel like they belong," Claire added, voice softer. "Makes me wonder how someone like you ended up so... guarded."

Callan smirked, sipping his coffee. "That a polite way of saying I'm difficult?"

Claire laughed. "I didn't say that. But you're not exactly the open book type."

Callan looked out the window at the quiet street. "Isabelle's always been different from me. More... grounded."

Claire studied him. "You worry about her?"

"No, not really." His eyes stayed on the glass. "She's a survivor. We both are. Just in different ways."

"She seems happy," Claire said. "Talks about you like you're the best brother in the world."

"She's biased," he replied, irritation flickering at the edges. He could go months—years—without thinking about Isabelle. He was not "the best brother" by anyone's standards.

The mood shifted—less flirtatious, more real. Claire didn't push. She just let the silence settle comfortably between them. Later, outside her apartment: "Wanna come up?"

Callan considered it. Then declined. Whatever he and Tricia had, this felt too close to something else. He kissed Claire goodnight—innocent. And pretended not to notice the relief on her face. Casual sex might've been normal these days, but Claire wasn't wired like that. Neither, tonight, was he.

As he walked down the steps into the humid night, he was already thinking about the conversation he'd had with Isabelle before his flight.

The Winnipeg air hung thick with honeysuckle and warm asphalt. But as he neared his car, something caught his attention.

Across the street, under a flickering streetlight, sat a silver sedan. Older model. Worn bumper. Cheap hubcaps. On the surface—harmless.

But the engine was idling. Exhaust curling in the air. The driver sat too straight. Buzzcut. Ex-cop or ex-military. Left hand tapping anxiously on the wheel. Near the dash vent, a faint red standby light blinked—body cam or dash-mounted recorder.

Sloppy.

Callan didn't stare. Didn't give him anything to latch onto. He lingered by his car, adjusted his jacket like he hadn't noticed a thing. But the driver kept glancing—once at his phone, once at the mirror.

Callan smirked. Low-rent surveillance. Whoever hired this guy hadn't paid for someone with Callan's résumé.

Cute.

He got into his car, snapped a picture of the sedan's license plate, and pulled away. The sedan stayed put, taillights still glowing in his mirror.

But Callan was already shifting gears. Someone was watching him.

And they'd just made the mistake of stepping into his world.

***

The next morning, he pretended to sleep in, hurried through the farewell breakfast Isabelle made, let her hug him—but wouldn't let her drive him to the airport.

At the terminal—quiet compared to MIA—Callan leaned back in a stiff chair. Boarding calls crackled overhead, footsteps echoed across polished tile. He stared at Ellen's texts, a dull pressure building behind his eyes.

Ellen: David betting again. Thousands gone. Dangerous people.

He should've expected it. With David, self-destruction was never far.

Callan sighed, thumbs typing before he could overthink it.

Callan: So, were you cheating on him?

Her reply came fast. Sharp.

Ellen: Seriously? That's what you're going to ask me right now?

Callan smirked faintly. Typical fucking Ellen. Cornered. Still biting.

When she finally answered, "No. I am NOT cheating," Callan didn't relax. He just shifted the weight lower in his chest.

At what point had he become all things to everyone?

Ellen was fun when she was up. But crisis-mode Ellen was not something he wanted—or needed. At least not outwardly. Still, his gut twisted. If he took the good, he had to take the bad.

His thumb hovered over the call button. Then he hit it.

She picked up on the second ring. "So, we're doing this properly now?"

Callan's voice stayed level. "You're pulling me into this, Ellen. You don't get to do that over text."

She exhaled hard. "You think I wanted to? I've been sitting on this for weeks, hoping it would go away. But it's not. And I'm scared, Callan. I need you."

The tension between them stretched—brittle and frayed.

Finally, he asked, "Where are you now?"

"My new place," Ellen replied, voice softening. "He doesn't know where."

Callan scanned the crowd in the terminal. Parents. Laptops. Kids.

"So, you guys are finished?"

Her answer came with trademark Ellen confidence. "Yes."

CHAPTER 51

After a ten-hour travel day, Callan found himself back in the familiar confines of his condo, fully embracing the hermit lifestyle.

Three days. No returned calls, no meetings scheduled, no obligations met—just him, Beckett, and the quiet hum of the city outside.

He cooked when he felt like it. Ignored Ellen's texts. Dodged David's calls. Claire got a pass—for now. Everyone else could circle the drain as far as he was concerned.

Even Beckett seemed impressed. The cat sprawled across the couch like the two of them had struck an unspoken truce: no bullshit, no noise, just space.

"Nesting," Isabelle had called it. A quick Google search made Callan laugh. Sure. He was nesting.

Couldn't argue with the timing either. The Grafton gig paid out like a busted slot machine—the client more than happy to shell out for the Harold issue, and corporate passed the entire bonus to him without question.

He closed the banking app, took a sip of coffee, and sank into the couch beside Beckett, who—as always— was doing his best impression of a professional napper.

Callan unlocked, thumbing through messages until he landed back in a familiar thread.

Claire: So... have you recovered from the emotional trauma of leaving Winnipeg behind?

Callan: Barely. I keep looking for mediocre coffee, but Miami is failing me.

Claire: That was artisanal *coffee, thank you very much. I handpicked that café just for you.*

Callan: Artisanal is generous. Pretty sure the barista hated me.

Claire: He hated everyone. It's part of the charm.

Callan: Ah, so you were testing my tolerance for passive-aggressive latte art?

Claire: Exactly. You passed. Barely.

Callan: Good to know. Next time, I'll just order an espresso and glare back.

Claire: Oof. Intimidating. Very Miami of you.

Callan: I'm versatile. Miami glare, Winnipeg patience. Depends on the company.

Claire: Hmm. I liked the guy who didn't flinch at striking out and still held the door.

Callan: I still owe you for that dinner.

Claire: You tried to pay, remember? I'm stubborn. You'll have to plan your revenge carefully.

Callan: Working on it. Might involve sunshine and better coffee.

Claire: That sounds dangerously like an invitation.

Callan: Maybe it is.

Claire: Okay, so... since you maybe just invited me to Miami, I should probably say this now before I overthink it at 2 AM.

Yes, you're older than me. We talked about it at dinner, and I'm not pretending it's nothing, but also... it's not exactly keeping me up at night. You're not some cliché midlife crisis guy driving a red convertible and quoting Hemingway. You're just you. And I like how you are.

Honestly, you seem more grounded than half the guys my age who still think "meal prep" means surviving off protein shakes.

So, yeah. I'm good with it—if you are.

Callan: I do own a red sports car. But to be fair, I bought it in my thirties during an actual midlife crisis.

Claire:

Callan: I wasn't losing sleep over it either, but I'd be lying if I said it didn't cross my mind. I'd hate for it to be something that trips us up later.

Claire: I get that. It crossed my mind too. But honestly? I don't feel weird about it when I'm with you. It's easy. And I'm not looking for reasons to overthink something that feels good.

So yeah, I'm not blind to it, but I'm also not worried—unless you are.

Callan: I'm not worried about us now, but I've also learned not to ignore things that could matter later.

And since we're being honest... are kids something you see in your future?

Because I am at a point where I'm sure that chapter is closed for me, and I'd rather be upfront than pretend it's not in the back of my head.

There it was. Her out card. A fastball right down the middle.

Claire: Well, since we're sharing TMI... I was diagnosed with endometriosis a few years ago. It's made the whole kids thing uncertain for me too. I've come to terms with it, but I get that it's a lot to unpack.

Fuck me, that didn't work! Callan mused, rubbing his hand through his hair.

Claire: Anyway, I should probably get back to pretending to be productive now. Thanks for being upfront with me—seriously. We're good.

Talk later?

Callan set the phone down on the coffee table, staring at it like it might disappear.

He'd launched the age grenade. Tossed in the kids salvo. He's tried—subtly—to dissuade Claire from deepening her attachment. But there she was, sweet and grounded, a softer, less needy version of Tricia. No pressure, no games, no dramatic strings.

The condo was still again. Except for Beckett. The cat had climbed onto the arm of the couch, tail flicking lazily, golden eyes fixed on him with a judgemental intensity only cats— and older sisters— could pull off.

Callan raised an eyebrow. "What?"

Beckett didn't blink. Just sat there, still as a gargoyle, gaze unwavering.

Callan huffed a laugh. "You're imagining me doodling hearts in a notebook, aren't you?"

Beckett's tail flicked harder. Punctuation.

Callan leaned back, rubbing his jaw. "I am *not* leading her on. I can kill most men with my bare hands, but I can't seem to set boundaries with women lately," he muttered, channelling what Beckett's stare seemed to say.

The cat, naturally, offered no rebuttal. Just more withering silence.

Then he stretched, yawned, and hopped down from the couch—strutting toward the kitchen like he had better things to do than supervise his human's emotional crisis.

Callan chuckled to himself and grabbed his coffee. "Jerk."

Still, as he took a sip, he couldn't help but feel Beckett wasn't wrong. He was getting soft.

And soft is how people end up dead.

He set the mug down and stared at the empty space Beckett left behind—then sighed, his thoughts drifting straight to Tricia.

It didn't make sense. They'd barely spoken while he was away, but somehow, even back home, her presence hung over him like cigarette smoke. Faint. Persistent. Impossible to shake.

With a quiet curse, he crossed to the table and opened the work laptop for the first time since stepping off the plane. The familiar hum of encrypted boot-up filled the silence as he logged in.

No updates.

His request for intel on Tricia—backgrounds, ties, buried dirt—was still sitting idle. No movement. No flags. Nothing pulled.

Unusual.

The system was fast. Faster than most governments. Either someone was stonewalling... or Tricia had more layers than he thought.

Callan leaned back, jaw tightening, as a new wave of contracts loaded on screen. Dozens. Each more violent—and more profitable—than the last. He barely looked at them.

He shut the laptop. The weight of unanswered questions settling deep in his chest.

It was time to clear his head. Callan stood, grabbed his keys, helmet, and riding gear and made for the door.

The Triumph was calling.

CHAPTER 52

The palace was quiet. Just the way Beckett liked it.

Golden rays stretched across the hardwood floor, claiming the coveted patch of warmth by the living room window—his throne, naturally. Beckett loafed there, paws tucked neatly beneath him, surveying his kingdom like the benevolent dictator he was.

Outside, the world buzzed and glittered beneath the hot light. Metal beasts crept along winding paths, their blinking eyes pulsing in strange rhythms. Tiny humans darted below, scurrying like prey with too many legs—always rushing somewhere pointless. Always moving. Often forgetting the simple wisdom of a good nap.

The Human had left an hour ago—helmet under one arm, motorcycle jacket slung over his shoulder—off to wherever humans went when they needed to outrun their thoughts. Beckett had flicked an ear in acknowledgement. The Human always came back. Predictable, like clockwork.

So, Beckett lounged, basked, and did nothing.

As was his right.

Until the lock clicked.

His ears swivelled forward.

That wasn't the Human's smooth, practiced entry. No muttered curse. No jangle of gloves hitting the floor. This was slower. Hesitant. Wrong.

Beckett didn't move. Yet.

The door creaked open, a draft stirring his fur.

Intruder.

Silent as fog, Beckett slipped from his throne, muscles coiled. He darted beneath the couch, settling into the shadows with the grace of a jungle predator. Golden eyes sharpened, tracking.

Boots. Gloves. Masked face.

The scent hit next—cold sweat, leather, and something metallic. Beckett flattened his ears, tail twitching, slow and deliberate. Someone had breached his palace.

The stranger moved with caution, but not the Human's kind. This was unfamiliar. Clumsy in its confidence. Beckett watched them drift through the space—*his* space—with unsettling ease.

They weren't just trespassing. They knew the terrain.

Into the bedroom, they prowled. Past the Human's chair, the kitchen counter, the bookshelf Beckett liked to topple when feeling dramatic. The intruder sidestepped every creaky tile and familiar landmark without hesitation.

Insulting.

They returned, drifting toward the living room with quiet calculation. Beckett ghosted along the baseboard, belly low, every inch of him bristling with territorial fury.

The stranger crouched by the Human's end table—Beckett's end table—and opened the drawer.

Beckett's eyes narrowed to lethal slits.

There it was.

The shiny.

That silver bauble the Human had carelessly stashed days ago. Beckett had been keeping tabs on it, as any self-respecting monarch would. It was his. His shiny.

The intruder plucked it from the drawer, holding it to the light like they'd just unearthed buried treasure.

Beckett's patience snapped. He exploded from the shadows—seventeen pounds of claws, teeth, and royal vengeance.

Fangs sank into fabric and flesh. His claws raked down the intruder's arm with surgical precision. The figure cursed, staggering back, nearly toppling the table.

Beckett clung like a demon, hissing and snarling, daring them to fight for their life. His growl vibrated through the room—a battle cry fit for a king.

The intruder flailed, finally shaking him loose, but Beckett landed on all fours, tail fluffed like a bottlebrush, eyes blazing.

This was not over. Another sharp hiss and he lunged again, forcing them to retreat. The intruder stumbled, yanked the door open, and vanished into the hallway, leaving behind a trail of shredded fabric and wounded pride.

Beckett stood victorious, chest heaving.

His palace. His victory. He padded forward and spotted the shiny, abandoned in their escape. A swift paw sent it skittering across the floor, metallic clinks echoing like applause. One final bat and the shiny vanished beneath the dishwasher.

Beckett sighed.

Lost forever. Typical.

With regal indifference, he flopped onto the couch, stretched luxuri-ously, and began cleaning his paws. A warrior's reward.

His palace. His shiny. His rules.

CHAPTER 53

The Triumph pulled hard down the coastal highway, the early morning air biting through Callan's jacket like glass needles. The engine purred beneath him, a low, steady thrum that unravelled the knots behind his ribs as the city blurred past.

He wasn't running. But when questions stacked too high, Callan knew better than to let them topple inside four walls.

Back in town, Java Junction pulled him in like muscle memory. The scent—burnt espresso and overworked air conditioning—hit him as soon as he stepped through the door. Wanda slid him a coffee without a word, reading the weight in his shoulders better than most.

Then they walked in.

Two men. One built like a bulldozer, leather-skinned and slow-moving. The other still shiny—badge gleaming, shoes that hadn't learned to whisper yet.

They made a beeline for Callan. "Mr. McWard," the older one said, voice like asphalt and bad bourbon. "Callan McWard. Mind if we join you?"

Callan's gaze swept over them slowly, unhurried. "You're already halfway to sitting. Seems like you made up your mind."

The older cop claimed the chair across from him. "Detective Grayson," the bulldozer said, with a tilt of the head toward the kid. "O'Halloran."

O'Halloran. Soft edges of the accent, faint but lingering. Callan arched a brow. "Let me guess: Dad wanted a prizefighter, got a college dropout instead."

The rookie smirked, but his thumb rubbed at the corner of his notebook. Nervous. Still learning what the badge actually weighed. O'Halloran straightened his shoulders. The twitch didn't fully die.

Callan sipped his coffee. "This about parking violations?"

Grayson didn't blink. "More serious."

"Mind coming with us?" O'Halloran added. Softer. Practicing his grit but not there yet.

Callan tilted his head. "Do I get to pick the playlist?"

O'Halloran leaned in, rehearsed. "Sure. Long as you like Springsteen."

***

The precinct reeked of cold coffee and cheap antiseptic. Linoleum gleamed underfoot—scrubbed too clean, like someone thought you could mop the blood out of a city like this.

Inside the interview room: four walls, one bulb, same old dance. The air squeezed his ribs. No charges, not yet, but the cops were circling like they smelled blood.

Callan sat in the metal chair, eyes tracing ceiling tile cracks. His thoughts drifted—Diego barking orders in sun-baked pits, sand sticking to bruised knuckles.

They wouldn't break him with good cop, bad cop. Too basic.

Grayson and O'Halloran entered. Grayson clutched a file like it had teeth. They circled first. Small talk with handcuffs.

"Busy week," Grayson said.

"Just got back into town," Callan replied.

Questions followed. Callan volleyed them back clean, slicing answers into perfect halves. Never lies. Never the full truth. He leaned forward slightly. "Do you two shitheads always double-team the coffee runs too?"

A jab. Bait. Grayson didn't flinch.

Then came the file. It scraped across the table. Callan glanced down.

Dwayne.

Dead-eyed in an alley. Head at a tilt. Throat carved open—deep, deliberate. Not fast. Not sterile. Personal.

His chest stayed calm. But behind his eyes, the gears clicked.

Not a junkie hit. Not rage. This was clean. Brutal. Pro-level, or someone Dwayne trusted long enough to get inside the wire.

Could be Tricia. Could be worse. Someone like Callan—with his training, minus the patience. He stared at the photo gain. Sloppy work would've made a mess. This was surgical.

In every police interview room everywhere, silence never gets you arrested. So, Callan said nothing.

O'Halloran leaned in, overeager. "Jogger found Dean this way."

Dean. Callan clocked it. Rookie move. Deliberate slip. See if he'd bite.

He didn't blink. Didn't correct it.

Just let the air hang heavy.

"Looks familiar," Callan said. "Think I met him once."

O'Halloran shifted. Disappointed. Still trying to hold steady.

More questions. Motives. Connections.

Callan parried like a boxer slipping jabs. Calm. Detached.

Then O'Halloran stumbled again.

"And the fight," he blurted. "We've got video evidence."

Grayson's glare cut sideways. Too late.

Callan leaned back, the smirk lazy, shaded by weariness. Reflex.

Tricia, you lying bitch.

"Do you, now?"

He stood slow and easy. "I'll take my phone call. You've wasted enough of my morning."

Chapter 54

Montgomery "Monty" Caldwell never looked the part. His suits were cheap and ill-fitting, and it always seemed like he'd cut his own hair. Monty carried himself like someone used to being overlooked. There was a perpetual tiredness to him, a worn-in quality that made him blend into the background. Until recently, it mirrored Callan's own quiet, mundane existence.

But beneath the scuffed-up exterior was a sharp, calculating mind that thrived in the margins. Monty worked quietly, making deals in out-of-the-way places, steering clear of attention. His wins weren't showy, but they were consistent. In Florida's underworld, when things got complicated, Monty was the one you called—not because he looked the part, but because he always delivered.

He had Callan out of the precinct in less than an hour.

***

They sat in Monty's Maserati—his only outward indicator of his success—parked at the curb, windows fogged from Miami's thick humidity. Callan stared ahead, but his mind was miles deep.

"Did you do it?" Monty asked, blunt as always.

"No."

"Good enough. They were fishing. Only reason you got hauled in was cos you had a beef with the deceased." Monty's confidence didn't match his appearance, but it never had. "Need a ride someplace?"

"My bike's at the coffee shop by my place."

Monty nodded and pulled away from the curb.

***

The café was mellow, familiar. The hum of conversation, the hiss of the espresso machine—it gave the place its usual easy rhythm. Callan slipped inside, grateful for the hit of air conditioning.

He ordered without thinking. "Half-sweet mocha."

The barista gave him a distracted nod before moving to make the drink. Callan drifted to the end of the counter, eyes distant, his mind tangled in the day's mess. The sun outside filtered through the large windows, casting soft patterns across the floor, but he felt no comfort in the warmth.

When his drink was ready, he took it to a small table by the window. The seat gave him a view of the street and its lazy swirl of traffic. He took a slow sip—the sweetness cutting through the bitterness—then pulled out his phone.

No point in sitting on it. He tapped Tricia's name and hit *video call*.

She answered fast, sunlight behind her casting sharp angles on her face. "Hey handsome, what's up?"

He didn't bother easing into it. "The video didn't disappear."

Her brow knit. Genuine concern? Maybe. Maybe not. "Wait... what do you mean?"

"It resurfaced," Callan said, voice low. "So, either it was never deleted, or someone else had a copy."

She tilted her head, like she was sorting through mental files. "No, he deleted it. I watched him do it, hun. But you know how these things work—someone else probably recorded from another angle. Happens all the time."

Hun? Handsome? The sweetness was too smooth. Rehearsed. And still, somehow, disarming.

"You're positive?" he pressed.

"Yes," she said, firmer this time. "I'm police, Callan. I don't fumble."

He nodded slowly, eyes fixed on hers. "All right."

She smiled. Relaxed a little. "Good. Anything else?"

"No," Callan said. "Just wanted to clear that up."

"It's good to see your face. Call me if you need anything, okay?" She blew him a kiss. Her wrist, he noticed, looked scratched—like she'd gone five rounds with an angry cat.

"Yeah. Sure."

He ended the call, staring down into his mocha. A quiet frustration simmered. If Tricia wasn't lying—and that was still an *if*—then someone else had been watching. Closer than he thought.

He tapped his fingers on the table, thinking. His phone buzzed. "Yeah?"

Monty's voice came crisp. "Just heard from the coroner. Dwayne Callister's been dead since last week."

Callan exhaled through his nose. "Excellent."

"Jesus, Callan. Ice cold. How the fuck is that excellent?"

"I was in Canada," he said. "I'll send you my trip details." A pause. "How'd you find out so fast?"

"Easy, kid," Monty said. "I'm burning your retainer like taxpayer money. Oh, one more thing—your big 'video evidence'? It's just grainy parking lot footage. Nothing there."

Callan hung up and let the silence settle. The noise of Java Junction faded to background static—clinking mugs, quiet talk, the hiss of espresso.

But his mind wouldn't be quiet.

Dwayne wasn't some corner-store thug. Someone slit his throat. Messy, yes, but it had nerve. Whoever did it had planning and guts. Not the signature of one of Callan's people—but not some street player either.

And Tricia hadn't lied. That's what gnawed at him. He expected a lie, but she'd been clean. That meant someone else was watching. *Someone else knew!*

He thought of Tricia. Then David. Then all the blurred edges still circling out there in the shadows.

Callan leaned back, exhaling slow. Someone was making ghosts. And this time, it wasn't him. And that, more than the rookie's slip or Grayson's stonewall act, left a chill at the base of his spine.

CHAPTER 55

The door creaked open—familiar, grounding—as Callan stepped into the condo. Beckett was already patrolling the living room, tail high, moving with the kind of self-satisfied swagger that suggested he'd won some invisible war while Callan was out. His steps were light, but his ego? Heavy. A conquest, no doubt.

Callan paused to watch his boy. He never tired of it. A small, quiet gratitude settled in his chest.

"Yeah, yeah," he murmured, tossing his keys on the counter. "You're the king."

Beckett chirped and hopped onto the sofa armrest, casting him a sidelong glance like he was waiting for applause.

"Love you, big boy." Callan scratched his chin.

The work laptop booted with its usual encrypted hum, bathing the room in its cold glow. His fingers moved fast—muscle memory guiding him through the layers of Dwayne's flagged file.

He dug deeper this time, peeling back the next layer.

Buried beneath the standard dossier was the real prize: metadata from black-market comms logs, surveillance captures, leaked satellite reports. Dwayne's burner was sloppy—bouncing signals too frequently between tower clusters.

But Callan knew how to read the noise. He ran a heatmap and waited as patterns surfaced—one cluster centred on a high-end neighbourhood. Gated. Exclusive. The kind of place where ballplayers and crypto millionaires buried their secrets in six-car garages.

Callan smirked. "You really liked to play dress-up, huh?"

He shut the laptop.

Beckett still watched from his perch, silent and steady.

"Stay," Callan said, grabbing his go-bag and heading out.

The house wasn't hard to find—tucked behind manicured hedges and wrought-iron gates, one of those modern palaces with too much glass and too little soul. What surprised him wasn't the house. It was how easy it was to get inside.

There was security, sure. Cameras on the corners. Motion lights. A keypad by the door.

But the keypads were dusty, like no one had touched them in weeks. A side gate was ajar, not just unlocked. Like someone had left in a hurry and never came back. The back patio door was shut, but the latch was broken. Forced open once, never repaired

"Professional or sloppy?" Callan muttered as he slipped inside, quiet as a whisper.

The house was dark. Silent.

Too silent. Inside, it looked like a real estate listing. Furniture expensive enough to sell the image of wealth, but no soul. No family photos. No clutter. The kind of house you owned when you didn't want to leave fingerprints on your life.

Callan moved across the hardwood like a shadow, every step deliberate.

Something was wrong.

According to the file, Dwayne had been embedded here for months—maybe longer. But there wasn't a trace of personal history. No receipts. No mail. No signs of a life lived.

Callan's gut twisted. He scanned the living room—eyes landing on a scuffed patch on the floor where a rug had clearly been rolled up recently.

Someone packed this place in a hurry.

"Or someone cleaned it," he whispered. And if it was cleaned—it wasn't Dwayne. It was whoever was tying up loose ends.

He knew the signs. Whoever had sanitized this place wasn't a burglar or some flunky. They were methodical. Precise. Like him. Or a cop. Either way, Callan wasn't convinced he'd find anything.

He gave it an hour, combing for removable media or overlooked details.

Nothing.

He stepped back into the Miami night, unsettled by the neighbourhood's sterile stillness. Too clean. Too curated. Too perfect—like a showroom nobody actually lived in.

He swung a leg over the Triumph Street Triple and fired it up. The engine growled low and sharp as he rolled down the tree-lined street.

A glance in the mirror.

There.

A dark SUV pulling from the curb a block back. Headlights dimmed, not off. Keeping distance, but sloppy—too steady on the follow. Amateurs.

Callan shifted gears, the growl beneath him flaring into a snarl. He weaved through the affluent streets with surgical precision. Palm trees blurred. A yellow light turned red behind him. The SUV hesitated, fell back.

By the time he hit Biscayne Boulevard, the tail was struggling.

He hooked a sharp right, ducking into a narrow alley too tight for a full-size vehicle. Tires kissed the pavement. The SUV vanished.

Gone.

He didn't slow until he looped back toward the mainland, threading through low-traffic backstreets. By the time he reached his garage, the adrenaline had faded, replaced by the usual hum of focus.

Inside, he killed the engine and peeled off the license plate with practiced ease, replacing it with a clean one from the stash behind the workbench. No fingerprints. No scuffs. Sterile as a scalpel.

The elevator ride felt eternal. He missed the lock twice before the key slid in. Callan hardly noticed Beckett, who crossed the condo like a returning general, tail flicking, clearly convinced the place had remained secure solely because of his watchful presence.

Callan gave the cat a sidelong glance. "You get your win today, buddy?"

Beckett flicked his tail and strutted off.

CHAPTER 56

Callan slept most of the next day. He rose around dinner time and went through the motions of being human. A few hours later, the condo felt too small. He needed air. Movement. More time in the saddle.

So, he decided to check in on David.

Carving lanes between traffic like the laws were just background noise, Callan tore through the Miami night. The Triumph roared beneath him, tethered to his pulse, like muscle and bone, as he wove past red lights, ignored speed limits, and treated stop signs like polite suggestions.

"Why don't I ride this thing more often?" he murmured into his helmet.

The wind peeled at his jacket—warm, thick with humidity—but his focus stayed razor sharp. Every block felt like a fuse burning too fast.

David's McMansion wasn't exactly subtle. Gated neighbourhood. Palm trees trimmed within an inch of their lives. Homes that screamed "midlife crisis" louder than the convertibles parked out front.

He cut through a side street and parked the Triumph at the end of the driveway.

The soft touches of suburban wealth filled the air—distant lawn sprinklers, the muted hum of AC units. Too quiet. Too still. Too staged.

Callan adjusted his jacket and walked up the driveway with casual confidence. No creeping, no crouching. He'd been here too many times for that. Neighbours had seen him—at barbecues, pool parties, tense Sunday dinners where David's temper bled through expensive wine and Ellen's carefully structured charm. Callan was part of the scenery here.

He rang the doorbell, waiting beneath the porch light's soft glow. No tension. Just another late-night drop-in.

The neighbourhood hummed its usual lullaby—TV murmurs, a spoiled golden retriever barking in the distance. Everything normal. Everything still.

But Callan's gut whispered otherwise.

When no one came, he knocked—twice. Firm, not impatient. "C'mon, David. Don't make me break into your house like we're strangers."

Still nothing.

He glanced at the front windows—curtains drawn tight. Lights on in the back, but the air felt wrong. Too quiet. Too careful.

He tried the handle.

Unlocked.

Exhaling through his nose, he pushed the door open with the ease of muscle memory. No tension. Just the practiced ease of someone who'd done this a hundred times before.

The familiar scent hit him immediately. Leather couches, the faint citrus cleaner Ellen swore by—now dulled beneath something sharper—stale takeout. The bitter edge of spilled liquor. The kind of mess that lingers when no one's around to care.

"David?" His voice carried through the foyer, steady but edged.

Silence.

He moved past the entry table—where David usually tossed his keys. Empty. Past the art deco mirror Ellen left behind, streaked with fingerprints like no one had wiped it down in weeks.

The living room was chaos.

Scotch bottle on its side. Couch cushions displaced. An empty pizza box curling at the corners. A sharp contrast to the clean, curated space Ellen once ran like a tight ship.

David's prints were all over this—a downward spiral Callan had seen too many times. And yet... something about it felt off. Not just neglect. Something sharper.

His eyes swept the room like it was a crime scene.

The glass of Scotch still had a faint halo of condensation.

The TV remote lay shattered on the floor.

A poker chip sat half-hidden under the coffee table—scarred, worn.

It wasn't just messy. This was frantic. A storm passed through—and Callan had arrived late to the wreckage.

"Where the hell are you, David?" he muttered.

Light from the kitchen bled into the living room, casting uneven shadows. He moved toward it, boots whispering against the hardwood.

The kitchen was worse. Counters cluttered with takeout containers, stained coffee mugs, unopened mail. A sharp contrast to Ellen's surgical precision. Now it felt hollow. Abandoned.

Then he saw it.

The back door to the pool deck— ajar. Curtains swaying in the warm breeze.

His gut coiled.

The silence outside was louder than anything inside.

He stepped onto the deck, scanning the yard. The pool sat still beneath the sodium light. Perfectly calm—except for the figure floating face-down in the water.

David.

Half-submerged. Arms slack. Shirt ballooned in the water. A dark bloom just above the temple.

Gunshot.

Callan's pulse held steady, but his chest tightened. He crouched at the pool's edge, scanning the scene. No weapon. No spent casing. Clean shot. Close range. Execution, not panic.

"Jesus, David…"

The water rippled softly, a dark mirror reflecting the lifeless sky. Callan's hand gripped the pool's edge, the texture of the rough tile biting into his skin. He remembered a younger David—reckless, cocky, trying to hustle him at a poker table. A ghost of a laugh echoed and vanished.

David had always been a slow-motion disaster. But this wasn't a collapse. This was demolition. Controlled. Intentional.

The chill that settled deep in Callan's bones had nothing to do with the night air.

This wasn't random. It wasn't desperation.

It was a message.

Callan forced himself to focus. No time for sentiment. No room for mistakes.

Tricia.

He was on her board now. A part of her game. And this? This felt like a chess move. Like someone removing liabilities.

He looked down at David's body. The blood blooming in the water like ink across tile. Silent. Final.

His jaw tightened. Whoever did this knew what they were doing. No drag marks. No prints. No signs of entry or escape.

A pro. Or someone who wanted Callan to find the scene just like this.

The instinct was there—leave. Fast. Quiet. Before anyone saw him.

But his feet didn't move.

His thoughts drifted to Ellen. The panic in her voice during that last call. The quiet tremor when she'd said David was in deep.

She'd loved him. For better or worse. And now?

Now she'd get a phone call. Maybe tonight. Maybe tomorrow.

It'd wreck her.

"You idiot," Callan muttered to David's corpse. "Dragged everyone down with you."

The sympathy surprised him. Mostly for Ellen. Maybe for David too.

He scrubbed a hand over his face.

Not now. Not here.

He moved to the sliding door, careful not to leave prints. No alarms. No cameras. Whoever did this either wiped it clean—or knew Callan would come looking.

He left like he'd done countless times before. Helmet on. If someone had clocked him earlier, there wasn't much he could do now—but it was better than nothing.

Before he swung a leg over the Triumph, he gave the cul-de-sac one last scan.

No porch lights flicked on. No curious eyes behind curtains.

Still.

He knew how this worked.

Even if no one saw him, someone might've heard the bike arrive.

"Too late to worry about it now," he muttered, starting the engine.

It came to life quiet but eager. By the time he pulled onto the main road, he was just another shadow slipping through the sprawl of Miami night traffic.

Ellen's inevitable grief rode shotgun all the way home.

CHAPTER 57

The city was pressed in behind the condo windows like a silent threat. They felt too thin now to keep the crush of life out. A faint hum of Beckett grooming himself in the corner was the only sound. The glow of Callan's laptop cast dark shadows across his face as he moved with quiet purpose.

He shut the laptop. The click echoed louder than it should.

His gut churned—not from the files he'd just scoured, but from the nagging thoughts of Ellen. He rubbed his temple, willing her out of his mind, but guilt crept back in like smoke under a door.

"Focus," he muttered.

Beckett paused his lazy grooming long enough to give Callan a bored glance, then resumed, as indifferent as ever.

Callan stood, pocketed his phone, and grabbed the small trash bag from the kitchen. He needed air. Something grounding. Taking out the trash solved nothing, but it gave him a minute away from the slow swirl of dread.

The hallway outside was dead quiet. The building always carried a faint smell of mildew—humidity's signature, the scent of a place where nothing ever truly dried out. His flip-flops whispered against the marble as he made his way to the service elevator.

The doors yawned open. He stepped in, trash bag dangling loosely from one hand.

On the eighth floor, the elevator jolted to a stop. A snowbird and her rat-sized dog stepped in. *Lunch for Beckett*, Callan mused.

The woman—leather-skinned, sun-drenched—gave him a second glance and edged to the far wall. It was like she could sense something off in him. And whatever it was, she didn't want to catch it.

The doors slid open on the ground floor.

Detective Grayson stood stone-faced, cradling a steaming travel mug. O'Halloran, arms crossed, towered beside him like an impatient bulldog.

Callan's pulse didn't blip. He just sighed. "Gentlemen," he said flatly. "I'm flattered you're checking in again. But do you really want to deal with Monty this early?"

Grayson's mouth twitched—barely. "Funny. You're under arrest."

"For what?" Callan asked, handing the trash bag to the stunned snowbird. She took it without question, enthralled with the live-action crime drama unfolding in her building.

"Dangerous driving," Grayson said, stepping in. "Specifically, reckless endangerment. Around 2:30 this morning."

Callan kept his hands visible, relaxed. "You guys seriously burn gas for a misdemeanour now?"

Grayson leaned in. "Let's just say this is the easiest way to get you in the room." He gave Callan what he liked to call *the gotcha wink*.

Callan smirked. "Once again, boys—I'm flattered."

"Don't be," O'Halloran rumbled. "You're burning daylight, Callan."

Callan lifted his wrists voluntarily. "Let's not make a scene."

Grayson cuffed him—quick, practiced. O'Halloran retrieved the discarded trash bag like it might be evidence.

As they led Callan into the humid Miami morning, he could almost hear Diego's voice in the back of his mind. *Control the room, or the room controls you.*

Today, it was the room, but he had time to change that.

***

The interview room felt smaller this time. Same cold concrete. Same buzzing overhead light. Same cheap chairs.

Callan sat still. Arms crossed. Eyes on the chipped edge of the table. Hours passed—no questions, no conversation. Just Grayson and O'Halloran playing the long game with silence and stares.

Grayson's weapon was patience, letting the clock grind down. O'Halloran twitched, pen tapping against his knee, casting glances at the two-way mirror like he was waiting for cues.

Callan didn't bite. No yawn. No fidget. Just stillness.

Let them simmer.

Then—the door crashed open like a gunshot.

Monty stormed in. Tie loose. Jacket creased. Fury sharp.

"That's enough of this bullshit," he snapped, voice slicing through the tension like a blade.

Grayson sighed, annoyed. O'Halloran shifted like a kid caught past curfew.

Monty jabbed a finger at Grayson. "My client's been boxed up for hours. No charges. No warrant. He walks."

Grayson grinned like a cat that swallowed the canary. "No charges. *Yet.* But your boy's headed out to Biscayne Bay. Seems the detectives out there want a word."

Callan gave Monty a slow nod but felt the shift. *Biscayne Bay.* The words echoed like a warning bell.

Grayson stared at his folder. "Transport's en route. Bay PD's got questions. Seems your client's name came up out there, too."

As the detectives filed out, Monty leaned in, voice low and sharp.

"One blink for guilty."

Callan blinked. Twice.

Monty frowned. Rapped his knuckle against the table. "Anything you're not telling me?"

Callan's jaw flexed. He could feel the noose tightening. But the words stuck—caught somewhere between pride and ghosts he wasn't ready to exhume.

"They're reaching," Callan said quietly, though he didn't believe it.

Monty pursed his lips. "We won't know until they start asking. I'll see you out there. Be smart."

Before Callan could reply, the door creaked open again. A young uniform stepped in with a clipboard. "Transfer detail's ready."

Callan stood. The cuffs clicked back on, heavy against his wrists. As they led him out, Monty followed close, voice low and steady. "Keep your head down. Don't say a damn thing until I catch up."

Callan nodded, but his thoughts had already jumped—toward Biscayne Bay. Toward the storm waiting for him there.

Not just the case.

Her

As they moved down the corridor beneath flickering lights, Callan clenched his jaw tighter. He knew exactly who he was about to face.

And he wasn't sure what would sting more—the questions...

Or the betrayal.

CHAPTER 58

The holding cell of the Biscayne Bay police station smelled like the gym room at a country club. Callan knew the smell from a job he'd done in Palm Springs five years earlier. A very lucrative gig, where he'd quite literally scared a known con man to death. George saw Callan, saw the knife, pissed himself, and dropped dead. A hilarious story—one he couldn't tell anyone.

His trip down memory lane was interrupted.

"McWard."

"Present."

Biscayne Bay PD clearly had a gaudy operating budget—and processed very few criminals. The office was pristine. The interview room, palatial compared to Miami PD. Callan eased into the metal chair and prepared for another broody interrogation.

He didn't wait long. The door creaked open.

Detective Tricia Langley.

"Tricia."

"It's *Detective* Langley."

Called it, Callan lamented inwardly. He leaned back in the chair, arms folded. "Right. *Detective.*"

She slid into the seat across from him. Dressed down, but unmistakably on duty—dark jeans, a leather jacket parted just enough to flash her badge and sidearm. Casual, but calculated. Her makeup and hair, however, made her look ready for a date or a photo shoot.

Even under the sterile interrogation room light, she was gorgeous. And each time he saw her, Callan found himself more drawn in. She sat calm, collected—but her eyes were cold. Calculated.

"So," she began, voice smooth as silk but laced with steel, "we should talk about what happened on County Road 17."

A chill crawled up his spine. "What are you talking about?"

She tilted her head, that same playful smirk she used behind the wheel—but now it felt like a dagger.

"You know. The night you decided to take control. When you didn't take no for an answer."

His breath caught. "No? You never said—"

"Didn't I?" she cut in smoothly, leaning forward, voice dropping—intimate, dangerous. "Or maybe you just weren't listening. Maybe you were too busy proving how good you are at pushing limits."

His stomach twisted. The memory replayed like a warped film reel: The hunger in her eyes, the way she'd taken the lead, the deliberate brush of her fingers along his jaw, the whispered challenge. None of it fit the picture she was painting now—but that didn't matter.

She straightened, unreadable. "Doesn't matter what you *think* happened, Callan. What matters is how it *looks* when I tell my version." She gave him a pointed look, voice a whisper. "And right now? You look like a man who loses control behind closed doors."

Callan's fists clenched at his sides, nails biting into his palms. "You're lying," was all he could manage.

For the first time in years, Callan McWard was speechless.

Her eyes widened, shimmering with sudden, perfect tears. She shook her head, her breath hitching. "God, listen to you," she whispered. "I trusted you."

Callan froze. The whiplash between predator and trembling victim left him disoriented. But it was a performance. And a damn good one.

She let the silence stretch, then buried her face in her hands—just long enough. When she peeked through her fingers, her voice had dropped to a sly whisper.

"Tell me, Callan," she purred, crocodile tears still glistening, "when this goes to trial... who do you think they'll believe?"

His heartbeat thundered in his ears.

She wiped her cheek, leaving the faintest smear of mascara. "A decorated detective. A woman in a dangerous profession. Trusted by the badge. Or a middle-aged loner, deep in a midlife crisis? The man whose only friends are a washed-up model and her sleazy ambulance-chasing husband?"

Her voice broke again, tremulous. She rocked slightly in her chair. To anyone watching behind the glass, she looked like a woman barely holding it together.

But Callan saw it—the glint in her eye. Sharp as broken glass.

"You're bluffing," he said.

She leaned in closer. He could see the wicked curve at the corner of her mouth.

"Am I?" she whispered. "Or did you finally lose control... just like they always said you would?"

Callan felt cornered. Not by guns. Not by enemies on the road. But by a woman who knew exactly how to spin the truth—and how fragile it could be in the wrong hands.

Tricia's voice dropped to a velvet razor. "I have your DNA on my clothing, baby."

His blood froze. She was so close now, he could feel her breath—warm, sickly sweet, and deliberate.

Her lips brushed the shell of his ear.

"Everyone saw me walk back into the bar alone... crying."

His throat went dry. The room shrank around him. He could already hear it—cops of every stripe, drunk after duty, whispering, nodding. The narrative writing itself.

Tricia met his gaze. Her eyes glassy, sharp beneath the shimmer.

"I've written the ending for you, Callan," she murmured. "And the jury's going to eat it up."

He shook his head, fury clawing at his ribs.

She let it hang for a beat, then smoothed her jacket and stood.

"You're lucky I care about you, lover," she said. Almost affectionate. Almost. "Otherwise, I'd let them rip you apart."

Callan didn't flinch when she reached into her pocket, produced a key, and stepped behind him. The cuffs clicked open.

"You're free to go," she said softly, lips curling into something between a smile and a sneer.

He stood slowly, rubbing his wrists. "Just like that?"

Tricia tilted her head, eyes narrowing as she read him. "Consider it a gift."

He stepped past her toward the door but couldn't stop himself from asking. "Why?"

Her smirk widened. She touched his cheek, gentle. "You know why, silly."

She wasn't just winning this round—she was keeping score.

She opened the door. The station's waiting area gleamed—polished tile, modern furniture, expensive art. Callan barely noticed. His attention locked on Monty, arguing with a young patrol officer by the vending machines.

Monty turned, blinking in disbelief. "You've gotta be kidding me," he muttered, striding over. "What the hell just happened?"

Callan barely had time to respond before Tricia joined them, cool as ever. "Counselor," she said smoothly. "All cleared up. Your client's free to go."

Monty blinked. Suspicious. "What did you do?"

Callan just shook his head. "Let's go."

Monty nodded once, clipped. "Fine." He turned to Tricia. "We're done."

"Are we?" she asked, just loud enough.

Callan didn't look back as Monty pushed him toward the exit. But he felt her eyes, burning into his back like knives.

Outside, as the humid night wrapped around him, Callan exhaled.

"She let me walk," he muttered. But even as he said it, he knew the truth.

She hadn't let him walk. She'd moved him exactly where she wanted.

And then, a curveball.

Leaning against Monty's car: Mel.

"I believe you already know FBI Special Agent Williams," Monty said, uncharacteristically sheepish. A notorious mob lawyer introducing a Fed was nearly comical.

But the way Callan's month was going, he refused to be surprised.

"Hello Callan," Mel said, grinning like a wolf.

CHAPTER 59

Monty's Maserati glided through Miami's cluttered streets, heat radiating off the asphalt in waves. Callan sat in the backseat, eyes pinned to the skyline like it owed him something.

"Langley," Mel said. "Her real name's Langston."

Callan's gaze cut over. "Tricia Langston."

"Daughter of Judge Philip Langston," Mel confirmed.

Callan's pulse ticked up. "Didn't peg her for a nepotism baby."

"Not exactly," Mel said flat. "Married a cop in Tampa years back. Kept the name after the split—keeps the locals guessing."

Callan's voice dropped, edged with venom. "How does this impact me?"

Mel's jaw tensed. "It's not just her. It's a whole syndicate—politicians, judges, fixers. Langston's the spine. Tricia's the teeth."

Callan's lips pressed into a hard line. "And you've been circling?"

"For years."

Callan gave a humourless smirk. "So, what—you want me to spy? Flip her? Black-bag her into an FBI van?"

Mel let out a dry chuckle. "Close. I need you in her head."

Callan arched a brow.

"She won't trust a badge," Mel continued. "But you? You're off the grid. And you've already rattled her more than you think." He hesitated. "She's got blind spots. Especially with men."

Callan's stare sharpened. "You're asking me to seduce her."

"I'm asking you to earn her trust. Then tear it down."

Callan sat still, the tension rising behind his eyes. "Yeah," he muttered. "Noticed."

Mel let the silence hang.

Callan shifted in his seat.

Mel sighed and continued "You can't touch Langston yet. But Tricia's the crack."

He sat quiet, images flashing—dark alleys, surveillance stills, David's blood making abstract patterns in the water.

"Let me guess," Callan said. "This is you asking nice."

Monty snorted. "Could've fooled me."

Mel ignored it. "Help me flip her; I'll make the rest disappear."

Callan's jaw clenched. He already knew his answer. But damn if it didn't taste bitter. His eyes flicked back to the window.

"All right," he said.

Monty glanced over his shoulder, eyebrows raised. Mel sat straighter, waiting for the sting.

"I'll help you burn their little empire to the ground."

Mel blinked. "You're serious?"

Callan's smirk cut slow, razor-thin. "Serious as a heart attack."

Mel leaned in slightly, voice cautioning. "UC work isn't for everyone. FBI's got ways to prep people."

Callan nodded slowly, steel behind it. "Sure. We'll go with that."

Mel's stare sharpened. "Don't get cocky on me."

Callan met his eyes in the rearview. Calm as a loaded gun. "If you want Tricia to crack, let me handle it my way."

"What way's that?"

Callan leaned forward, voice quiet. "The way that leaves a mark."

Monty chuckled, tapping the s wheel. "Told you he plays 'em close."

Mel's suspicion deepened, eyes narrowing. "You're not just some accountant."

Callan leaned back, folding his arms. "Never was."

Mel cursed under his breath. A quiet, involuntary thing.

Callan's smirk didn't waver. "Relax, Fed. I've got this."

Mel shook his head. Suspicion and respect trading places behind his eyes.

Monty grinned, eyes back on the road. "Man's already halfway inside."

Callan looked out the window, the skyline drifting by in a heat shimmer. "I'll give you what you want," he said quietly. "But be ready for what it costs."

CHAPTER 60

The condo walls were closing in again. This was usually a safe space, but now it felt intimately similar to the police interview rooms he'd recently visited.

Callan shut the door behind him, the soft click ricocheting louder than it should have. The place was still—too still. Beckett was still camped out at Lucy's, leaving the space stripped bare of its usual friction, that subtle chaos Callan had grown used to.

He tossed his keys onto the counter. Stood there watching the empty room like it might change under his stare. The low hum of the A/C filled the silence but didn't help. The walls felt closer tonight.

Rolling his shoulders, he moved to the corner desk and cracked open his work laptop. The glow from the screen spilled shadows across the condo, long and sharp.

Langley file—still pending.

Callan cursed under his breath, pulled up the secure line to IT.

"Langley file request still pending. Expedite. Today. –Lucian." He hit send and stared at the blinking cursor, the silence pressing heavier now.

The tension from the drive with Mel still buzzed beneath his skin—sharper in the quiet, no distractions to blunt the edges.

He leaned back, eyes drifting to the window. Neon bled against glass, streaks of pink and blue smeared across the skyline like someone scrubbed the day away too fast.

The phone buzzed.

Callan sighed, rubbing his face before checking it.

Claire: [selfie—flirty, playful, oversized sweater slipping off one shoulder, smirk barely contained]

Claire: Miss me yet?

Callan: Define miss.

Claire: The part where you can't stop thinking about me. Or where you wish you weren't brooding alone in your bougie condo.

Callan: Guilty on the condo part. For the rest, I plead the Fifth.

Claire: Lame. But I'll allow it... for now.

Callan: For what it's worth, you look dangerously good in that. Distracting, even.

Claire: Distracting, huh? Sounds like I'm doing my job. Want me to up the ante?

Callan: Tempting. But if I let you win, I'll be up all night. And I've got people to disappoint in the morning.

Claire: Boring. But fine, go be responsible. For now.

Callan: That sounds like a threat.

Claire: No, babe—that's a promise.

His thumbs hovered, thoughts tumbling faster than the words could keep up.

Callan typing:

I've been staring at this screen too long, trying to figure out how to say something that won't sound like a goodbye. But if it did... you'd need to know I'm better for having had you in my life. Way better.

You've been light where I usually sit in the dark. Too comfortable there, probably. So yeah... I miss you. More than I should probably admit right now.

If things shift, if I go quiet for a bit, just know it's not because I don't care. It's the opposite.

Stay safe, Claire.

Delete.

Callan sent: I'm out for a bit. Catch up with you later.

No time for more.

On to Ellen. *Callan: We need to meet. Send me your address.*

Send. No soft edges.

The reply came back too fast. Address locked in. Callan's gut tightened. He tapped *Call* and raised the phone to his ear, eyes sweeping the condo like it might whisper secrets back.

Ellen picked up on the first ring. "Callan?" Calm, clipped, like she'd been waiting. He stayed silent, listening. No voices. No static. Just her breathing.

"You alone?"

A beat. "Yeah. You think I'd send my address if I wasn't?"

His jaw ticked, but he let out a breath. "Just checking."

"Relax," she said, softer now. "It's me."

Callan gave a small nod to no one. "After dark, stay sharp."

"No problem," Ellen replied, steady as stone. "I'll be here."

He ended the call without a goodbye.

And now—the devil.

Callan: Call me.

No grey area. Just a line in the sand. His stomach knotted tighter. He'd already stood too close to her flames. Now he was about to walk right into them.

The laptop chimed.

"Request received. Escalating priority."

Not fast enough.

He rubbed the back of his neck where tension coiled like a wire. The condo felt colder now, like the walls were leaning in.

He moved to the kitchen, poured a finger of whiskey, sipped. The burn barely touched the ice creeping through him.

Buzz.

Tricia.

Callan answered. Silence—heavy and thick, like breath caught in a throat. Then her breathing, slow and careful, brushing against his nerves like a blade.

Her voice followed, sweet and rotten all at once. "Hey you," she purred, dragging the words out like she wanted to taste them.

The memory slammed back—her across that metal table, stone-cold under buzzing fluorescents. No cracks. No warmth. Just ice beneath the rage. Now she sounded like someone disciplining a bad pet.

Callan let the silence stretch, feeling her bristle on the other end.

"You don't have to be scared," she murmured, conspiratorial, like they were tangled up in something dark and secret. "I've been thinking about you today. Every. Single. Minute."

You're the one that should be afraid, Callan thought. His grip on the whiskey glass tightened. "Is that so?"

A girlish laugh—sharp, brittle, like glass breaking underfoot. "Mmmhm. I was thinking about the last time we were together. You left me... unfinished. Like I didn't matter."

She was rewriting history. That bar. That night. *You wanted to go back alone, not me.*

"I'm sorry, baby," Callan said, voice steel.

"That's okay, Callan." Her tone softened, almost reverent. "You're always so... closed off. But I see you. I know what's beneath it. I remember how you touched my arm... how you pushed my head down onto you."

Her sigh, full of breathless longing, twisted like a knife. "No one sees me like you do."

"When can I see you again?" he asked, voice low.

"Oh, I knew you'd ask," she crooned, elated. "There's still so much to finish. You left such a mess." Then softer, disarmingly. "I ache for you."

She meant it. Whatever this was—delusion or something worse—it was locked in deep.

"You're quiet," she taunted, the sweetness slipping into something sharp. "You're making me impatient." Her voice paused. "Are you punishing me?"

His jaw flexed. "I'm not punishing you."

"Good." She let the hook sink in. "Because waiting makes me... impulsive."

The whiskey burned, but the cold stayed.

"Where?" she snapped, tone razor-sharp.

"What?"

"Where do we meet, darling?" Then sugary again. "Or should I just find you? I know where you sleep."

Callan exhaled slow. "I'll be in touch."

"Oh, Callan," she sang, voice sliding like silk over glass, "you don't get to decide that."

His patience snapped. "Tricia."

The way she whispered it back, soaked in triumph, made his skin crawl.

"I knew you'd come around," she whispered. "You're mine, Callan. You just don't see it yet."

The glass cracked beneath his hand as he set it down.

"You're not in charge, lover," he warned, voice a growl. "I'll let you know."

Her brittle laugh scraped the line. "Oh, yes Daddy. Love it when you take charge."

Callan ended the call. The silence that followed felt colder than the call itself.

But it wasn't just her voice clinging to him—it was the memory of her eyes across that table. Cold. Certain.

And the sickening sense that this was only the beginning.

The laptop dinged again.

CHAPTER 61

Moving on autopilot, Callan gathered his laptop, recon bag, and phone. He had to get out—*move*—before he lost it.

Outside, the streets were washed in dull neon and rain-slick reflections. No music. No radio. Just the swipe of the wipers, and tires slicing through wet asphalt.

The silence pressed like a vise.

Ellen's neighbourhood wasn't much better. Tucked away. Too quiet. Shadows stretched long beneath tired streetlamps—the kind of street where the dark felt like it watched you.

He parked two houses down. Habit. The motion-sensor light above Ellen's door flickered as he approached, casting her porch in a sickly glow. She cracked the door just enough for him to see half her face—messy hair, dark circles under her eyes, her skin pale like she hadn't slept in days.

"David's dead," she whispered, like she was still trying to believe it.

"I know."

She let him in without another word.

The air inside was thick and humid. Ellen grabbed him, burying her face into his chest, her body trembling. Callan stood stiff at first, then wrapped his arms around her, grounding them both.

"He was supposed to be safe," she murmured, voice raw.

Callan exhaled. "We need to figure out why."

They moved to the kitchen. Ellen slid her laptop onto the table, hands still unsteady.

"He emailed me right before he died," she said, pulling up her inbox. "It's... strange."

Callan leaned in.

From David: Ellen, just in case. Don't trust anyone but Callan. Love you. Attach: TSF file.

"TSF," Callan muttered. The chill was instant.

"You know it?" Ellen asked.

"Yeah. Military-grade encryption. Tradecraft stuff."

Ellen blinked. "David wasn't military."

"No, but whoever passed him this file was."

His instincts surged—David had been holding something hot. Something people killed for.

"Can you open it?"

Callan nodded, already sliding his work laptop onto the counter. But before he could decrypt the file, a new notification blinked from The Archive.

Tricia Langley's sealed file.

Callan clicked *OPEN*, and lines of text unravelled faster than he could read. Suppressed records. Redacted notes. Black ink someone powerful had worked hard to bury.

Then the lock broke.

JUVENILE INCIDENTS (SEALED)

• Age 15: Aggravated Assault. Victim hospitalized.

• Age 16: Felony vandalism targeting ex-boyfriend.

• Age 17: Stalking, harassment, unauthorized break-ins.

• Age 17: Animal cruelty—extreme. Victim: family pet.

It wasn't just the crimes—it was the *feeling*. A cold, clinical detachment seeping from the reports like a faint, metallic scent.

He remembered the way she'd looked at him in the interview room. Not with lust. With something closer to... curiosity. Like a collector eyeing a rare specimen.

Callan's gut twisted. She didn't just hurt people. She *liked* it.

His eyes flicked to Ellen, who was chewing her lip, watching him.

"That bad?" she asked quietly.

Callan's voice stayed flat. "It's worse."

He scrolled deeper.

ADULT INCIDENTS (SEALED)

• Domestic battery. • Excessive force in custody.

• Stalking a former partner using department databases.

• Officer-involved shooting—no weapon on the suspect. No indictment.

Callan leaned back, pulse sharp.

Mel had called Tricia *the pit bull*, but this wasn't about loyalty. This was pathology. A dangerous person with a badge—and far too much insulation from the world's consequences.

"She's broken," Callan muttered.

Ellen's voice wavered. "Is she the one who killed David?"

His jaw worked. "No."

His instincts said no. "But she's circling whatever's behind it."

He stared at the sealed file, fists curling tight.

Tricia Langley wasn't just a crack in the armour.

She was the fault line.

CHAPTER 62

Leaning over his work laptop, Callan scanned the decrypted contents of David's email. The screen glowed cold and clinical in the dim motel room, casting a blue light across his face.

Lines of data spilled like rot—photos, time-stamped surveillance logs, financial records. Every line whispered the same word.

Blackmail.

He knocked back the last of his whiskey. It burned just enough to keep his thoughts sharp—though not sharp enough to cut through the dread curdling in his gut.

"Pack your shit," he said, voice flat.

Ellen, curled up on the couch in a loose sweatshirt, legs tangled beneath her, didn't even look up. She swirled her half-finished wine lazily, the ice cubes clinking like wind chimes.

"Why?"

"I have a safe house out in Jacksonville."

She wrinkled her nose. "Jesus. I'd rather be dead." A beat. "Wait—why the hell do *you* have a safe house?"

Callan shut the laptop hard. The plastic snap cut through the silence. He didn't answer her second question.

Ellen stared at him, eyes narrowing. Then came the sigh—heavier this time, resigned.

"I'll go pack."

***

The drive was quiet. Rain ticked against the windshield in uneven rhythms, streaking through the headlights like falling sparks. The air in the car was thick with road funk—wet asphalt, cheap coffee, the faint burnt-plastic smell from the dashboard vent he kept meaning to fix.

Eventually, Ellen broke the silence.

"You know, David never really had any friends," she said, voice small. "Not the kind who stuck."

Callan adjusted his grip on the wheel. His knuckles popped.

"He had you."

Ellen gave a bitter smile. "Yeah, well. I never had male friends who didn't want to sleep with me. Except David. He was too busy screwing himself over."

The road stretched endlessly ahead. Callan checked the rearview mirror for the fifth time in as many minutes.

Taillights. Mist. Still, the unease stuck like fog.

***

The Jacksonville condo was bare bones, like everything Callan didn't want to get attached to. The front door creaked like an old violin. Inside, the overhead light buzzed faintly, revealing pale walls, a sagging couch, and the faint musty tang of disuse. The air was stale, overlaid with air freshener and something old beneath it—dust, maybe. Or time.

He handed Ellen a manila envelope, thick with cash. "Twenty grand. Don't go out unless you have to."

She flipped through the bills with a practiced flick of her thumb, then looked up, one brow raised.

"Trying to get rid of me?"

Callan didn't respond. He was already scanning the space—doorways, windows, sightlines. No exposed angles. Fewer reflections. He took in the room like it might try to betray him.

Outside, thunder rumbled low—pressing against the windows like a held breath. Still, the knot in his chest only twisted tighter.

Ellen was smart. She could vanish if she wanted. But this wasn't just about safety. Not really.

This was strategy. She was bait. Maybe.

***

Callan started the trek back to Miami alone, the miles piling up under a bug-smeared windshield. The rain had stopped, but the silence had weight.

Somewhere on that long, empty stretch of highway, the slow, gnawing truth caught up to him.

He'd always prided himself on being a professional—a gardener who pruned monsters from the world's rose beds. But tonight, with Ellen tucked away in a safe house, unknowingly prepped as bait, Callan saw it clearly.

He wasn't protecting what little he had left. He was hunting. Playing the long game like a predator.

The reflection in the rearview wasn't a ghost. It was him.

The monster.

And maybe—he'd been one all along.

CHAPTER 63

The humid morning air clung to Callan's skin as he left the condo's parking garage. He paused on the sidewalk, taking in the city as it stirred to life.

He started walking toward Java Junction, dialling Tricia's number as he moved. The ring cut through the silence.

When she picked up, there was no greeting. Just breath—steady, deliberate.

"I need to know something," Callan said, voice low, careful. Like a man threading a needle with broken hands.

A faint rustle on the other end. Then her voice—calm, but unmistakably sharp.

"Is this your way of asking for a favour, Callan?"

"No." His pace slowed. "I just need to know what you want from me."

Silence stretched, long enough to pull the tension tight. Then came a laugh—not amused but measured. Dark. "*What I want?* You make it sound like I'm some kind of predator."

"Isn't that what you are?" His tone was flat, but there was something underneath—something pointed.

She didn't answer right away. He could almost hear her smile.

"I didn't start this game, Callan," she said, the words drifting into his ear like smoke. "But it seems like you and I have been playing by the same rules all along, haven't we?"

"Maybe." His eyes narrowed, pushing past her voice's pull. "But the difference is, I'm done pretending I don't see you coming."

"And *that*'s what you've always done, Callan," she said. *That* —velvet and venom. "Pretend. Pretend you don't care. Pretend you don't need anyone."

Callan stopped walking. Stared at the sidewalk like it might offer answers. She saw him. She saw *through* him. And didn't look away.

"So what?" he asked. "You're just gonna keep playing this game? Make me chase you? What's the end of it, Tricia?"

"Maybe I'm not the one playing," she whispered. Her voice was glass now—cutting, cool. "Maybe you've been chasing something you don't even understand. You think this is about us? About me? It's about control. It always has been."

His jaw clenched. The weight of it settled on him, but he didn't flinch.

"Then what do you want?" he asked. Still, but with something beneath—curiosity, real and raw. "You've got all the pieces. You've played your hand. But what's the endgame, Tricia?"

Her reply came soft. Measured. Too calm. "I already told you. I want what I've always wanted." A pause. The air between them pulled tight.

"I want you, Callan. I want you to stop pretending you don't need me."

Callan exhaled sharply. The breath felt cold on his lips.

"That's what this is? You think I need you?"

"No," she said, almost kind now. Almost. "I think you don't have a choice."

The line went quiet. Callan could feel it—the space between them folding inward. Not distance, not really. Something else. Something neither of them had ever named.

"I guess I'll have to figure out what the hell I'm supposed to do with that," he said finally.

"I'm sure you will," she replied. Her voice soft. Knowing. Like the last piece of a puzzle sliding into place.

He said nothing. Just stood there, staring down the clean, polished street, the conversation pressing against his ribs like a weight.

Then—"I'll be seeing you soon," she murmured. A promise. "I want to see you," she added. A breath. "9:30 PM. I'll text you the details."

Callan didn't respond. He ended the call, the disconnect sharp in the quiet.

He stood there a moment longer. Then walked.

The neighbourhood stretched ahead—quiet, orderly, gleaming.

But the air behind him felt heavier now.

Like something was following.

Chapter 64

The low hum of soft jazz played in the background, barely audible over the clinking of glasses and the quiet murmur of other patrons.

The lighting was dim, casting long shadows across the polished wood floors, steeping the space in a hush of intimacy. A place where people came to talk, to linger in their thoughts—and sometimes, to let their secrets spill.

Callan sat in the far corner, hands folded neatly on the table. His eyes swept the room, practiced glances—never lingering, never still. His posture was relaxed, but alert. He wasn't here for dinner. He was here to see if Tricia was playing another game.

The door opened with a soft chime. And there she was.

Tricia moved like she owned the air around her. Even here, even now, she pulled attention like a riptide. But something about her was different tonight. The dress was calculated—tight black silk that clung like it had been stitched onto her. Heels clicking softly across the floor. Her perfume hit before she reached him: dark, sweet, intoxicating.

She smiled as she approached—slow, deliberate, lingering. She slid into the seat across from him, crossing her legs as the fabric of her dress shifted. Just so.

"Nice place," he said, voice low and neutral. "Didn't expect you to pick somewhere so... quiet."

Tricia met his gaze evenly. "Figured you'd appreciate the atmosphere."

Callan's eyes flickered over her once but didn't linger. He wasn't about to get pulled under.

She tilted her head, smirking. "I'm sure you're used to places with a little more... noise." "Depends on the noise," he said, not missing a beat.

Her eyes sparkled with something dangerous. She reached out, fingers trailing slowly across the table—stopping just short of touching his. The space between them buzzed like static before a storm.

"I think you know exactly what I'm talking about," Tricia purred, voice dipping, velvet soft. She leaned back, giving him a full view, her posture open, her gaze even more so. "You're not great at pretending, Callan. You like the chase. But you've got to admit..." Her smile deepened. "I'm hard to resist."

Callan didn't flinch. "You don't know me as well as you think."

"Oh, I think I've got you pegged." She leaned forward, her breath brushing his ear. "You *like* the tension. That little edge... it gets you going, doesn't it?"

The words hung in the air like smoke. Callan held still.

"You're playing a dangerous game," he said at last, voice quiet but hard.

Her smile didn't fade. If anything, it sharpened. "What's the fun in not playing?"

She ran a fingertip along the rim of her glass, never breaking eye contact. "You've been running from me for a while now. I'm just curious… how long can you keep pretending you don't want this?"

The heat between them was no longer just about proximity. It was layered now—mental, psychological. A knife-edge connection. Tricia was pulling him in. And part of him was letting her.

"I'm not interested in playing games, Tricia," he said, voice steady. "What do you really want from me?"

She tilted her head slightly. "I think you know," she said softly. "I think you've always known."

The words were barely above a whisper, but they landed hard. She sat back, crossing her arms, watching him with eyes that saw too much. "I want you to stop running. Stop pretending. I want you to come to me, Callan. Just like you always do."

He didn't move. Just stared at her, eyes unreadable. Her words had struck something deep. But he wasn't ready to step off the ledge she was offering.

"Maybe I'm not running," he said quietly. "Maybe I've been standing still long enough to see you coming."

That made her smile—not the flirty kind. The kind that said she'd just won something he hadn't even realised he'd bet.

And then, just as the tension seemed to peak, she leaned in and whispered:

"I need you to kill my father."

Callan didn't move. Didn't breathe. His hand still rested near hers, the heat from her skin almost searing him. But her words dropped like ice into his bloodstream.

He pulled back, eyes locked on hers. Searching. Testing. Looking for the tell.

But she wasn't playing. Not this time.

"I need you to kill him," she repeated, slower now. Measured. Absolute.

The restaurant faded around them. He could still hear jazz, the soft clink of cutlery, but it all felt distant. Unimportant. All he could hear was her voice, playing on a loop.

His voice came low. "Why?"

Tricia didn't flinch. "Because I need to be free. I have to be rid of him. Of everything he's ever made me."

Something shifted in her face then. The predator pulled back. For the first time tonight—maybe for the first time ever—she looked fragile. Not weak. But stripped bare. A girl in too much lipstick and too little armour, sitting across from the only person who might see her clearly.

"I've never been more serious in my life," she said.

"Will you do it?"

Chapter 65

Tricia's voice begins...

"It's funny, isn't it? How we convince ourselves we're not monsters. How we whisper that we're justified. That we've earned our place in the world. That the things we do—the people we hurt—are just collateral damage in the name of survival.

"I used to think I hated my father. But that wasn't it. Not really. The truth? I deserved him. I was his pawn. Moulded. Sharpened. Broken and put back together, just to fit the shape of his vision. The daughter who needed to be perfect. Who needed to bend. Who needed to *break* and then smile like nothing ever hurt.

"Love? No. It was never love. It was control. A constant test I was born to fail.

"He ruined my mother. And then he ruined me. She stayed silent. Fragile. A ghost in her own skin. But me? I became something else. Strong. Dangerous.

"I *wanted* to love—I really did. But how can you, when love was a currency, when affection was a prize you earned only by being useful?

He taught me that I was only worth what I could give. What I could sell. Piece by piece.

"I spent my whole entire life trying to make him proud. I thought, maybe if I could just be good enough, he'd finally see me. Finally love me. Stupid, right?

"I remember the first time I caught him. My father, the great and mighty man. So corrupt, so slick, so vile. The mob, the feds—they all paid him. They all feared him. And me? I was a bystander. A toy. He twisted my mother. Twisted me. Turned every truth into a weapon.

"But it wasn't until he destroyed the one person I loved that I finally saw it. He framed him. My lover. The only one who looked at me like I was more than just a pawn. And my father took him away. With a smile.

"A few well-placed lies, and he was gone. Locked away. Forgotten.

"I still remember how that felt. The helplessness. The *rage*. That's when I knew—he would never let me go. I would always be his. His puppet.

"Unless I cut the strings.

"I killed him in my mind a thousand times.

"He was a chain. And I broke it. And when I finally stood over him, his blood cooling, his eyes still and empty... I felt it. Freedom. For the first time in my life, I wasn't afraid.

"I didn't just *want* him dead, Callan. I *needed* him dead. For me. For the girl I used to be. For the woman I am now.

"And I'm not the monster. He was. He always was."

CHAPTER 66

Tricia was curled against him like a cat, her warmth pressing into his side, the soft rise and fall of her breath matching his own. For a moment, everything felt still—too still, like the calm before something inevitable. His hand rested loosely around her waist and, as much as he wanted to ignore the chaos that awaited them, he couldn't.

He rolled over, propping himself up on his elbow, and looked down at her—half-sleeping, half-aware.

"I've got a better ending in mind for Philip Langston," he murmured, his voice low, weighted in the quiet morning air. "But you're going to have to flip to the FBI."

Tricia's eyes fluttered open at his words, but she didn't move. She just lay there, like she was figuring out if he was serious—or testing her. It didn't take long.

She shifted slightly, nestling closer into him, her body pressing into his like proximity alone could anchor her. "That is fucking priceless," she muttered. "Let the old man rot in prison instead of yachting and playing golf."

She didn't laugh. Didn't even smile. She just breathed him in like she was absorbing the moment. Then, in that soft, almost lazy tone she used when she was about to say something ridiculous—or dangerous—she added, "Dead or in a cell, either way, he loses. And I win!"

She pulled back just enough to look at him, her eyes gleaming with something unreadable. "He's had his turn. Now it's mine."

Callan stared down at her, trying to decipher the glee behind her words, but the pieces wouldn't fit.

"So, you want to take his place?" His voice was flat, but the idea tasted bitter.

Her expression softened, patient, like he should already understand the rules of the game.

"I just want this behind me so I can move forward."

The way she said it—so casually—like this wasn't about murder or incarceration, but just... closure. And in that moment, something clicked. The way she talked about control, about power—it had always been her endgame. She didn't want to play second to anyone. Not to Langston. Not even to him.

And now, she was ready to make her move.

"I'll do it."

The words left her lips with unsettling ease. Her breath was warm against his ear, her mouth staying there as her hands moved slowly, deliberately, over his body.

Callan didn't respond. His thoughts were spinning, trying to make sense of the offer, of her. But as she shifted against him, her lips brushing his skin, clarity slipped through his fingers.

Her hands traced across his chest, slow and certain, like she was mapping him—owning the moment. He didn't move. Couldn't.

Her lips found his neck, soft and teasing, and the heat between them rose. Still, his mind stayed tangled in doubt and desire. She wasn't waiting for him to catch up. She was already moving forward. Already in control.

He didn't know what to say. Didn't know how to react. All he could do was close his eyes and try to shut out the overwhelming truth: He had already said yes. And there was no going back now.

CHAPTER 67

The hum of city life murmured in the background. Callan stared at the thumb drive on the table, his mind looping through Tricia's unexpected shift.

Not long ago, she'd been hunting him down with vicious determination. Now, she was the one offering him the key to an empire built on lies.

The arrest of Philip Langston—was it too good to be true? Nothing about this felt clean.

His phone buzzed. Unknown number. He answered. "Callan."

Mel's voice came through, low and cautious. "I've sent you the intel David Crawford compiled. Tricia Langley has a lot to say."

Callan leaned back in his chair, the tension settling behind his ribs like a storm on the horizon. The game was about to change.

CHAPTER 68

The small café was the kind of place where deals got made in whispered tones and urgent glances. Tricia sat across from Mel, posture rigid, the weight of her truth already sinking in. Callan slid into the seat beside Mel, his gaze flicking to Tricia. She hadn't changed much—same sharp eyes, same guarded expression. But now, something in her was fractured, barely held together.

She sat like a prisoner without cuffs—rigid, ready, waiting to detonate her own life.

"We've got an hour," Mel said, eyeing Callan. "Start talking, Tricia."

Tricia exhaled, eyes darting between them. It looked like she was about to speak, then stalled—chewing on the silence.

Finally, her voice came, tight but steady. "I've been working for Philip Langston for years. You have the files Callan sent over, so you know I'm not just a cop on the take—I was deep. He didn't just pull strings. He *was* the puppet master. Every move, every decision in this city... his fingerprints are all over it."

Callan didn't flinch. He'd known Langston was dangerous. But this—this was rotten down to the bone.

"He had David killed. And Dwayne. The workups David compiled are in there. Surveillance, evidence—you can see it for yourself," she said, knuckles white around a cup of untouched coffee.

Callan felt the shift. Langston wasn't just a kingpin. He was a black hole—and everything circled him.

Her voice softened, guilt bleeding through. "I helped cover it up," Tricia said. "I had the evidence, but I didn't know how far he'd go."

Mel leaned in, voice low and sharp. "And now?"

"I'm done." Tricia's voice hardened. "I'm giving it all up. You want Langston? You've got him. Everything. Files. Recordings. Proof of more bodies than I can count."

She slammed her palm on the table, silverware rattling. "I know you don't trust me, Mel. Hell, I wouldn't either. But it's enough to bury him."

Callan studied Mel as Tricia unloaded years of corruption. She wasn't just flipping—she was detonating her own life.

"He's got people everywhere," she continued. "Politicians, judges, cops—you name it. He's been laundering money, setting people up, cutting deals that ruin lives."

Mel sat back, tapping a finger against the tabletop. "You want immunity?"

Tricia's glare was tired but unflinching. "I want protection. I'm not walking out of this just to catch a bullet. I'm giving you Langston's empire. But I want out—clean."

Silence closed in tight.

Callan could see it—the blur between victim and accomplice. Tricia was both. A product of Langston's poison.

Mel finally spoke. "You're on a short leash. Slip once, and there's no deal."

"I don't slip," she shot back. "Not anymore."

As the tension lifted, Callan pushed back from the table.

***

The restroom stank of bleach and humidity, sharp against the heat pressing in from outside. Callan splashed water on his face, stared at the cracked mirror. The city clung to him like a warning.

He hated leaving them out there. But he needed a breath. One second to think. Tricia had just handed him dynamite and asked him to light the fuse.

Callan wiped his hands dry.

Then the shots split the air.

Bang-Bang! Bang!

He recognized that shot cadence. Two in the chest. One in the head. Professional work.

Callan surged back through the door as chaos erupted. Tables overturned. People screamed. Bodies pushed past him—panic crashing through the café like a wave.

Through the fogged window, he saw the black Suburban.

Mel lay crumpled on the sidewalk. Blood pooling beneath him.

Tricia fought—Callan could see it in her frame—but a brutal punch to the liver dropped her. One of the shooters cuffed her wrist to his belt and dragged her toward the Suburban.

Callan slammed out the door just as the Suburban fishtailed onto the street. The heat shimmered off the cracked pavement, the SUV barrelling away.

For a second, her eyes found his through the rear window.

Terror. Wide-eyed and raw. Like a child.

Not the Tricia he knew.

It froze Callan more than the gunfire ever could.

"Motherfuckers," he hissed.

Then it was gone—swallowed by the Miami heat and chaos.

Callan stood there, breath shallow, sweat stinging his eyes as the copper tang of death settled over the street.

It was the same SUV that had tailed him from Dwayne's. It hadn't been Tricia following him that night.

It took him less than five minutes to scan the scene. Mel was dead—shot in broad daylight. And every set of eyes inside that café had seen Callan sitting with him just moments before.

He needed to move. Fast.

CHAPTER 69

The city felt heavier than usual as Callan steered through the Miami afternoon, heading back to the condo. Humidity pressed against the windshield like a second layer of glass. His shirt clung to his back, damp and uncomfortable, but he left the AC off. Let it simmer.

He ran it over again in his mind, slow and deliberate.

Tricia—hauled off by Langston's people. Or if it wasn't Langston, it was someone worse. Odds were, Langston had found out she had flipped and decided she'd outlived her usefulness. His own daughter. A clean subtraction. Callan could see the logic in it. Hell, he was open to the idea that loose ends tie themselves if you're just patient enough.

And truth be told, Tricia was exactly where she belonged. In the meat grinder. She wasn't a good person. And her death would solve Callan's problem.

What was that, exactly?

That someone out there in the universe had seen through his aloofness and wanted him anyway. Tricia was bad. But she made Callan feel something. Wanted? Loved? Was any of this actually a *problem*?

He drummed his fingers on the steering wheel at a red light. Somewhere in the back of his skull, a small voice whispered: Tricia flipping on Langston could've solved half the puzzle. And maybe her disappearance still would. No Tricia, no blackmail. No messy courtrooms. No more games.

The light turned green. Callan didn't move. Couldn't move, his mind stuck in a feedback loop.

He let the engine idle while the city flowed around him—angry Floridians honking and shouting as they swerved past. Probably all armed. Probably all pissed off. Miami.

The practical part of him whispered: Let it happen. Let Langston squeeze her for what she knows and dump her in a ditch. No muss. No cleanup.

But then the counterpunch landed. He'd told her to go to the Feds. His words. His advice. *Walk away from Langston. Cooperate.* She'd taken the deal. And now she was probably in a trunk, bleeding out somewhere.

Callan shifted in his seat, jaw tight.

"The fuck am I gonna do? What *should* I do? Are those different things?" He was talking to himself like someone might answer. The light had turned red again.

It wasn't about morals. Wasn't about loyalty. Tricia said it herself, more than once—it was always about control. And right now, he still had some.

At the next green, he hit the gas, weaving into traffic. The glow of Miami pulsed against the slick streets like an open wound.

Whether Tricia survived... that decision might no longer be his to make. But maybe—just maybe—he could control the room one more time.

***

The condo was dark when Callan slipped inside. The soft whir of the ceiling fan, the low hum of the fridge, and Beckett's lazy stare from his perch by the window were the only greetings.

The Miami skyline beyond the glass cut the dusk like a jagged scar.

Callan dropped his keys on the counter and rubbed the back of his neck.

The cat blinked. Tail twitching like a metronome. Then, a low, unimpressed *meow*.

Callan crossed the kitchen and collapsed into the chair. His arms felt heavy, weighted with the past few hours. Mel's corpse. Tricia's disappearance. The illusion of control slipping through his fingers.

Beckett padded across the counter like he owned it, parked himself next to Callan's phone.

"What's your take, Beck?" Callan asked, voice flat. "Let Langston clean up his own mess? Or throw myself into a dumpster fire?"

The cat stared at him like he was the dumbest creature in the room. Then he meowed again—sharper this time—and jabbed a paw at the phone.

"Wish I could speak your language, my guy," Callan muttered. Then louder, "Get off the counter, you ape."

But Beckett, true to form, didn't move. Just stared like a professional nuisance.

Callan reached for the cat and froze when the phone lit up beneath Beckett's paw.

It was ringing.

Isabelle.

"Goddammit."

He considered letting it go to voicemail. Be he answered anyway.

"Well, hello stranger. How's it going?" Her voice was alive and lovely, all musical lilt and familiarity—knocking him slightly off-centre.

Callan stared at Beckett, who stared back, utterly unbothered.

"Yeah, actually," Callan said finally, "I've been better."

He leaned back in the chair, eyes to the ceiling as Belle's voice hummed quietly in his ear.

"You sure you're okay?" she asked again.

Callan hesitated. "Define 'okay.'"

"You've never sounded so... I dunno, *broken*. What's up, buttercup?"

He didn't answer right away. Just stared at Beckett, who was now grooming himself like none of this was his problem.

Finally, Callan exhaled through his nose. "Can I ask you something hypothetical?"

She chuckled, but it sounded a little tight. "I would love it." A beat passed. Quiet, but not uncomfortable.

"Shoot," she said.

Callan swirled the glass of water in front of him, thinking.

"Let's say you knew someone, call them Person A, who's done some pretty dark things. Now Person A is in serious trouble. Trouble they earned. The easy move is to let the universe handle it."

"But?"

"But there's a version where stepping in helps," Callan admitted, voice low. "Even if it's risky. Even if they possibly don't deserve it."

Isabelle didn't respond right away. When she did, her voice was soft but clear.

"I always try to leave the world better than I found it."

Callan rubbed his jaw, listening.

"And if that means helping someone who's hurt me—or someone who probably deserves what's coming—that's just the cost of being me."

He let her words hang there. Simple. Sharp. Cutting in a way she hadn't intended.

"You don't make it easy, you know," he said quietly.

Her smile was audible. "Neither do you."

They'd always been like— two orbits that never quite aligned. Planets circling the same sun, never colliding, never drifting away.

"Thanks for this, sis. I mean it. But I have to run."

"Goodbye, Callan."

The call endcd, and Callan sat there, staring into nothing. Wondering if he'd ever hear her voice again.

CHAPTER 70

Callan ended the call, Isabelle's words lingering like the aftertaste of strong whiskey.

He glanced at Beckett, now loafed on the counter, eyes half-closed and wholly indifferent to the storm he'd just helped stir.

"Leave the world better than you found it," Callan muttered, shaking his head. "Easier said than done."

He powered up his work laptop, the screen casting a cold light across the dim room. The Archive awaited—a digital underworld of data brokers, black-hat hackers, and freelance information peddlers. No warrants. No waiting. Just a matter of credits... and conscience.

Callan navigated encrypted channels, punched in Tricia's cell number. Seconds later, a blinking dot materialized on the map. It pulsed faintly, west of the city limits.

Belle Glade.

He leaned back, staring at the map like it might confess something. Langston's people hadn't just stashed her. They'd buried her out where the roads turn to dust and the air tastes like metal and rot.

"Of course," Callan muttered. "Drag her out to the sticks."

Belle Glade—where the swamp swallowed mistakes and secrets got eaten by gators or meth-heads. Rural enough to stay quiet, lawless enough to stay buried. The kind of place where the cops showed up late, if they showed up at all.

Beckett meowed like he knew, still watching Callan through half-closed eyes.

Callan shut the laptop. Muscles coiled tight. This wasn't just Langston tying off loose ends.

It was a message.

His advice had walked Tricia into a death trap. Now he had to decide how much he gave a damn.

He stood, sliding the burner into his pocket. "All right," he told the cat. "Let's see if we can clean up someone else's mess."

He crossed the room toward the hall closet.

"I need to pack for a trip to the country, old man," he added, mostly for Beckett's benefit. The cat stretched, yawned, and went back to ignoring him.

Callan knelt at the safe, spun the dial, popped the door with a soft click. Inside, the old friends waited.

He picked up the Glock 19, checked the chamber. Set it aside.

The plate carrier came next—heavy, worn, the scent of sweat and Cordura clinging to it like a memory. Three spare mags rode on the front. He grabbed the short-barrelled M4, checked the holo sight, flipped it on. Still held a charge.

The Microtech switchblade slid into his pocket with practiced ease.

The rest—extra ammo, gloves, a cleaning kit—went into the black duffle. He zipped it shut and slung it over one shoulder.

The weight felt right.

"God forbid I run into that snowbird from a couple of days ago," he muttered, picturing the nosy retiree with the poodle and mirrored sunglasses. "Nothing says 'friendly neighbour' like plate armour and enough firepower to invade Panama."

He locked the safe, took one last look around the apartment, and headed for the door.

Diego always said control was about choosing your battlefield. But the Glades?

They weren't a battlefield.

They were a graveyard.

CHAPTER 71

Callan burned west on cracked, two-lane roads, past sugarcane fields and swampy nothing. The 90-minute run out to the Glades felt like a slow bleed. Belle Glade's outskirts blurred past—just a forgotten bruise on the map.

It took another agonizing hour to track down the site, tucked behind a line of cypress and razor grass. An old warehouse—corrugated siding flaking under floodlights that bled yellow into the murk. The kind of place built to store fertilizer and busted farm equipment.

Now it stored something else. Bloodier business.

He ditched the car a mile out, abandoned it behind a dead construction site. Switched to boots-on-dirt. By then, night had settled in thick and oppressive, draped over everything like wet canvas.

Two guys outside. Rusted-out pickup nearby. One lit a cigarette, the other slapped at mosquitoes. More shadows slipped behind the warehouse's slatted walls.

No patrols. No perimeter. Just locals playing enforcer in borrowed gear—shotguns and cheap carbines slung lazy over guts and boredom. Situational awareness: zero.

Callan ghosted through the tree line, breathing in the swamp's sweet rot.

One straggler—mid-thirties, patchy beard, high or just stupid—wandered too far off, pissing into the weeds.

Callan was on him before he zipped up.

A hand over the mouth. The blade pressed tight beneath the jawline, angling upward. The guy convulsed—grunted once—then sagged back into the dark.

"You're gonna tell me where she is," Callan whispered, voice surgical. "Or I'm gonna take you apart."

The man shook in his boots, stinking of sweat and chewing tobacco. "She's... she's in the warehouse," he stammered. "Back room. Langston's guys... inside."

"How many?"

"Four," he blurted. "Four more inside."

Confirmation.

Callan yanked the man's head back, exposed the throat, and opened it with one clean stroke.

The body slumped into the muck, gurgling softly into the earth.

This wasn't justice. And it sure as hell wasn't for *her*.

This was preservation.

Not of *her* life—but of his.

Because if he let this slide—if he let someone get butchered on *his* advice, without lifting a finger—then he wasn't a weapon anymore.

He was wreckage.

And he had to believe there was still a difference. Even if the line got redrawn every time he crossed it.

Callan wiped the blade clean on the dead man's shirt, holstered it, and crept toward the warehouse. No recon. No plan. Just movement.

The corrugated walls loomed—rusted and riddled with bullet holes and history.

Inside: Voices. Muffled. The thrum of bad country music leaking from a busted speaker.

Callan slipped through a side entrance—half-hinged, half-collapsed—rifle low, breath even. No plan. No mental checklist. Just that primal voice screaming, *assess—then act.*

He ignored it.

The kill box was waiting.

CHAPTER 72

Inside, the Quonset smelled like the rest of the Glades—mildew, gasoline, and rot. Callan moved low past stacks of crates and mouldy tarps, boots whispering across cracked concrete.

The main space was wide open. No partitions. No cover.

Four men clustered near the back, half-silhouetted by a flickering bulb that exactly exposed what they were up to.

Tricia was cuffed to a steel support beam. Clothes torn, wrists shredded. They were circling her—laughing, fumbling with belts, one holding a knife. It wasn't just intimidation.

They were torturing her. Stripping her down like some animal caged for sport.

Callan froze.

A half-second. That's all.

But in that breath, his stomach turned. Langston. This was *his* sanction.

Callan brought the M4 to his shoulder.

He didn't shout. Didn't warn. He just *fired*.

The first burst tore through a spine. The man collapsed like a puppet cut loose. The next pivoted mid-laugh—caught two rounds, chest and throat. Gone before he hit the ground.

The third fumbled, pants halfway down. Callan hit him centre mass. The man folded forward, bleeding out, with his hands still at his waist.

The fourth—barely turned before the round hit him clean through the face. His skull cracked like dropped porcelain.

Brass clattered on concrete. Smoke and heat filled the space. His ears rang from the noise bouncing off corrugated steel. He liked the ringing. It reminded him he was alive.

Callan turned—eyes on the main door—just as two more stumbled in. Stacked too close. Moving too slow.

He didn't even aim. Just dumped rounds through the entryway like it was Fallujah all over again.

When the dust settled, six bodies bled into the concrete. Piss and blood pooled beneath them. One moved. The gut-shot bastard. Moaning, crying. Calling for help. Calling for his mother.

Callan didn't flinch. Didn't speak.

He wasn't here for mercy.

Somewhere, a basement keyboard warrior would call it cowardice. Callan smirked at that. *"Never give a sucker an even break,"* his stepdad always said.

He moved to Tricia. Propped the rifle against the beam. She was shaking. Lip split. Eye swollen shut. Blood down her chin. But still upright. Still trying to fight the cuffs with what was left of her.

He pulled the key from the dead man's pocket. The cuffs came off easier than expected. She didn't thank him. Just rubbed her wrists and stared.

He thought he'd been fast. He hadn't. Langston's men had worked her.

Welts. Bruises. The kind of damage you don't come back from clean.

Callan had seen women like this before—but only in case files. Photos. Evidence. Cold and clinical.

This was *different*. This wasn't a briefing.

This was personal.

"It's me," Callan said, voice stripped down to gravel. "It's Callan. You're safe."

She didn't collapse. Didn't cry.

She leaned back against the beam, holding her ribs. Blood smeared across her fingers. She didn't even look at her hands.

Just breathing—deep and ragged—through a nose that was clearly broken.

Her one good eye locked on his. Then moved past him, scanning. Processing.

"Langston?" she rasped.

"Not here."

She nodded. Just once. Bone-deep. No drama. No sound.

Then, quieter,

"I want his fucking head."

Callan didn't argue.

She pushed off the beam. Wobbled. Stayed upright.

He moved to steady her. She shrugged him off. Not angry Just—*don't.*

"I'm not done yet," she said.

Her voice, cracked as it was, still had the edge. Still her.

Then she looked past him—toward the far corner.

The gut-shot bastard. Still alive. Still twitching in his own mess.

She stepped forward. Barefoot. Slow.

"Give me your sidearm," she said.

Callan hesitated. Not because he doubted her.

Because he didn't.

"Tricia—"

She looked up at him. Swollen face. Raw wrists. That *look*.

"Give me the fucking gun."

He handed it over. No words.

She took it, walked barefoot across the blood-slick floor. Stopped three feet from the man.

He whimpered. Begged. Swore he hadn't touched her. Swore he was just following orders.

Tricia said nothing. She raised the gun. Aimed low.

Pulled the trigger.

The shot echoed like judgement. The man screamed. Then he didn't.

Tricia stood there a moment. Breathing heavy. Then walked back, held the pistol grip-first.

Like a soldier.

Callan took it.

And she said, *"Now—let's go kill my father."*

Callan knew combat ineffective when he saw it. "We need to patch you up first. I have a kit in the car."

CHAPTER 73

The silence in the car wasn't just quiet—it was surgical. Like someone had bleached the inside of Callan's skull and left the smell behind. He drove with both hands on the wheel, eyes stitched to the road like a lifeline.

Tricia sat beside him, arms crossed, one leg jittering like a lie detector trying to stay neutral. Her face was unreadable—but he didn't need to look at her to feel it. The gap between them widened with every mile. Whatever they'd just survived had burned something down, and neither of them was pretending otherwise.

He should say something. She should say something. Neither did.

They'd left the warehouse like ghosts—slipping out through the swamp trail he'd memorized on the way in. Six bodies behind them. Gunned down like extras in a low-budget war movie.

His ears were still ringing. He'd forgotten his muffs. Unusual for him. There's no pension for hearing loss in his line of work.

He replayed the scene.

The carbine in his hands. The familiar heft. The squeeze of the trigger. Target to target. Controlled. Smooth. Like poetry.

He shook it off. Refocused.

They were heading back to Miami on a humid stretch of highway—miles and miles of nothing. Trees looming. Mosquitos plastered to the windshield like ghosts trying to hitch a ride.

He inhaled—slow, measured—like that might keep the guilt from getting traction.

They were alive. That was supposed to be enough.

He told himself that three times before Tricia exhaled next to him—long and low, like a door closing for good.

He didn't look at her. Couldn't. Her face was a wreck—her father's men had made sure of that. And still, she'd talked him into leaving the scene untouched.

That wasn't his style. Clean exits were his religion. No prints. No trace. That's how he'd survived two decades. She wanted Langston dead—too badly. She wasn't thinking clearly. Hell, she never did. Where he was all patience and precision, she was gasoline and spark. And the worst part? He let her. Let her talk him into walking away. Left the mess behind.

The warehouse had her DNA all over it. Blood. Clothes. Skin. Every inch a breadcrumb trail. Callan was clean—except for what she knew. Except for what he'd done for her.

And he still drove away. That wasn't strategy. That was weakness. That was *feeling*.

"That's the cost of being me." Isabelle's words, echoing. He clenched the wheel. Told himself again—*she's safe*. That was the goal.

Then came the look. Reflected in the side mirror—her eyes, levelled and flat. Not angry. Not betrayed.

Just disappointed. And that was worse.

He drove another mile. Then another. Then slammed the brakes hard enough to punch rubber into the air.

Tricia lurched forward, catching herself on the dash. "Jesus, Callan!" But he was already shifting into reverse.

"What are you doing?" she snapped, voice cracking like glass.

He didn't answer. The hollow in his chest had started to scream. And every mile he stayed away from that warehouse felt like cowardice with a gas pedal.

He spun the wheel. Gravel popped. Tires bit down like they were angry too.

He didn't look at her. Didn't have to. Whatever came next would break something between them.

But that was a price he could pay.

A small price for silence in his head.

Diego's voice looped through the noise: "There are a million ways to get hung. Don't give them more rope."

"You're serious," she said, her voice serrated now. "You're actually going back?"

He didn't respond.

"You just can't follow a simple plan, can you?" she hissed. "You need everything to be a moral crusade because God forbid you sit still long enough to *feel* something."

Still, he drove.

She laughed—short and sharp. "You think going back fixes it? You think Mel gets to come back because you showed up late with a gun and a guilty conscience? You're not better than those men, Callan. You're just *tidier*."

That one landed. But she wasn't wrong. And he wasn't ashamed of it.

"You should've just kept driving. Straight into the ocean. Do us all a favour."

He didn't hear her.

She leaned in. Closer now. Voice like poison in a wineglass.

"You know what the worst part is? I *still* wanted to believe in you. I listened to you about the Bureau. You got me raped, Callan. You almost got me killed. Where were you when they were fucking me?"

He gripped the wheel tighter. Said nothing. Swallowed everything.

"With your cat," she spat. "While I was bleeding, you were spoon-feeding that fucking animal."

That did it.

He slammed the brakes again—hard. The car jerked to a dead stop. Tires screamed. Gravel sprayed.

She slammed back into the seat, one hand on the dash, the other curled into a fist.

"What the fuck is wrong with you?" she shouted.

Callan didn't answer. Just stared out the windshield like it owed him something.

Then—quiet now. Controlled rage.

"Say it," she goaded. "Blame me. Hit me. Go ahead."

Still nothing.

"You think this was ever in your control?" she pressed. "You act cleaner. Like you're safer. You're not. You're just a coward with rules instead of courage."

Still nothing.

She sat back. Eyes cold. Voice soft. "You know, Callan? You owe me... for not killing that little slut up in Canada."

Claire.

The last time he saw her, he'd clocked a tail. Tricia's doing. Of course it was. Something cracked inside him.

He turned on her.

Fast. Brutal.

One hand on her collar. He slammed her back into the seat, knuckles white against her throat.

She didn't fight. Just stared at him. Smiling.

The kind of smile that knew it had won.

He'd seen it before—Lois Grafton, the night he took her life. Same smile. Same rot behind the eyes.

His grip tightened. Her breath caught.

"I should've left you there," he growled. "Let them finish. You're radioactive, Langley. There's no redemption for people like us. But at least I have a *code*."

His hands locked harder around her throat.

And then— her fingers came up—not to fight. To touch his cheek. Like a lover would.

That took the air out of the car.

"You don't win by being the bigger monster," Diego's voice said, clean and cold in his mind. "You win by being the last one standing."

It hit like a slap. He yanked back, like she was fire.

Tricia gasped, coughed—but didn't cry. Didn't move. Just sat there. Throat bruising. Eyes feral. No tears. No victory.

Callan leaned back in his seat. Chest heaving. Hands shaking on the wheel.

Then, from beside him—low and certain: "You're just like me."

He looked at her. She sported a gruesome grin, her busted face a visceral reminder of his recent failures.

And that, somehow, was the worst cut of all. Because for one breathless second, he didn't see her.

He saw himself.

Chapter 74

This was the part Callan hated. The aftermath. The mess. He'd built his career on clean jobs—quiet exits, no trace. But this? This was different. This time, there was no choice.

They had to clean up.

Tricia didn't fight it in the end. All it took was one look inside the duffle bag their attackers had brought—restraints, blades, a bone saw—and she got it. If Callan hadn't shown up when he did, she'd be mulch in the swamp.

She knew it. He saw it in her face—not gratitude, but recognition. The kind of understanding that only comes after death brushes your jaw and decides to keep walking.

Eight hours later, the last piece of the assholes was in the Everglades. Dinner time.

They washed off in swamp water, dried with whatever wasn't soaked in blood. Every textile went into the fire with ritualistic urgency—shirts, socks, Tricia's shoelaces. Even the strip of towel he'd used to wipe the carbine clean.

Callan watched the smoke curl into dusk. The air was still. No birds. No insects. Just gator wakes moving slow through black water, patient and heavy.

Tricia sat barefoot on a rotted log, arms locked around her knees. She hadn't spoken since the second body hit the water. Just worked. Efficient. Mechanical.

He wondered what was going through her head. Not grief. Not fear. Something quieter. The slow dissolve of illusion.

When the fire finally collapsed into wet ash, he stood. She looked up. Not soft. Not angry. Just... a nod.

A battlefield truce.

Callan looked toward the tree line.

"They were the easy part," he said.

All she offered for a response was silence. The kind that knew exactly what was coming next.

"Good enough," he muttered. "Time to roll."

The car sat where he'd stashed it—tucked behind the warehouse, nose half-buried in palmetto brush and guilt.

The walk back was slow and sticky. The swamp clung to their ankles like regret.

Tricia still hadn't said a word. She moved like a ghost playing along. Following, but not *with* him.

At the trunk, Callan popped it open and reached for the backup kit—burner phone, clean shirt, bottled water, keys. Everything folded once and packed like a Plan B you never wanted to use.

He was about to speak—maybe say they'd split, maybe offer her an out—when it hit.

Sharp. Left side. Just under the ribs.

He staggered back, hand clamped to his side.

Warm. Wet. Spreading.

He blinked.

Tricia stood two steps away.

Knife in hand. Small. Serrated. Not his.

It was red now. Not gator red. *His* red.

"What the fuck—" he rasped, stumbling into the bumper.

Blood soaked through his shirt, fast but shallow. Superficial. She missed the vitals. She fucked it up.

She came again—blade high, ice pick grip. But she was sloppy. Always had been.

He caught her wrist mid-swing. Twisted hard. The knife hit the gravel. She hissed but didn't scream.

"You're out of your goddamn mind," he growled, shoving her back.

She slammed into the car but stayed on her feet. Glared at him like *he* was the traitor.

"I won't let you ruin this for me," she spat. "I can't stand the idea of them winning."

Callan narrowed his eyes. "Them?"

She took a breath, like a smoker trying to hold something in. "I'm this close to taking the crown from my old man."

And there it was.

She didn't want justice.

She wanted the throne.

He wasn't helping her escape.

He was helping her usurp.

Something turned cold in his gut. The wound pulsed.

"You're not okay," he said. "You need help."

"I needed help *then*," she snapped. "Not now."

He didn't argue. Didn't try to fix it. Instead, he punched her. Clean shot to the gut. No hesitation.

She dropped to her knees with a groan. He stepped over her, grabbed his Glock from the trunk, and spun.

She was already moving—staggering around the building, fast for someone who'd just eaten a punch.

He fired twice. Missed both. Pain dulled his aim.

Or maybe the part of him that could kill her was offline.

He limped forward, cleared the corner—Empty.

The warehouse door creaked. She was inside. Gone.

Callan cursed, low and vicious. His shirt was soaked now, blood thick around the hem. Manageable. But not for long.

He slammed the trunk shut, slid behind the wheel, turned the key. The engine roared to life. Gravel kicked like teeth as he peeled out.

He drove.

Bleeding.

But alive.

And this time, he left her behind.

Chapter 75

The ER was understaffed, underlit, and already two hours behind. Callan didn't mind. He wasn't in a rush anymore.

The bleeding had slowed. He kept pressure on the wound with an old
T-shirt he found in the trunk—he didn't recognize it. Maybe someone
dead. Didn't matter.

When they finally called his fake name, he stood and walked like he
hadn't just been stabbed by someone he used to trust.

The triage nurse didn't look twice. Nor did the doctor, middle-aged,
overworked, more concerned with paperwork than pain.

Callan told them he got into a bar fight in Fort Lauderdale. "Wrong
guy. Bad night." They asked for ID. He handed them one—laminated,
scuffed, real enough to pass.

Name:

Anthony Crane

Blood type: AB

Birthday: Someone else's.

Nine stitches. Local anesthetic. No cops.

The nurse offered a Vicodin. He shook his head.

By the time he stepped out under the humming fluorescent overhang, it was close to 3:00 AM. Miami humidity clung to his skin like old sins.

***

Home wasn't really home. Just a condo under a trust name, triple-locked, with no pictures on the walls.

Beckett met him at the door, tail twitching, eyes narrow. Judgemental little bastard.

"Still alive," Callan muttered, crouching to scratch behind the cat's ears. "Barely."

He moved on instinct—efficient, practiced. Stripped off the bloody shirt, shoved it into a garbage bag. Packed it with the emergency duffel: Cash, clean IDs, passports, burners, spare plates, cat food, one day of litter.

The second duffel was clothing, toiletries, meds. Toothbrush still in its wrapper.

One last walk-through. Lights off. Drawers closed.

The condo fees were on autopay. No mortgage. The housecleaner would keep showing up. The place would look lived-in. His cars downstairs—low mileage, zero curiosity. His money was legit, taxes paid. The paper trail was clean. He was a wealthy man with nowhere to be.

Beckett meowed, short and sharp.

"Yeah, yeah. You're coming."

He dropped the carrier on the couch and zipped it halfway. Beckett climbed in on his own.

The apartment already felt hollow.

***

Callan pulled out one of the burners and scrolled to Ellen's number.

Stared at it a long moment.

Then hit CALL.

She picked up on the second ring.

"Callan?" She sounded half-asleep. Not scared. Just surprised.

"I'm heading to you tonight," he said. "I'll text when I'm close." He hung up before she could ask questions.

***

Beckett curled in the carrier, unbothered.

Callan zipped it up, slung both duffels over one shoulder, cat in the other hand.

One last trip for the Mazda.

He drove to a nondescript auto body shop in Little Haiti. Didn't say a word. Just handed over the keys and a thick envelope of cash.

They gave him a Hyundai SUV. Silver. Unremarkable. Wouldn't outrun anyone. But it wouldn't get noticed either. That was the point.

Callan climbed in, adjusted the seat, checked the mirrors. Then he pulled out—slow, smooth—and disappeared into the Miami dark.

CHAPTER 76

The miles blurred like a bad dream left out in the rain. Callan kept one hand on the wheel, the other near the fresh stitches. Every bump reminded him of Tricia's blade. Not deep enough to kill—but deep enough to remember.

Beckett stirred in the carrier beside him. The cat wasn't much for small talk, but Callan had gotten used to the rhythm of their drives: Silence, eye contact, judgement.

"You ever get the feeling we're just collecting more ghosts?" he asked.

Beckett blinked. Slowly. That cat could make a death row inmate feel like the guilty party.

Callan shifted, wincing at the tug of skin against thread. "Yeah. That's what I thought."

The Hyundai purred beneath him. Clean ride. Paper plates. No digital trail. He'd picked it because it blended in—and because it had room in the back for everything he might need to vanish. Again.

Jacksonville was still hours off, but the roads were open. Dark. Quiet. Just the low hum of tires and Beckett adjusting like a king who deserved better.

"You'll like this one," Callan said. "It's clean. Quiet. Doesn't smell like mould or failure."

Beckett yawned, unimpressed.

The Jacksonville safehouse was a relic from a different life. Not his name on the lease. No paper. No cameras. He'd set it up back when he believed in long games and quiet exits.

Before Ellen.

Before Miami.

Before the rot came home.

He hadn't let himself think too hard about her. Ellen. She didn't know everything. But she knew enough.

Enough to ask the right questions.

Enough to not ask at all.

"Just keep it together a little longer," he muttered. Mostly to himself. Beckett flicked his tail once against the carrier's mesh wall.

***

The condo sat at the edge of a cul-de-sac where the streetlights buzzed louder than they glowed. Three stories. White siding. Weathered roof. It looked like nothing. That was the point.

Callan parked two blocks away and approached on foot—duffels in one hand, Beckett in the other. No cameras. No neighbours watching. Just crickets and the low hiss of Florida heat bleeding into the dark.

The door opened before he knocked.

Ellen stood in the frame, backlit by amber kitchen light. Tank top. Shorts. Hair up. Barefoot, just like he pictured.

She looked at him. Then at Beckett. Then at the bloodstain.

"I said you could come," she said. "Didn't say you had to show up stabbed." Silence. "Not that it surprises me."

Callan gave her a tired smile. "Didn't want to come empty-handed."

She stepped aside without a word.

Inside, the place smelled like lemon cleaner—the same one she swore by when she still lived with David. Last time Callan smelled it was the night he found David's body.

The furniture was basic but not cheap. No photos. No clutter. Just function.

Beckett jumped out of the carrier as soon as it hit the floor.

Stretched like he'd stepped off a transatlantic flight and expected applause.

Ellen handed Callan a glass of water and nodded toward the couch. "Sit. I'll get the med kit."

He didn't argue.

While she moved through drawers, he scanned the space. Still secure. Still clean. Everything where he left it a week ago—except now there were groceries on the counter and a paperback on the table.

She'd been living in it.

"You been all right?" he asked as she knelt beside him, gauze and tape in hand.

She gave him a look. "That depends. You counting the part where your girlfriend's father had my husband killed?"

He exhaled. "Yeah. Counting that."

The silence held. She cleaned up a leaky bandage with smooth, practiced movements. Didn't ask who stabbed him. Didn't ask why.

"I burned some bridges," he said.

"You ever not?" A flicker of a smile. Gone quick. "Tricia?"

"She's in the wind. I just need a day," he said. "To regroup. Figure out what's next."

She stood, tossed the gauze into the trash. "Take two."

"You're still a smartass."

She jabbed a finger into his stitches.

"Ow."

"You deserved that."

She headed toward the hallway, pausing in the doorway. "You can stay as long as you need. But if anyone comes looking..."

"I know."

She hesitated. "You running?"

Callan met her eyes.

"Yeah. Too much heat in Florida."

"Take me with you?"

He didn't answer right away. Just watched her. "You clear of David's murder?"

"Yes. The guy who pulled the trigger was shot in Texas. They found David's Rolex on him. The gun, too. Case closed."

Callan nodded. "Then pack a bag. It's a long drive."

She disappeared into the bedroom without another word.

Callan leaned back on the couch. Let the quiet settle.

Beckett jumped up beside him. Tail flicked once against his arm. Then the cat purred.

Chapter 77

The condo had finally gone still. Callan was asleep on the couch—shirtless, stitched, breathing like someone who didn't trust rest to be harmless. Even unconscious, he looked ready to flinch.

Ellen stood at the edge of the kitchen, one hand on the counter, the other wrapped around a lukewarm glass of water she'd refilled twice and never drank. She let herself watch him. Just for a moment.

He was older than she remembered. Pushing fifty now. Five years, maybe six, ahead of her. Still broad-shouldered. Still that same half-feral calm he'd had the first time she saw him.

She hadn't liked him then.

David brought him around once for Sunday dinner. Callan had shown up late in a Porsche, with some wide-eyed thirty-year-old clinging to his arm. The girl had a laugh like a windchime and no idea what room she was standing in.

Ellen had hated them both, instinctively. Callan—for the quiet arrogance of men who collect younger women like they're proof of relevance. And the girl—for being the version of Ellen she was supposed to miss.

But she didn't miss her. Not really. And Callan? He'd grown on her.

Not because he tried. Because he didn't. He had that rare thing—stillness. Not the performative kind. The kind that comes from having already imagined the worst and accepted it.

She and Callan had become fast friends. Real ones. David never seemed to mind. Which, in hindsight, should've been a red flag.

She'd found Callan attractive, sure. Who wouldn't? He had that battered, old-world thing some men carried without trying. A face built for secrets. A body that looked like it had chopped some wood.

But it wasn't lust. Not exactly. It was that quiet ache you get when someone shows up already broken in ways you understand.

Beckett was curled behind Callan's knees, tail twitching every time he exhaled, like the cat was testing him for signs of life.

Ellen stood in the kitchen, lights low, drinking tepid water from a chipped glass she hadn't meant to keep. The quiet in the condo felt too arranged. Like a waiting room for something she hadn't named yet.

Her phone buzzed on the counter.

Unknown number. Delaware area code.

She didn't know anyone in Delaware. That was exactly why she answered. "Hello?"

A man's voice. Measured. Government-shaped. "Hi, is this Ellen Crawford?"

"Yes," she said. "Who's this?"

"My name is Emerson Dahl. I'm an agent with the FBI. I'm following up on a case out of Miami. I'm reaching out to schedule a short interview. Nothing complicated."

"What kind of interview?"

"Informal," he said. "We're just tying off the remaining threads on an active file. Your husband's name came up in an older contact report."

Goddamn David.

"Could be nothing," he added.

His tone was polite, but she heard the scaffolding underneath it.

"And what exactly do you need from me?"

"Just a few questions. I'm in Miami for a few days, working out of the field office. If you'd prefer, we can meet somewhere else. Shouldn't take more than twenty minutes. Tomorrow or the next day, if that works."

She turned toward the living room.

Callan hadn't moved.

Beckett was watching her like he'd already filed a report.

"Let me get back to you," she said. Then added, "Will I need a lawyer?"

Dahl chuckled. No push. No hesitation. "That's really up to you. You're not suspected of anything, Miss Crawford."

Miss Crawford. A not-so-subtle reminder that David was dead.

"All right. I'll contact you tomorrow. Is texting okay?"

"Absolutely. Thank you, Miss Crawford." *Click.*

Ellen set the phone down and stood there for a moment. Then dumped the water and poured herself a glass of wine. Walking past the sofa, she caught Beckett watching her. Something in his gold-green eyes stopped her cold.

You shouldn't have taken that call, they seemed to say.

CHAPTER 78

The kitchen smelled like coffee and bacon—an old trick Ellen had once read about in a real estate guide: Make the place smell like home, even if it isn't.

She was barefoot, hair tied back, moving in quiet arcs between stove and counter. Callan sat at the table; Beckett stretched long across the windowsill like a loaf of judgement.

"You didn't have to cook," he said.

"I didn't," she replied, flipping the bacon. "I made enough for two and let you wake up near it. That's strategy. Not charity."

Callan almost smiled.

She slid him a plate and took the seat across from him. No small talk. Just eggs, toast, and the sound of Beckett occasionally thumping his tail against the wall like a metronome.

"Got a call last night," Ellen said, after a few bites. "FBI."

Callan set his fork down. Not alarmed but interested.

"Name?"

"Emerson Dahl. Said he's out of Miami. He's following up on Mel Williams. Wanted to talk."

Callan exhaled. "Shit."

"I didn't tell him anything. He kept it vague. Said David's name came up in a contact report."

"That tracks."

"You know him?"

Callan shook his head. "No. But if he's chasing Mel's trail, he's about to start tripping over Langston's."

"You want me to ghost him?"

"No," Callan said. "You should meet. Keep it normal."

Ellen raised an eyebrow. "You want me to talk to an FBI agent whose interest in me is a mystery?"

"You've got nothing to hide. And he hasn't connected anything yet, or he wouldn't have called you polite."

She nodded slowly. "All right. Still feels a little... exposed."

"I'll make a call." Callan pushed back from the table, pulling out his burner. "Take someone with you."

"Who?"

"Monty."

Ellen blinked. "Monty?"

"You will love Monty. He's a lawyer, but you'd never believe it. This will be fantastic."

He stepped onto the small back porch to make the call. Beckett slipped through the cracked door and curled up in a patch of sunlight like none of this involved him.

Callan shook his head and dialed Monty.

The phone rang twice.

Monty answered, voice dry as ever. "You calling this early, I'm guessing it's not about brunch."

"Nope." Callan paused.

"Mel?"

"Yeah."

Silence for a breath.

"Damn shame," Monty said. "He was solid."

"He was better than solid."

Another pause. No sentiment. Just that shared ache from men who don't grieve out loud.

"You think it was Langston?" Monty asked.

"I'd bet the house."

Monty exhaled through his nose. "You calling for backup?"

"I need you to sit in on a meeting. Ellen's talking to an agent—Emerson Dahl. New face. Bureau-issued. Doesn't know what he's walking into."

"He clean?"

"Don't know yet."

"You trust Ellen?"

"I do."

"That'll do for me."

Callan gave him the time and place. Monty didn't ask for notes. Never needed to.

***

"All set," he said to Ellen. He sat down and finished his breakfast.

"I am as ready as I'll ever be. To leave, I mean." Ellen set her fork down, brow knitting. "I've never lived anywhere but here."

"Think of it like a road trip. Miami'll be here when you get back."

***

Callan walked the quiet street, leash in one hand, burner in the other. Beckett trotted a few feet ahead, tail up, silent as ever.

He dialed the number. Wasn't sure it would still work. But it did.

She picked up.

"Detective Langley."

"Tricia."

A pause.

"I didn't kill you," she said.

"Because you missed," Callan replied. "Not because you stopped yourself."

She exhaled. Not a laugh. Not a denial.

"Fair."

Silence. "I know you're not in Miami anymore," she said. "Where'd you run to this time? North?"

He didn't answer.

"What do you want, Callan?"

"I want to make sure you're done."

"Done with what?"

"With whatever the hell you thought you were going to build out of that fire."

Another long pause. "I was never going to win," she said. "But I wasn't going to let him win either."

Callan slowed his steps. Beckett circled a tree, oblivious. "And now?"

"And now I disappear for a while."

"That a promise?"

"It's a truce," she said. "I don't come after you. You don't come after me."

Callan let that sit. Felt the edges of it. It wasn't peace. But it would hold.

"For now," he said.

"For now," she agreed. Another pause. This one almost warm. "Tell Ellen goodbye," Tricia added. "She deserved better men."

"Yeah," Callan said quietly. "She did."

"Oh Callan?"

"Yeah?"

"When I chose you for this... game, I never knew how dangerous you really were. You were a loner the world wouldn't miss when I was done with you."

"Okay, Tricia."

Click.

Callan stood in the street for a moment, phone dead in his hand. Beckett sat down beside him, tail curling neatly across his paws like a period at the end of a sentence.

The sky was cloudless. Northern air already touching the wind.

Chapter 79

It was Wednesday afternoon. Ellen chose a coffee shop outside Jacksonville.

Ellen picked the place. Bright, loud, public. The kind of chain café where everything smelled like cinnamon syrup and spilled milk. Where no one looked too closely at anything.

Monty looked like a man who'd woken up on someone's couch. Wrinkled T-shirt, unbrushed hair, cargo shorts with too many pockets and not enough dignity. But his eyes were sharp—scanning exits, corners, reflections.

Dahl showed up alone. Business casual. No jacket. Rolled sleeves. Bureau notebook in hand. He didn't try to charm. Just nodded once and sat.

"Miss Crawford," he said. "Thanks for meeting."

Monty grunted into his oversized coffee. Said nothing.

"I'll keep it short," Dahl continued. "I'm reviewing the last case connected to Melvin Williams. Your husband, David, shows up in a few places. Most notably—a payment to a private investigator named Dwayne McAllister. The subject of that surveillance was Philip Langston."

Ellen held her cup with both hands. Calm, but careful.

"I didn't know anything about that," she said.

"No idea why David would've been interested in Langston?"

She shook her head. "David didn't tell me things. He had... debts. Gambling. I always figured he was trying to fix something without letting me see it."

Dahl studied her. Then nodded. "McAllister's a name we've seen before. Not a great sign."

Ellen sipped her tea.

Monty scratched something on a napkin, then used it to clean his glasses.

Dahl glanced at him. Then back to Ellen.

"Did you know about any of David's contacts inside the Bureau?"

"No," she said honestly. "He didn't treat me like someone who'd need to know."

Dahl flipped to a new page. "You staying in Jacksonville?"

"Actually, I'm heading to Canada," she said. "Just for a while."

That surprised him.

"Where in Canada?"

"Haven't picked yet."

"I used to spend summers in Ontario," Dahl said, softening a little. "Lakes, trees, people leave you alone. You'd like it. There's this one spot near Tobermory—clear water, blue like glass. Cold as hell, but worth it."

He smiled, almost sheepish.

Monty dropped his coffee lid with a snap. "Agent."

Dahl cleared his throat. "Right." Clicked his pen closed. Stood. "Thanks for your time. If anything comes up—"

"Go through me," Monty said.

Dahl nodded. "Understood."

He left without another word.

Ellen stared at her cup for a long second.

"You all right?" Monty asked, already digging through his pockets for gum or a receipt or both.

"Fine," she said. "We didn't lie."

"Not really," he muttered.

CHAPTER 80

The road had thinned out into farmland and faded highway signs—the kind that looked like they'd been forgotten on purpose. Wheatfields in the distance, sun caught low behind them, threw shadows like stories too long to retell.

Callan drove with both hands on the wheel, silence like a co-pilot. Ellen sat beside him, feet on the dash, picking dried honey from the corner of a gas station granola bar. Beckett was in the back seat, sprawled across a duffel bag like he'd paid for the spot.

Callan clicked the burner on and scrolled to the contact marked "I." He hit *CALL.*

Isabelle picked up on the first ring. Her voice was light but not surprised. "Callan."

"Hey. Just letting you know—we're heading up to the lake. Should be there tomorrow night."

A beat. Then warmth. "You're really going."

"I am."

"You bring company?" she asked.

"Yeah. Ellen and the cat."

He glanced at Beckett in the mirror. The cat blinked, unimpressed with the seating, and slowly batted a water bottle off the console.

"Tell Ellen hi," Isabelle said.

Callan smirked. "I'll pretend she didn't hear that."

Ellen leaned closer to the phone. "Hi, Isabelle. He's driving like we're being chased, and Beckett just committed water bottle murder."

"I wouldn't expect anything less," Isabelle replied.

There was something in her voice—joy, maybe. Or just relief. It made Callan's grip on the wheel ease. Slightly. But not all the way.

"You sure the place is stocked?" he asked.

"Property manager's good. Firewood's stacked. Place'll be cold when you get there, but clean. Quiet."

"Right."

"You all right?" she asked.

"Getting there."

Another beat. "I'm glad," Isabelle said. "It's been too long."

"Yeah," Callan said. He didn't add anything. Didn't need to.

"Be safe," she said, and hung up.

Callan set the phone down.

Ellen shifted beside him. "You okay?"

"Yeah."

"You don't sound okay."

"I'm going back to a place that hasn't seen me in a decade."

"And?"

"And that place remembers more than it forgives."

Beckett let out a low meow. Not a complaint. Just a reminder he was listening.

The sky ahead was starting to darken, soft and heavy. Wind picking up through the wheat. The kind of dusk that knew something was waiting just past it.

Callan didn't speed up. Didn't slow down.

He just drove.

Warren Flynn writes psychological noir and character driven thrillers about obsession, loyalty, and the private bargains people make to live with what they have done. He started writing in the late 1980s, then set fiction aside while he built a career and a complicated adult life. In September 2024, a broken leg forced him into stillness, and he returned to the page. He lives in Edmonton, Alberta, Canada with a deeply approving cat and is currently working on his debut psychological thriller series.

HOWLING WOLF PRESS

WWW.HOWLINGWOLFPRESS.COM

Stories that howl through the night...

At **Howling Wolf Press**, we publish bold, imaginative fiction with heart.

From whimsical fantasy to haunting adventures, our books are crafted to enchant and endure.

JOIN THE PACK

Discover unforgettable stories or share your own.

HowlingWolfPress.com

Follow the call

www.ingramcontent.com/pod-product-compliance
Lightning Source LLC
Chambersburg PA
CBHW051311300726
48976CB00002B/363